Peter's Daughter

Helen Wilkinson's *Dying to Live* attracted wide critical acclaim when it was published in 2002. Peter's Daughter is her first novel for adults, following the children's novel, *The Missing Peace* (2002). It was in 1999, after a career in Human Resources and Training, that she began to write full time. Within a year Helen won seven national awards for short stories. She is married to Jim, has three children and lives in Shropshire. For more information on her books, visit www.sticklebackbooks.com

'Truly wonderful work – Helen's words paint a picture that I can see.'

'So powerful.'

'Where did these remarkable words come from? Filed away in my mind is the phrase 'Dictated by angels' - which applies to Helen's book Peter's Daughter.'

'Superb. It engulfs you right to the end. I couldn't put it down until I'd finished. I share your great desire for Christian fiction.'

'This book blew me away.'

Cover painting *Lake Galilee* © Helen Little 2003,
Cover photograph © Jo Smith 2003

PETER'S DAUGHTER
A STICKLEBACK BOOK

Published in England 2003 by Stickleback Books
an imprint of Ichthus Ltd
10 Park Plaza
Battlefield Industrial Estate
Shrewsbury, SY1 3AF
Tel. +44 (0)1743 718314
sticklebackbooks.com

ISBN 0-9543105-1-9

Printed and bound in Great Britain by Biddles
Limited

PETER'S DAUGHTER

A novel by

HELEN WILKINSON

stickleback books

Acknowledgements

My heartfelt thanks to everyone who has helped make this book a reality;

Peter and Alison; for your prayers every day that I was writing, Helen; for the single-hair paintbrush, Hannah, Jo and Simon; for breathing life into Ben and Susannah, Becki; the perfect (adopted) editor, Ju; for your antique book which made the Holy Land come alive, Helen Hinton; for endless support and advice, Kevin; for checking the theology, Dave Thompson; for the picture of a river which began it all, Clive; for being there when my lights blacked out, Everyone at Stickleback – thank you for your faith in this book. And Jim – the re-inforced concrete in my life. You underpin everything I do. I love you.

For my sisters,
Win
Joyce
And Eva

Love bade me welcome; yet my soul drew back,
Guilty of dust and sin.
But quick-eyed Love,
Drew nearer to me, sweetly questioning
If I lacked anything.

George Herbert 1633

Part One

Galilee

Et-Tel, Israel
23rd June 2003

Digging in the dust. All I've ever done, or ever will do.

Every day here, Lucky Doug and the other diggers are pulling out lead weights from throw nets. Fish hooks, net needles and domestic pottery. So trust me to be in a trench that's empty as a pauper's larder - three months trowelling for diddly-squat.

Diddly squat until 11.45 this morning.

That's when I saw it.

And it was pretty much like all my fantasies have ever been.

* * *

Until now, my life's been thin on fantasy and would make a better pamphlet than a book:

Ben Henshaw. Born 2nd June 1962.

Fell in love with ancient history at the bottom of my garden, 1968, after finding a greenish thrupenny bit.

Disappointed it wasn't Roman, but smitten enough to read Archaeology at York 1981 to '84.

Discovered the second love of my life, Carys, 13th August 1984 on my virgin dig as a Field Archaeologist in Egypt.

Married Carys 1985.

Unemployed for a total of six years between 1985 and 1996.

Carys fell out of love with me, and into bed with an accountant 1997.

Oh, and I failed to get promotion in 1995, which could explain the appeal of the accountant.

I'm a hot-headed, passionate child grown into forty-one year old cynic, with dreams as dead and dry as the bones I pick over. And that's on a good day - a regular 24 hours out here is stale as the air in a Pharaoh's tomb. I'm so out of touch with my school-boy ambition, that I can't even remember it. No doubt some kid is sitting in the UK watching *Time Team* and feeling a hint of what I once had, before real life buried me under layers of disappointment and failure.

9

So here I am, watching the fee-paying hobbyists who arrived last night. Israel is one of the few places where novices and enthusiasts can pay a huge amount to play at being archaeologists - they even get to stay in the luxury Ginosar Kibbutz in dirty dormitories – just like us.

This latest party spewed out of the air-conditioned coach like a bunch of hungry hyenas yesterday evening, their excitement sickening me. It's made worse by the pain of remembering that I was like them once. But I refuse to believe that I still am, not even in the lowest substratum of my ancient self.

I remember my first crushing week at York University when I was a fresh-faced nineteen year-old, longing to soak up anything about archaeology. The wizened Professor Sterne came into our first lecture on Palaeolithic sites, his crumpled tweed suit giving the impression that he lived in a time-warp. He honoured us with a word of welcome, and we strained forward eagerly to learn what the next three years promised.

'Well hello,' he sneered, 'I'm here to warn you to forget any ideas you may have that archaeology involves discovering fossils, examining dinosaur remains, or discovering un-robbed tombs. It's sheer bloody hard graft - detail, mind-numbing hours of cataloguing, and physical labour that will wreck your back and your brain. You'll be out of work more than you're paid, because there are more archaeologists than there are digs.'

I had put down my pen and felt a slow, dull ache begin in the pit of my stomach.

'The lucky ones here will go on to be Field Archaeologists and do it for forty years without honour or even recognition. The rest of you will be unemployed until you drop the dream and become librarians. So welcome to York, and I'll hand you over to Mrs Clark.'

Nothing of Mrs Clark's lecture has stayed in my memory. But the chill of disappointment had begun to creep.

The dig here isn't the worst I've worked on, at least the

weather's hot and dry. But it does remind me of the other curse of my life - that I seem to spend all my time on digs associated with religion. I try to avoid them, as I'm a committed, fully paid-up atheist, but they follow me around. Mostly in the Holy Land, but I've done Iona and many others.

And I've been here before. We're based at Et-Tel, one and a half kilometres off the northern shore of the Sea of Galilee, at the point where the river Jordan used to flow into the lake. Tel means hill or mound, and we're here trying to prove or disprove that this one is the historical site of Bethsaida which means 'House of the Fisherman' in Hebrew.

It's one of the three ancient cities that rejected Christ and were cursed by him. All three have disappeared from history – which you could take one of two ways. Either there was a Christ and his curse worked, or the places never existed and the scholars, who made up the New Testament decades later, invented them for the purposes of their legend.

Anyway, last time I was here, the site directors decided the lack of 1st century domestic finds from Et-Tel suggested this sight couldn't be Bethsaida of the gospels, but there was enough uncertainty to bring us back to try again.

In case you haven't heard of Bethsaida, it's the place where Jesus was said to have fed the five thousand, healed the blind man and walked on the water. As you do. So I'm looking for the wet sandals.

* * *

If I'm completely honest, all I ever wanted was to make the ultimate find. Unearth Excalibur's sheath, or Cleopatra's milk-stained bath-tub. And a flicker of that desire has remained inside me, beneath all my disillusionment.

Every morning as I remove the tarpaulins from the day before and start to scrape tiny particles of dust with my twenty-year old trowel, a speck of hope rises within me. Will today be the day? Could it happen?

Ten minutes later my back aches from all the yesterdays, sweat has soaked my tee-shirt and I'm back in the real world of Professor Sterne. So the old git was right after all.

Today began just like all the others. The Site Director had already told us this was the last before we closed my empty trench on the extreme south of the site nearest the lake. This afternoon I should have been moving on to a trench looking for the eastern tower of the 9th century BCE city gate.

Since my last dig here in 1987, there's been something of a monumental shift in thinking about the site. Seems the guys who said Et-Tel was Bethsaida were right after all. Recently they've discovered an entire town of fishermen's homes from the 1st centuries BCE and CE. The finds just keep on coming – mostly from Lucky Doug.

I was supposed to have come out of the trench, but was enjoying the shade and well hidden from prying eyes, so I carried on trowelling. Flicking little bits of dust. Each flick the same as the last - dried silt, devoid of artefacts.

Then my trowel caught on something. A small piece of stone, it had to be. I carried on flicking, more carefully now, and dropped my eyes closer to the ground. The stone got bigger, flatter, smoother. Until it wasn't a stone any more, but a shard of pottery, at least 13 by 8cm. For me this was good enough, my first find in six mindless weeks. Because it was clearly a large piece of 1st century CE domestic pot.

I didn't want anyone to share the precious moment, so I kept quiet, recorded its position diligently, then lifted the shard as gently as a surgeon removes a kidney, and turned it over in my leathery hands.

The second word I said was 'ostrakon', my first word is unprintable. Because on the underside of the shard were letters, inscribed in black inky script. Aramaic script. At my first heady count, at least thirty Aramaic words.

Ostrakon is the Greek word for potshard - I've seen some corkers in museums of course, my favourite was found at the Red Sea and was a contract about Domitian's imperial titles.

And now I had one in my hands that will send every ostrakon ever found into oblivion.

The rest of today has been a whirl. As soon as I had placed my piece in a plastic bag, I shrieked, 'Eureka!'

That's when every digger, researcher, volunteer and team leader invaded my trench and leaped on me. The shard was passed from guesser to expert, then rushed to the site director. But it was mine. All mine. I found it, and it will always be because of me.

Immediately people began to treat me with respect - for the first time this dig, or ever. Unlucky Ben just got lucky. My trench is going to be extended and opinion about the limits of the site expanded.

By noon we had a translation.

It *is* Aramaic, written with ink made from soot and sun-dried glue. And it's better than anyone on earth could have hoped. A rarity, a gem of a find saying,

FORGIVE ME, I HAVE NO PAPYRUS....

NAME OF JESUS TO SUSANNAH DAUGHTER OF SIMON ....

THE LORD WILL PROTECT ME FROM THE WRATH OF ALBINUS .....

I MUST STAY IN ROME....

Ironic that an atheist has to be the one to explain. And of course it doesn't prove or disprove anything. But,

- Bethsaida has always been known as the birthplace of Saint Peter, that's Simon Peter of course, who as you may notice has the first name Simon....and this is from a Simon...OK so you've got it.
- Any first century document which may be referring to Christ is of international importance. This is without doubt a first century potshard. Believe me, they can prove it.
- It's written to a woman, and that's as rare as finding a French fry in a health food bar.

By 4pm we had a camera crew on site – something to do with the Israeli News Agency, tipped off by our Site Director. I didn't want to be involved, but wasn't given any choice, they pushed and pulled me until I was back in the trench, retrieving a fake piece of pot from the ground for the camera - with a fake grin.

'No-one will know what you're really holding,' the Producer said glibly, 'It could be a piece of plastic for all the viewers know. We'll cut to the bagged shard in the next shot.'

A young reporter shoved a mike under my nose, 'So Mr Henshaw, how does it feel to make the greatest archaeological find for a hundred years?'

I studied her empty, ambitious face. Today a dig, tomorrow a suicide bomb. What the hell's the point?

Pushing her mike aside, I vaulted out of the trench and made for the trees.

Maybe I'll feel better in the morning. The shard is going to Jerusalem for examination, and I'm rejoining it tomorrow. Israeli/Palestinian conflict permitting. The find of my life. My fantasy.

Jerusalem
25th June 2003

The professors and experts at the Hebrew University of Jerusalem have given me access to the distinguished gang who are examining the shard.

The Archaeology Institute is a fairly un-prepossessing place, a disorganised rabbit warren - just like a thousand research departments across the civilised world.

As I approached the building this morning, I knew my find was within these walls, and every fire-door and corridor was taking me closer to her.

We were re-united in the Archaeology Institute where one of the big noises introduced me to Taylor Denton. With a first name like that, I guessed she was American as soon as they introduced me, before she opened her mouth and proved it.

She's tanned, slim, full-breasted - the sort of girl who wouldn't give me two minutes in a bar if I tried to chat her up, but she's giving me her full attention here. Her eyes are blue as tea-cups of Californian ocean, and she's drop-dead gorgeous. God only knows what she was thinking about me – skinny, wiry, tall and unshaven for three days. Specs, fine lines around the grey(ish) eyes caused by screwing up my face against the middle-eastern sun. I could go on, but I don't want to depress myself.

'Hi, I'm Taylor, nice to meet you,' she said, utterly genuinely.

Nice – everything's *nice* in the U.S. but if Taylor said it, I wasn't going to hold it against her.

'Ben Henshaw – Digger, pretty chuffed Digger since yesterday.'

I shook her hand and savoured the cool firmness of her hold, against the sweat of the streets I had brought in on my own hand. I wiped my palm on the back of my shorts – but it was too late then of course.

'You must be *totally* thrilled!' she enthused, pouring out the blueness of those little oceans into my eyes. She smelled as good as she looked.

'Yup, yesterday was the best day of my life – no contest.'

'Tell me – how it felt, what you thought...... everything.'

The big cheeses were busying themselves, jawing. I guessed we had a couple of minutes and lowered my voice, 'It was just like you pray for – except I don't pray – I'm an atheist.'

She smiled, 'An atheist on a major dig at an early Christian site who's just found what may be the most significant Christian evidence of the last century. A note written by Simon Peter himself. That's pretty funny!' she drawled.

'But Simon was a very common name in first century Palestine,' I protested.

'And how many Simons of Bethsaida would be writing in the name of Christ from Rome? Three, two....one?' she mocked.

'So it's an early fake, we all know that's the most likely explanation.'

'Hey you found it – shouldn't you be defending its authenticity?'

'A first century fake obviously,' I insisted, 'the ink and style of pot prove that.'

'Then it's still unique. The early Christians didn't do fakes.

15

They just weren't bothered about material things, and gave no thought to the future. Because they believed Christ would come again in their life-times, they didn't bother about evidence for future generations who would never exist. And we don't know many guys called Albinus.'

'Yeah, I'm out of my depth with Albinus - who was he?'

'A friend of Caesar's and twelfth prefect of Judaea 62 to 64 CE. The New Testament mentions him, as do other non-Christian texts. He had a wife Xanthippe who became a Christian under Peter's teaching, and then refused to sleep with her husband and his concubines.'

'I bet Albinus was pretty pissed off with that!'

'So pissed off he teamed up with Agrippa II – Roman prefect of Galilee - and ordered Peter's execution.'

Suddenly I wanted proof this was really happening to me. 'Can I see the shard again?'

Taylor turned to the lab bench behind her, and I was so absorbed at the thought of seeing my shard again, that I didn't notice her gorgeous rear view – hardly noticed.

She passed me a pair of new cotton gloves and then my find in a tray.

It was perfectly clean, paler now, larger than I remembered.

I held the broken edges gently between thumb and fore-finger, and read the Aramaic words again. I already knew them by heart.

FORGIVE ME, I HAVE NO PAPYRUS....

NAME OF JESUS TO SUSANNAH DAUGHTER OF SIMON ....

THE LORD WILL PROTECT ME FROM THE WRATH OF ALBINUS .....

I MUST STAY IN ROME....

Susannah, Simon, Albinus, Jesus. Names leaping across a bridge of two thousand years. Such history, such power.

'Ben?'

I looked up into Taylor's California-blue eyes.

'What are you thinking – can you tell me?' she asked.

At that moment Taylor's boss slapped me on the back, 'Well, well you must be pleased with yourself.' He laughed loudly and turned to his colleague.

I reckoned I had about ten seconds and whispered to Taylor, 'Would you have lunch with me? Today?' It was the first time I've asked a girl for any reason except wanting to get her out of her clothes.

And maybe that's why she said yes.

* * *

We went to a bar Taylor knows in the old town. It's cool and quiet, and looks too dingy to attract tourists. So they miss the courtyard at the back, shaded with vines – perfect for a long, slow lunch. Taylor chose our salads, and we both had chilled beer.

'This is a wicked place,' I encouraged her, looking up at the dappled noon-light illuminating the leaves above and around us.

'Now can you tell me what you were thinking?' she asked over the rim of her green glass.

'I'm thinking - I want to know who Susannah is.'

'Simon's daughter I should imagine – if the shard's genuine.'

'But I want to know what she looked like, how she moved, who she married, what she believed. All the things archaeology can't teach me.'

Taylor looked at me with her head tilted slightly to one side, as if I was speaking a foreign language.

She let me go on, 'Last night I lay in my bunk and realised I've just achieved what every Digger dreams of, what I came into this profession for. But it isn't enough. Anything I dig up in future will be a disappointment. After twenty years I've realised archaeology can't teach me the answers.'

'So research them. Someone, somewhere will have other pieces in the jigsaw. Maybe there'll be more finds at Et-Tel. Maybe there's a reference to a Susannah in an obscure text. Recovering this shard should be making you happy, not morose,'

Taylor persuaded.

'I'm very tired. Tired and confused.'

'Confused about religion?'

'No, not that at all – why do people bring everything back to religion? Even if the shard is genuine and there was a Simon writing home from Rome, and Albinus had him killed because he believed in Christ – that doesn't affect my life here. No it's not that. But I'm rocked somehow – and feeling tired with my life.'

'Are you married?'

'Divorced.'

'I'm sorry.'

'It's history.' I sipped my beer. 'Taylor that's it – it's history – but it's real, real to me. I want to follow my shard. Want to find Susannah.'

'What do you mean?'

'I don't know. I don't bloody-well know. I'm sick of my life, sick of being a Field Archaeologist – and just when I should be rushing back to the trench, fired with enthusiasm because I've made the best find out here for decades – instead I feel weary of it all. The dirt, hard work, the particle by particle disappointment. I want to be real, and live real life. I'm sorry, it's the feeling of the day after, and the beer. Sorry.'

Then the weirdest thing happened, Taylor reached across the metal table and put her small hand on top of mine. 'Ben, it's OK. Do it, go after her, find Susannah.'

'Find, fall in love and marry her. Yeah, right! Chase a relationship with a two-thousand-years-dead girl. That's weird even for me.'

Her eyes were wide open and clear, 'You've been hurting a long time haven't you Ben?'

'So who isn't?'

'Me. Millions of people. Go after her, but promise me one thing. Come back and tell me. Write me. I'm looking at you and seeing so many things - a slim, nearly middle-aged Brit with yearning eyes and a perfect body. Who's as short on peace as anyone I ever saw.'

18

Perfect body. She had said it. I smiled in spite of myself.

'I promise. I'll come back and tell you.'

Et-Tel
26th June 2003

When I reached the site the place was full of journalists – crawling around the perimeter like so many ants in a panic. A very helpful amateur pointed me out to a bloke with a camera the size of a Volkswagen Beetle, 'That's Ben Henshaw – the one who found it!'

So all the ants started to home in on me. I had no time to think, and legged it to the site director's cabin. The man I could never get access to until two days ago. I burst in and asked for a minute of his time. Now it was almost too easy.

'Ben, yes, of course. Sit down.' He motioned to his spare chair and rubbed beads of sweat from his balding head. 'What can I do for you?'

'I've come to let you know that I'll be taking some time off.'

'To research in the University Department? We're more than happy for you to do that, but we're hoping you'll take on more responsibility here and head up a team too.'

'That won't be possible – I want a complete break.'

He removed his reading glasses, rubbed his head wearily, and looked at me long and hard through blood-shot eyes, 'For starters we've arranged for you to be interviewed by CNN at 15.45, then there will be a piece to camera with you in the trench, reconstructing the scene of your find for BBC History. And Ben, you won't want to take time off until you've worked on the extended trench – I don't need to tell you that there may be another piece of that shard waiting to be discovered near the first.'

'Sorry, no. I need to get away.'

'Until when?'

'I don't know. But it could be a long time.'

'Can you afford it?'

'No, but what's new.'

'I don't pretend to understand – just when your last twenty years will start to pay off. But I can't stop you. Obviously.'

I came out from the stale heat of the cabin into the bowl of fire of Palestinian sun. Israeli sun. Whatever, it was bloody hot. Pulling my baseball cap down tight over my eyes, I walked quickly as I could to the road, just glancing at my trench on the way. It was totally surrounded by the ants.

'Anyone seen Ben?' I heard above the general hubbub.

I looked across the site with a weird hint of fondness, especially for the eucalyptus trees that seemed to connect me to the past - their shade had been good for many a lunch time beer.

A taxi was parked at the roadside – waiting for a journalist I guess. It's the first time I've ever left the site in comfort.

Kibbutz Ginosar was deserted. The dorm was empty as I chucked my few possessions into the ancient backpack. I've always had a reputation for losing things and leaving them, I blame it on Mum who left home when I was seven, so no-one taught me how to look after myself. At least packing never takes me long.

I regretted that I hadn't used the laundry for days, but hell, clothes are filthy in five minutes here, so who cares?

One rucksack, weighing fifteen pounds. My whole life in a space that would fit in any kitchen cupboard in the UK. And it felt good.

After my rashness with the taxi I caught the bus for the 8km ride into Tiberias where I withdrew enough cash for a month. Perhaps I should clarify - that's all the cash I had. I bought a postcard and sent it immediately,

Dear Taylor
I've done it. Cleared out.
My email address is boogyhen@onetel.co.uk - what's yours? Damn it - I could have been famous. Love Ben.

There was one more job to do. Tiberias has a great bookshop for tourist archaeologists. I never go in. To be honest I would have struggled today if there had been anyone about.

I knew exactly what I was looking for, and found it without having to ask – translate as; I only had to look for twelve minutes, during which no member of staff came up and offered to help.

The book is a modern reprint of a journal written by a guy called David Roberts who was one of the first tourists to visit Palestine after major nineteenth century conflict.

When he returned to the UK in 1839, he published the journal with a remarkable set of lithographs based on his sketches. He was a stunningly good artist. The prints are heavy on the use of ochre and sandy tones, and recapture a land that by 1839 hadn't changed in twenty centuries. I need those prints, to get a feel for the places I'll have to visit.

I made my way to the site of the ancient harbour, produced my professional ID card (it's going to be handy having that), and walked to the waterside. The excavations here aren't yet open to the public, but include the harbour walls built by Herod in 20CE.

I sat on a basal stone and leafed through my new volume, reading Roberts' archaic, twee words, 'We came in sight of the Sea of Galilee, embosomed in surrounding hills. Here at a glance, lay before us the scenes of our Saviour's miracles. The lake presents a beautiful sheet of limpid water, in a deep, depressed basin. A little boat with a white sail, gliding over the waters; the only one, as we afterwards found, upon the lake.'

I raised my own eyes to the lake, looking east towards the Golan heights which were pretty much unchanged from Roberts' print. In spite of myself I could feel a lump in my throat. God knows why, I don't.

Then I thought of Susannah and realised I don't know where to start. I've walked away from my job to chase a piece of history (arguably). Not helped by the fact that I've never taken much notice of current archaeological thinking on New Testament issues outside of my own site. And I've never owned a Bible – and am not going to start now.

I stared across the ruffled blue waters and dredged the bottom stratum of my brain. There wasn't much to go on. Et-Tel is, (unconfirmed – or ironically confirmed by me), Bethsaida, birthplace of Simon Peter and a couple of the other disciples.

And Capernaum, about four miles north along the lake shore is where Peter lived and where Jesus preached, and did miracles tra la la.

So if Susannah was Peter's daughter, she would have lived in Capernaum.

I got on the next ferry.

My mobile phone buzzed as an email came through – funny, it's been doing that a lot since the find.

Date 27.06.03
To boogyhen@onetel.co.uk
From taylordenton.arch.instit@hebron.com
Hi Ben, I have a parcel for you. Will mail via Site Director at Capernaum excavations. You should start there.
Keep in touch – thinking of you,
Taylor

Date 29.06.03
To taylordenton.arch.instit@hebron.com
From boogyhen@onetel.co.uk
I *have* started there. The place is looking derelict – another one that Jesus cursed. (Joke). Thanks for the Gospel of Mark. Heavy stuff. I don't own a Bible, and you can have this back when I've finished. You shouldn't have written to me inside the cover because you're only lending it. So Peter dictated to Mark? Who was Mark? Was he related?
Love Ben

Date 29.06.03
To boogyhen@onetel.co.uk
From taylordenton.arch.instit@hebron.com
Hi Ben

Hey – you're the archaeologist. Find out!
Love Taylor

Capernaum, Galilee
29th June 2003

So this place is having an effect on me. Or I'm going mad. I keep thinking about the bloody thrupenny bit I found at the bottom of my folks' garden. The heat is going to my head.

Capernaum is totally mind-bending. I've been here before of course, and admired the extent and state of preservation of the two thousand year old excavations. But I never *felt* anything before.

The lake has receded in the last 2,000 years, but I've been sitting today trying to imagine the scene Susannah may have known.

They've excavated a row of first century houses that ran along the shore-side, opposite the stone jetties and harbour entrance. On market days, villagers would have set up booths along this unpaved area, because there weren't any permanent shops or civic amenities. Unusually, there's a total lack of first century inscriptions here, which proves what a lowly sort of place Capernaum was in Susannah's time. They've found a lot, but not a gram of marble, fresco, plaster or mosaic. And no expensive red roof tiles.

Beyond, they've uncovered a whole village, which in Peter's time would have had a population of between 600 and 1,500, a medium sized village for Galilee.

The modern building above the excavations houses a display. Normally I avoid museum displays, but for the first time I read every word.

Apparently Jesus may have chosen Capernaum as HQ of his ministry because it was Jewish, but close to the border of Herod's tetrarchy, and beside the multi-racial kingdom of the tolerant Philip. That made it;
1. politically safe,
2. a religiously broad-minded sort of town. Gentile villages

were close, and Gentiles travelled through every day,
3.   geographically well placed. Traffic would have been heavy
     in the 1st century as Herod had just built Tiberias due south,
     and Capernaum was bang on route. And the main highway
     from Damascus to Caesarea was a stone's throw away. If
     you were an Olympic javelin thrower.

And it was perfect because he could stay with Peter – whose house was found decades ago. This building must have been Susannah's home too. And they've found a boat exactly contemporary with her father.

I stood for at least ten minutes looking at the pictures of the excavated 'Jesus' boat – very unusual because it's big enough for thirteen guys. Twelve plus one. And even I know how many apostles Jesus had.

Then I knew it was affecting my brain and went to the lakeside. First I sat squinting at Mount Hermon, still snow-capped in June, with deep ridges on top that would have harboured wolves and cave bears in Susannah's time.

So what have I got? A guy called Simon who writes in the name of Jesus. A daughter called Susannah. A couple of dozen words in Aramaic. Words that are buzzing in my head like so many wasps.

Then I just lay back on a rock for a minute, to turn my brain off.

Capernaum, Galilee
CE 30

The day my world blew apart started like any other day.

Dad and Uncle Andrew were out in the cold mid-winter dawn, using the throw net from the boat.

I was sitting on my favourite flat rock at half-light, watching and waiting for the fish to take home for breakfast. I was thinking I'm a woman now – because two months ago I celebrated my thirteenth Feast of Tabernacles. It's no use behaving as if I'm still a child.

Dad can make the throw net look as graceful as a dance of the veil. I watched him that morning with new eyes, seeing eyes – he's big and burly, and a million times more real to me than the God of our fathers. Strong, with a slight stoop, like a big bear who's restraining his strength.

He coiled the net over his brown arm, watching the water always, then threw it – as light in his hands as a spider's web. The net fell into the water like a bride's skirt sinking to the floor at the end of the wedding dance. All the little lead weights hit the water together – so when Dad throws the net exactly right, I hear one single plop from the shore, not many little ones.

I must have watched Dad throw the net a thousand, thousand times. He's never happier than when he's casting, watching and pulling in the loaded net. If it returns empty, he hauls it by the centre rope and begins all over again. Dad loves to be active, he couldn't be cooped up all day indoors, like Levi the tax collector - he would go mad.

The lake is his life, just as it's mine.

Dad and Uncle Andrew, with James and John, have turned the fishing into a really successful business. We have more boats than anyone around the lake shore, and extended our houses to make quite a family settlement. My little world consists of work, family and basking in the beauty of Galilee.

Every Sabbath I thank the Almighty that I was born in Capernaum, not Jerusalem or any other dirty, busy place.

The only cloud on my horizon is fear of betrothal – because Dad and Grandpa Jonah have got their hearts set on me making a good marriage. Zebedee, Dad's business partner and distant cousin, has an office in Jerusalem where he runs the contract to supply fish to the High Priest's palace, and he knows several rich families. Zebedee told Dad all about the youngest son of some temple guard who sounds just right for me. It would mean I have to move to Jerusalem when I marry, and leave my beautiful lake for ever.

Every time Dad brings the subject up, I tell him I'm too young to be betrothed, but his patience is wearing thin.

Last time we talked he said, 'Elias the Carpenter's daughter is betrothed, and she's three years younger than you. After Passover we'll arrange the betrothal, and that's the end of it. You're old enough to be married already. I've no idea why you've got it into your head to stay in this dead-end place when you could go to Jerusalem. Surely you don't want to be pickling and potting fish for the rest of your life? You're too headstrong for your own good my girl.'

'I wonder where I get that from?'

'You cheeky vixen – most fathers would beat you for

less,' and Dad chased me around the courtyard with his net needle and threatened to prick my tongue for answering back.

But last night's talk was different. Serious and frightening.

Momma started it, in the quiet, sideways manner she has. 'Simon, I've been speaking to my mother about Susannah.'

Dad hadn't been home long, and his brown eyes were tired. 'What's she done this time?'

'It's what she *hasn't* done, Susannah must be betrothed. She'll bring shame on us if we wait any longer – the people are saying no-one will have her because of her pale face and fiery eyes.'

'Nonsense, she's the prettiest girl this side of the Decapolis, with her mother's great looks.'

'And her father's obstinacy,' she retorted.

'I've fixed it all with Zebedee, he knows the man for her. We've spoken about the price, and it won't be cheap as Susannah works for me in the business. I'll need good compensation for losing her.'

'I'm her mother Simon, please let me visit Zebedee with you next time you travel to Jerusalem. I want to meet the boy's family.'

'That's settled then,' he said and rubbed his big hands together.

Something popped inside my chest. 'No.' I said, the power of my retort shocking myself as much as anyone.

'What?' Dad raised his voice and glared at me.

'I said no. I can't marry, can't leave Galilee.'

My mother leapt on me, 'Kneel before your father and ask forgiveness, Susannah daughter of Simon.' Her olive eyes were cold and hard.

Just then Uncle Andrew burst in, letting a gust of winter lake-breeze sweep into the room with his cloak. His height and curly hair make him an awkward adult who looks like an overgrown child. 'Evening Sarah. Evening brother. Ah – is this a bad time?'

He looked at the family scene, mother's arm raised to strike me, Joseph poking a moth with a reed, and father like a thunder-cloud descending over Gergesene.

Dad turned to Andrew, 'Don't ever marry and have a daughter Andrew.'

'I come with news,' my uncle persisted, 'to make you all laugh – the tanner's eldest son has left Capernaum and gone to Nazareth to follow the new prophet. The one I told you about who was baptised in the Jordan when the Dove came down and the voice from heaven.'

'Ha!' exclaimed Dad with a tone full of mockery, 'The idiot. That will leave his father short. You wouldn't catch me chucking in a good job and a quiet life to chase some half-baked excuse for a man who calls himself a prophet. Or even one who is a prophet.'

That's one of the things I love about Dad - his common sense.

He turned to Momma who was still holding on to my tunic, 'Let her go Sarah, we'll deal with her later. Stay and drink a jar with us brother. We'll celebrate Susannah's future betrothal.'

I looked up at Dad in horror as he turned towards the wine jars, and just as he caught my eye he winked at me, fair and square behind Momma's back.

As I watched him fishing this morning, I remembered

all our happiest times, and how I will do anything to escape baking and sweeping to be in the potting house working with the fish and the pickles.

The net was fuller this time, and even before full dawn I could see the flashes of silver that mean breakfast, and a day without Dad's anger.

I smiled as I remembered his pride when he caught me beating the hired hand for stealing. I was only ten or eleven when I caught Melech dipping in the chest where Dad keeps the coins set aside for the Roman tax-collector.

Melech didn't see me coming, but I'd already watched him stuff one handful into his tunic before I crept forward and bit him on the hand. The pain forced him to unclasp his fingers, and ten or more bronze coins and several shekels fell tinkling across the stone flags. I screamed and hit Melech with a broom, until he dropped to his knees with his arm over his head, 'Stop you little she-devil, leave me!' he was screaming.

Dad heard the noise and came running into the potting house just as Melech was getting away. Dad pulled him up by his hair and dragged him to the new harbour wall, dropped Melech over the edge and told him he'd just lost his job.

Dad came back and found me picking up the coins, 'You're a fighter Susannah – you should have been a boy! Your husband will need a strong arm to keep you in check,' and he ruffled my veil and laughed from his belly.

It is typical of Dad to trust everybody, keeping the tax money in a chest in the potting house. Typical of him to damn the whole system of Herod's taxation, then put the money aside for it. He's honest and just, but when somebody lets him down, his anger's frightening.

I want to please him in everything, and that's why I know I'll have to go to Jerusalem and marry the jeweller's son.

Dad, Galilee, my world. I don't want a single thing to change, ever.

All the time I sat, the waters had been grey as stone, the sky gradually etching with a faint glow of feathery pink clouds that quenched and snuffed the morning star. The palms and houses made the thinnest of shadows, and cock-crows echoed from hill to hill. Then villagers brought beasts to the shore for water while sparrows began to chirp and swifts soar.

Suddenly - and I can never believe it though I see it every day - the sun leaped over the eastern hills, bathing us in warmth, and turning the lake from grey to blue in an instant. Just like every other day of my life, I breathed in and felt the wonder.

That's the exact moment I noticed the stranger on the shore. He was watching Dad, just like me. He didn't look like a traveller, with no purse, back-pack or stick. And there was a stillness about him, as if he saw everything and was completely comfortable with himself.

Standing with his long hair and uncut beard, he called out to Dad and Uncle Andrew, 'You don't seem to be catching much – come with me and I'll teach you how to catch men!'

That line worked with Dad all right, getting the little hooks into him.

'I'll need a bigger net!' he laughed back.

Uncle Andrew yelled, 'It's Jesus – the one I told you about, the one the Baptist called us to follow!'

I could hear Dad's booming voice from my rock, 'Don't mention the Baptist - I can't respect a bloke who goes about in a hairy shirt, eating insects. He's a raving madman!'

'He's no lunatic Simon, he's the first teacher I've ever heard speaking any sense around here. To the Baptist, everybody's equal - he's calling us all to repent, rich and poor alike.'

'I'll do my repenting in the synagogue at the appointed times – not because some madman tells me I should.'

The stranger was listening intently. The light breeze stirred the hem of his cloak, lifting it occasionally so I could see his serious, compelling face. He drew me and frightened me at the same time.

Dad shouted at him, 'Join us for breakfast - friend of the Baptist, and you can teach us about your kind of fishing.'

The stranger tilted back his head and laughed into the dawn sky.

I ran ahead and warned Momma that we would have company. But then Dad came home without Jesus after all. He had met Dad's partners James and John – Zebedee's sons – further along the shore, washing their trammel net after the night's fishing. So he'd gone to ask them to help him fish for men too.

Eventually they all trooped back to our house and we ate the freshly caught, grilled musht with Momma's little flat bread cakes. Jesus ate piles. He'd been walking all the previous day from Nazareth.

Of course, I wasn't allowed to talk to him - I helped Momma by serving breakfast and hid my face inside my winter veil.

Just once, when I helped him to more cakes, Jesus looked up into my face and smiled with his eyes. They were the brightest blue I've ever seen, the colour of spring irises around the lake. I wanted him to smile at me again.

Uncle Andrew asked, 'Tell us about the Baptist, do people still say he's the Messiah?'

'He's preparing the ground - many have repented, but true baptism happens in the heart - not in the river.'

'Do you think he'll stir up a revolt against Herod Antipas?'

'John hasn't come to stir up a revolt. His time is almost finished.'

'Why - is he ill then - or moving on?'

'His job is done.'

When Jesus said that, I felt annoyed for the first time. I could tell he wasn't going to answer Uncle Andrew's questions, and I thought he was rude. Momma had brought us up to answer politely and fully - even my ten year old brother can do that.

'I've known for a long time that I must come to Galilee,' Jesus said, 'and my heart leapt yesterday when I left Nazareth at first light. History came alive as I crossed the very ground where centuries of chariots have thundered against our people.'

I stopped working and leaned against the cold wall. I've never left Galilee and I was gripped.

'Before my eyes were the brown southern hills where Elijah prophesied, with Naboth's Vineyard against the skyline, and the long ridge where the priests of Baal worshipped when Elijah called down fire from heaven. And as I dropped down toward the lake I saw Tiberias – Herod's new palace wall stretches for miles - so much new whiteness, covering up the dirt underneath. Modern ambition replacing centuries of simple Jewish life.'

I burst out, 'We can see his white statues in the palace gardens – they gleam when the sun catches them!' Momma hushed me just as I was putting my hand to my mouth.

But Jesus didn't ignore me, 'They're bigger than life-size. And I saw Herod's splendid harbour with marble steps down to his barges.'

I wanted to hear Jesus talk about Tiberias, drawing the people and wealth with his words.

'I couldn't enter the city,' he said, 'the Rabbis think the place stinks. Herod's cemetery is right in the middle of the city, and I haven't time for the seven days purification afterwards.'

Dad said, 'Herod is bribing ruffians to live there, and even though we Galileans aren't very strict, Tiberias is no place for a good Jew.'

Jesus went on, 'I followed the road in its long descent to the lake. After the rocky gorge, everything about Galilee seems gentle - green valleys, soft hills, trickling streams beside the road. The opposite shore seemed very near - it was only this morning I realised the lake is several miles wide.

'I watched the setting sun as it turned the hills to brown and gold, filling the valleys with blue shadows. The eastern hills held the light of the vanished sun for a long time, then glowed with white radiance. A pink afterglow tinged the western sky and it was very quiet except for the clapping of pigeons flying to their roost, and the screaming of swifts.'

My eyes were fixed on this stranger who spoke about

the beauty of our land with the tongue of a poet.

'I watched the first star appear over Galilee and wondered what would become of me here, and whom I would meet. I prayed to my Father to send the right ones. And you were the first – Peter the rock, son of Jonah the dove. You will be my solid ground. Follow me.'

I was absolutely horrified to hear Dad's answer, 'Yes, I'll follow you, wherever it leads.'

I saw Momma pause ever so slightly as she cleared the bowls. You could have missed it, but I didn't.

That's when I started to hate this Jesus who's going to divide our family - wreck us like a boat cracked right through the keel.

Last night we had an almighty row in our house. Dad had been in a bad mood all evening. He invited Jesus to stay with us because we have plenty of space. After supper, Jesus had gone out to pray, and Uncle Andrew came across the courtyard to talk. I knew Dad would pick a fight with him.

He snarled at Uncle Andrew, 'Why did you say you would follow Jesus – we can't afford to lose you from the family business?'

Uncle Andrew is as kind as anyone I know, but Dad's his big brother and drives him mad. 'That's totally unfair Simon – you're the one who said you'd follow him first, "wherever it leads!"'

'I was just being polite – he won't have taken me seriously.'

'You're a fool - that man looks as if he takes promises very seriously.'

'We've got a thriving fishing business here, so if you

think I'm going to walk away for some itinerant follower of the Baptist, you've got another think coming. I live to fish, and I fish so this family can live. And he hardly makes you think, 'Oh, here comes a Prophet!' For a start, he's nothing like the Jesus you described at the baptism in the Jordan. I haven't noticed any doves coming down from heaven or words from the clouds brother!'

'Look - I'm the only one who's actually *met* the Baptist – and I know something's afoot in Palestine for the first time in five hundred years. You can't let Jesus down, you heard what he said about you being his foundation.'

'I'll do what I damn well like – who does he think he is anyway – coming round here demanding people follow him?'

That's when I looked towards the door and saw Jesus standing there. His cloaked head was framed against the dark sky, and he was very still.

Dad and Uncle Andrew stopped talking. None of us knew how much he had heard.

Momma invited Jesus in and poured him a drink of leben yoghurt. Dad busied himself putting more thorn branches on the fire. He didn't look at Jesus at all.

Uncle Andrew broke the stony silence, 'Come and sit down Jesus, it's cold out tonight, the sky's clear as a pool.'

I was proud of Dad, he'd really stood up for himself, he isn't going to let Jesus push him around after all.

Then little Joseph came down the ladder and called for Momma, 'I can't sleep.'

'Hush now, have a drink of leben and go back to bed,' she replied, 'we'll be coming up in the shake of a lamb's tail.'

Jesus was quiet, and we could all hear Joseph

swallowing his milky drink in gulps.

Uncle Andrew tried to make conversation with the stranger, 'How long are you planning to stay?'

Jesus didn't answer him. Instead he asked Momma, 'May I tell Joseph a story?'

'Yes please, please!' begged Joseph.

'If it's a quick, settling down kind of story,' smiled Momma.

Joseph crept close to Jesus by the fire, almost touching his creamy woollen tunic. I could sense that not just Joseph, but all of us were waiting for the stranger to begin.

'There was once a rich ruler who had no son to succeed him. How he had longed for a child, and how his wife had grieved she was barren! One day, in the winter of his life, the rich man accepted that his wife had grown too old to bear him a child. He decided to seek out a good and noble young man to whom he could leave all of his fields, his slaves and his houses. This man had so much money, he had to keep it in his cellars in empty grain jars.'

Joseph's eyes were round and wide as pomegranates.

'And so the rich man set out on a journey to find just such a worthy step-son who could inherit his kingdom. He journeyed for many days and nights. When his chariot wheels broke upon the rocky road, the slaves put him in a covered litter and carried him, and when his slaves could go no further, the ruler walked on his own two legs. When his sandals were worn into holes, he walked in his bare feet.

All that long journey he was looking for a young man who was worthy to inherit his kingdom, and the longer he travelled, he looked dirtier and shabbier, and less like a rich man. Across the whole of the land, in every town and village, he looked for a boy who was good enough, and brave enough to be his son.

To each one he said, "Would you give up everything to come and be a son to me, to tend my fields, feed my flocks and live with me?"

One said, "No sir, I'm betrothed to be married and I cannot leave this village."

Another said, "If you come back after the Feast of Weeks sir, I shall be ready to go with you then."

And a third said, "I have a thriving farm sir, and my father needs me to work here with my brothers."

Nowhere could the rich man find anyone to be his son, and at last he set off for his home with a heavy heart.

When he arrived in his own country, he was thirsty, and he stopped beside one of his wells for a drink. He saw a young peasant girl sitting beside the well drawing water for the goats.

"Little girl, fetch me some water because I am thirsty," he said.

"Yes sir," she said, "and you may have my bit of bread too, because you look as though you have made a long journey." She didn't recognise the master, because he was so dirty and hairy after his long time on the road.

"But that bread is all you have to eat," said the rich man.

"But it's mine to offer," she said, and passed him the bread.

"Little sister, because of your goodness and generosity with the little you have, you shall inherit all I own," said the rich man.

And she did. In time he made her part of his own

family, and he passed his money, his house and all his lands to the peasant girl, and she proved to be a wise and noble ruler.'

Joseph blinked up at Jesus, 'But she can't inherit his kingdom because she's a girl!'

'It's my story, and that's the way it ends,' said Jesus, smoothing Joseph's hair as Momma beamed.

My head was filled with battling emotions. I loved the story, I loved it that the girl got to inherit the kingdom, but I hated the feeling that the story means more than it says.

Suddenly I turned and noticed Dad. He was leaning against the door frame and facing out to the night, his shoulders rocking. I assumed he was laughing, but then he turned to face Jesus and I saw tears streaming down his grainy face. 'Forgive me Master, I'm a foolish fisherman. I will follow you, if you'll still have me.'

'The catch will be so great, your nets will burst with the weight of it,' Jesus said.

Capernaum, Galilee
29th June 2003

When I woke I had the oddest feeling. As if someone was watching. I looked behind me on the flat rock, and a black lizard darted away. There was no-one about.

The afternoon sun was starting to lose its ferocity, but I really needed the bottle of water from my backpack. We're 200 metres below sea level here, and though winter is cool, summer's an inferno. I reached for my bottle and my hand touched the gospel from Taylor. Lifting it out gingerly, I opened the front cover,

'Ben, For you. Susannah's story is behind Mark's words. Find peace. x.'

It wouldn't do any harm to look at it.

I wondered if there was any direct mention of Susannah – but presumed Taylor would have told me if there were. As I flicked my eye over the first couple of pages, I looked for thou's and shalt not's. I couldn't see any.

But I spotted the name of Galilee right away. '*Jesus was walking near Capernaum by the Lake of Galilee and saw Simon and his brother Andrew throwing a net into the water, because they were fishermen.*'

Then the weird feeling came back. I looked across the aqua-blue lake. Maybe if Susannah's Dad was a fisherman, and they lived in Capernaum, Susannah might have sat near my rock and watched him. So close, but separated by two thousand heart-rending years.

I pride myself on my lack of emotion, so why the hell am I aching inside for a girl I can't reach?

Unsure what to do, I read more of Mark's gospel. Still the first chapter; '*On the Sabbath Jesus went to the synagogue in Capernaum and began to teach.*'

I knew women weren't allowed into the inner synagogue, but I wanted to be there. It was a short walk back to the main excavations.

Tourists can be easily confused here – though in my experience you can confuse a tourist anywhere – they'll photograph your big toe if you tell them Julius Caesar sucked it. But Capernaum has *two* ancient synagogues. I was interested in the older, a black basalt building dating to the first few years CE. The foundations of the gray marble columns and cobblestone floor still exist. This is the exact spot where Peter would have heard Jesus preach. Weird. Standing on the very same cobbles.

I wondered what Susannah would have been doing on a Sabbath morning. It was easier to imagine what she would have looked like. From the feet up I pictured her as a teenage girl, with cork and leather-soled sandals, embroidered or decorated with stones. An ankle-length tunic made of creamy linen, robed above with a plain coloured robe and girdled. The breast of her robe embroidered, and her head veiled.

Creamy-white with yellow embroidery, I could picture it, making her look as slender and pale as a lily emerging from its stem.

I could have gone for a girl like that. If she wasn't dead as the proverbial dodo.

Capernaum, Galilee
CE 30

Two days after Jesus arrived was the Sabbath. Usually I go to the Synagogue with Momma, and we stand behind the open-work screen watching the men and boys reading from the Law, rocking from side to side and praying aloud. But this week I stayed at home to nurse Gran, Momma's mother, because she was sick with a fever.

It's a chilly winter and I was spooning broth to her lips, but she wouldn't drink it and kept whispering, 'I'm hot Sarah, too hot.'

She was so ill she thought I was Momma. I sat beside her bed, singing psalms and songs, and wiping her face with a damp linen cloth to cool her down. Gran's mouth was dry as summer dust. I was afraid she may be too old to survive this time, especially as she's quiet and meek like Momma, not tough like Grandma Tabitha.

Suddenly, into the quietness burst the shrieking and calling of boys running along the shore. At first I couldn't make out what they were shouting, and then I thought I heard, 'He's cured Mad Daniel!'

Over and over I heard the name Mad Daniel. I stood and peered out of the tiny first floor window but couldn't see the boys, so I hurried down the ladder and ran out of the house, across the courtyard and straight on to Capernaum's main road.

People were flocking out of the black synagogue. I could hear them clearly now, calling, 'Jesus has cast out Daniel's demon. Jesus is a magician!'

I blinked into the low sun and watched as I saw Daniel's father lead his son by the hand out of the synagogue.

41

Mad Daniel was standing up straight and walking, just like any normal man. He was smiling, and his father wept.

Momma saw me and came rushing to my side, 'Susannah - Jesus has healed Mad Daniel. He called on the evil spirit to come out of him, and Daniel stood up and the madness left him at once. We don't understand it - Jesus didn't use any magic words or tools like the travelling miracle workers who come through here. He just commanded the demon to leave. And you should have heard him speaking in the synagogue - the Scriptures made sense when he read them. He's somebody special, he's going to change things.'

'Especially the things that don't need changing,' I said, 'He's a meddler. I'm going back to take care of Gran.'

I can't understand the anger that wells up in me every time Jesus is mentioned. And I can't believe Momma's so gullible. I know Jesus is a fraud and home wrecker and I wish he'd never come.

Gran was shivering when I reached her. I piled all of the covers from our beds over her and still she shook. It wasn't long until I heard a great number of people coming into our main room downstairs. I could hear Dad of course, his deep voice booming out 'welcome' to all and sundry. I didn't hear Jesus speak, but it was obvious from the commotion that he was there with Dad and Uncle Andrew.

Everybody was full of the healing - the neighbours, and people from Magdala and Bethsaida who had come to the synagogue. They were all trying to squeeze in through our front door.

I heard Momma inviting people to drink a glass of wine, and I felt left out, un-needed, angry. Joseph was squealing a sing-song above the general noise,

'Jesus is staying in *our* house,

we've got a magician in *our* house.'

I hated them all and wanted everything back to normal, and for me to be at the centre of family life once again.

Suddenly I heard the quiet deep voice of Jesus, 'Where is Susannah?'

My heart missed a beat. He'd noticed I wasn't there. Then I panicked because I knew Momma would call me and I didn't want to come down.

I heard her footsteps on the ladder, turned and saw with shock, not her familiar veiled head, but Jesus himself. 'Forgive me, your Momma said I could come up.'

I looked down at the wooden boards, expecting him to ask why I wasn't at the synagogue - I was preparing my answer in advance. But when I raised my head, Jesus wasn't looking at me at all. He was staring at Gran on her mattress. Slowly, he knelt down on the floor and covered his eyes with one hand. I wondered whether he was thinking, but he may have been praying. Then he stood up, knelt beside Gran, and lifted her hand in his. He said, 'Get up!'

I couldn't believe his stupidity, and retorted 'She's ill - Gran can't get up, she's really poorly.'

He ignored me and said again, 'Mother of Sarah, get up.'

I felt a physical pain at his command, but as I watched, Gran's eyes opened and she came back to her senses.

She sat up and peeled back the coverlets, 'Why on earth am I swaddled in all the family's blankets? – I'm warm enough to roast! It's good to see you Jesus, what would you say to a nice little bit of yesterday's cold mutton for your dinner? I'll have it ready in a trice,' and Jesus lifted her to her feet.

'Gran, you're ill. You have a great fever and you mustn't get up,' I said.

'Nonsense girl, I've never felt better in my life. A good sleep was all I needed.'

Jesus smiled, kindly, and helped her to the ladder. He didn't follow Gran downstairs, but leaned against the rafters and watched me folding the bedding. My anger would have been obvious even to the Galilee idiot.

'Would you prefer Gran to be ill Susannah?' he asked me, his eyes alight.

'Of course not.'

He waited for me to say more. I knew he wanted me to incriminate myself.

'It's just I was perfectly capable of taking care of her, we were fine thank you.'

'She was dying.'

'Oh and now she isn't? You just hold her hand and she's skipping around like a lamb is she? Well that's great – thank you *so* much – how *did* we manage without you?'

Jesus paused, then said, 'I have only come to mend what is broken – not to break what's already whole.'

'Well we're all fine, as whole as a brand new denarius, so you needn't bother yourselves with us.'

I knew that I deserved a whipping for speaking to a man in that way, for speaking to a guest of my father like that. I've never been so vicious to anyone outside of the family. The tightness of my anger felt like a hot brick in my chest. If it would have got rid of him, I'd have slapped Jesus right there in the upper room. I expected him to tell Dad to beat me.

But what he said took my breath away, 'When you understand the truth Susannah, this passion in your heart will set Galilee alight for me. Your fire will turn the lake to gold.'

He held his broad hand out to me across the room. But I was too angry to take it. I looked straight at him, and was shocked by the expression in his eyes. There was no anger there, only love.

Jesus went down to the family, and I sat on Gran's mattress and replayed the entire scene again in my head. I could hear Gran downstairs, fussing and stirring and worriting. She sounded fine, back in her element, serving the Passover meal prepared before yesterday's sun-down, to our guests.

I couldn't accept what Jesus had done, but wanted to know what tricks he uses.

After a while I slipped quietly out of the house. It was a clear bright afternoon, with warmth in the winter sun. I went down to the harbour and clambered into one of Dad's small rowing boats. It was the Sabbath, so I couldn't row anywhere. I simply lay in the moored boat and looked up at the sky, watching the swifts circle and swoop above me, free as I longed to be. Unhindered by gender, law and tradition. They don't have to observe the Sabbath, or get betrothed. I could hear pigeons cooing from the rooftops, and sparrows tweeting monotonously in the olive trees.

I fell asleep and started to dream, I could see Jesus out on the lake in a boat and he was calling to me, 'Susannah, Susannah!'

Opening my eyes with a start, I saw Dad's brown face leaning over me in the boat, calling my name. His head seemed dark and brooding with its frame of bright sky behind.

'Oh Susannah, when will you ever learn? You deserve a beating for disobedience and for ignoring our guest. Why do you always live on the very edge of the law? It can't go on. I don't understand why God created you with a mind to think – you'd have been better with a woman's empty head.

Sometimes when I look at you, I see myself at your age, full of anger and impossible dreams. You must learn to accept things - if you lived anywhere in Judaea or Samaria you would have a terrible life, hemmed in by Scribes and Pharisees. You know what they say about us Galileans – that we're lawless yokels. I've been far too patient with you, and your betrothal is long overdue.'

'Oh Dad, please, please let me go on living here with you and Momma and Joseph. I'll be so good you won't regret it. And you need me to keep your accounts in order, to help with the business - and I would die of a broken heart if I ever had to leave the lake. It feeds my heart and I need it to breathe.' As I begged, I tugged at Dad's Sabbath cloak urgently.

'You know I understand Susannah, I love the lake with a passion too. I've lived and worked all my life on these shores and waters. I know every inlet, every twist of the shoals, every breath of breeze is like a mother's caress. But I'm going to have to leave too.'

'Where, go where? Why must you leave? That's crazy Dad.'

'If Jesus needs me to go with him, I'll go. I've promised.'

'Don't talk to me about that creep, that home-wrecker. I wish he'd never come here with his stories and his piercing stare.'

The tears welled up and pricked my eyelids. I couldn't cry in front of Dad. But the tears wouldn't stop, 'I love you Dad, you're the rock in my life, please don't ever go away.'

Even though it was the Sabbath, and any Pharisee would curse him for going near the tools of his trade, Dad climbed down into the boat beside me, and hugged me as if I were still his little girl. As I sobbed he squeezed me and said, 'Don't be afraid, be strong for Momma and Joseph. You'll be in charge when I'm away.'

I knew at that moment, with a certainty that will never leave me, that I've lost my Dad to the man from Nazareth.

I avoid Jesus now. When he comes into the room, I go out. When people start talking about him, I change the subject. I can't deny his power, the healings prove it, but I can deny him a place in my heart.

It didn't take very long for word to get around that Jesus can cure people. Nobody really cares whether his power comes from the prophets, or the devil of hell, or even whether he's a trickster. All they care is that it works. The people he cures, like Mad Daniel and Gran, stay cured.

Mad Daniel has taken to standing on the synagogue steps telling everybody what Jesus has done for him. He shows the scars from the manacles he used to wear to protect him from his evil fits, and makes people shake his hand and ask him questions to prove he's sane, 'Go on, ask me who's Emperor, and the names of the last three prefects of Judaea – I challenge you, ask me!'

More and more travellers have arrived from the surrounding country – we've had Jews from Bethsaida and Chorazin, brown Egyptians stopping by on the trade route to Damascus, but mostly sick people coming down from Tiberias. Out of the hill in Tiberias gushes a stream of hot mineral water which the Romans use for bathing and healing. Several famous Romans have been there to benefit from the waters, and the sick travel to Tiberias from all over Syria, hoping for a cure.

Now stories have spread that the sick have a much better chance of a cure in Capernaum - from Jesus the magician - than from the hot-spring.

* * *

In the first month after Jesus arrived, we were over-run with pilgrims. I spoke to a young Jewish girl, no older than me, who had travelled to Tiberias all the way from Beersheba in the south, to get healing for her sick mother.

She described the beauty of Tiberias to me, with its new marble palace walls contrasting against deep green palms, white roofs above eucalyptus trees and purple bougainvillea. The breeze from our lake reaches all the way to the new city, and shakes the eucalyptus leaves around the hot spring. But even though she had prayed to Yahweh, and raised her eyes to the distant pink and mauve hills in prayer, her mother hadn't been healed in the hot-spring.

So our house is always full. We have visitors sleeping in the potting house and the net store, out in the courtyard and the stable. Grandpa Jonah has almost as many at his house, and Zebedee even more, because he has the biggest home in Capernaum, even though he's away so much. And hundreds sleep in tents outside the village. After only a couple of weeks, I'm longing for the peace of our old life to return.

The thing I notice about Jesus is he doesn't seem able to help it. Someone only has to look up at him with big sorrowful eyes of pain, and he simply has to heal them. You honestly would think he feels sorrier about their pain than they do themselves.

The incident that turned the trickle of visitors into a deluge, happened in our house. Jesus had been away for a few days, hoping the fuss about Mad Daniel and Gran would die down. He returned to the lake at dawn and joined Dad and Uncle Andrew on the shore for breakfast. They ate their grilled fish and bread cakes, and no doubt Dad told him he was glad Jesus was back. But I wasn't.

By supper time that day, the crowd was as big as before, and Jesus suggested he should speak to the people to try and quieten things down. Dad opened up the heavy door into our courtyard from the main street and people flocked in. I was watching from the steps of Gran's ladder, horrified to see so many dirty, smelly peasants crowding into our nice clean rooms.

Our central room is different from the other houses in Capernaum. It's so large that we can't have the usual structure of arches supporting basalt beams to take the weight of a mud and clay roof. Dad and Uncle Andrew built it too wide for that. So our roof span has wooden beams covered with reeds cut from the lake-side.

Every spring, Dad takes me with Uncle Andrew and the hired hands to gather new reeds to re-roof that main room. It means we have a lovely big space for eating, sitting and working, but we also have more room for Jesus' visitors.

That day it was impossible to squeeze one more person inside, even the tiniest child, and Jesus started talking and teaching the crowd.

My heart sank as I saw another of our wall-lamps knocked to the floor by a fat visitor's shoulders, accompanied by the familiar sound of smashing pottery, and 'Whoops sorry!'

Jesus said a lot about the coming of the Kingdom and fulfilment of the prophets. Instead of listening to him, I sat on the ladder, scanning the crowd and watching the effect he had on them. Some people had their mouths open, some piped up and asked for healing right away, and others told them to keep quiet. There were even a couple of Pharisees looking smugly on.

All of a sudden I noticed a chink of daylight above my head which hadn't been there before. I looked up and was shocked to see the bundles of reeds on the roof being parted from above. Someone was on the roof and trying to dismantle it.

'Oi, what do you think you're doing?' Dad shouted.

Jesus stopped speaking and everybody looked up.

The patch of sunlight was getting bigger every moment. We could see a blanket-sized square of sky now. Then we saw two pairs of brown hands, a pallet and two spindly legs coming through the hole in our roof. The two pairs of hands lowered the pallet on ropes to Jesus' head height.

One of the helpers leaned through the hole and called down, 'Jesus, please help us, our friend is paralysed and we couldn't get him in through the front door. Please take pity on him Master. We know you can heal him.'

Jesus went through the usual routine. He sat, head bowed, the back of his hand resting on his forehead. Praying. No-one breathed or moved.

Then he raised his right arm and his face to the patch

of sky. 'Brother, your sins are forgiven. Stand up.'

There were two amazing things about that healing. The first was what happened to the man's body. From my position on Gran's ladder, I was close behind Jesus, and after he had spoken, I actually saw the change take place in the man's twisted body.

His legs and arms were so knotted and clawed, it was perfectly obvious that they wouldn't be able to support his weight. But I saw them un-knot. I saw the life flooding back into his legs.

Slowly, gingerly, he slid one leg off the pallet on to the tiny space of floor that people had cleared for him. Then he bent his arms to give himself leverage. It was all very slow. He pushed himself forward, and Jesus held out his hand to steady the paralysed man's rise. And he stood. Every one of us could see his legs were now as healthy and straight as Joseph's. They were a bit skinny mind you, but they weren't a bad pair of legs. He stood up straight, then started to jump for joy. He whooped, his friends yelled, and the entire place burst into a frenzy of wild excitement.

The second amazing thing was the reaction of Jonas the Pharisee at the back of the room. He went mad, calling Jesus all sorts of names and telling him only God has the power to forgive sins. I think Jesus must have regretted he'd said anything about sin in the first place.

An elderly net-maker from our village shouted out, 'I don't care what you teachers of the law think – I want some of the kind of power he has!'

The paralysed man picked up his mattress and beat a path through the crowd to the door and disappeared into the street, yelling 'I've been healed, it's a miracle!' as he went.

Everybody was cheering and reaching out to shake his hand as he passed.

I think the only person who didn't watch his exit and cheer, was Jesus. He sat, head bowed, and covered his face with one hand in that way he has. I actually felt a bit sorry for him, because no-one had thanked him.

Then I remembered I hadn't ever thanked him for what he had done for Gran either. So I slipped down the ladder and crouched beside him for a moment. 'Thank you,' was all I said.

The expression in his face un-nerved me, I saw joy mixed with sadness in his eyes, 'There will be many who never thank me,' he said.

I went out, following the hoards surrounding the paralysed man – I mean, the man who used to be paralysed – and I tried to make sense of what's happening in our house and in our village. Now, the crowds come in even greater numbers, and I have to row out into the middle of the lake whenever I need peace and quiet.

Capernaum, Galilee
29th June 2003

Suddenly it hit me I was totally starving. I hadn't eaten since breakfast, and it felt longer. The site was being closed up for the day, so I made for the gate and had a chat with the very attractive ticket girl.

'Hey, had a good day?' I asked her.

'Quiet. I think most of the tour buses have diverted to Bethsaida – they've had a major find. You may want to go there tomorrow.'

'Maybe. Actually, I've been.' I showed her my ID.

'Oh, you're a professional, then you don't have to leave now. Stay as long as you want.'

'I'm dying of hunger – any chance of getting food round here?'

'You can have this if you like,' she said, passing a Mars Bar and an apple from her bag. 'I'm off home now so you're welcome to it. You should look after that body.'

She was smiling at me in a way that can only be described as a come-on. Unbelievable. No-one has come on to me since 1999, even though I've tried really hard. Now I stop trying and they start coming. What's going on?

I smiled back, but couldn't focus on her, because Susannah was still in the front of my mind. So the moment passed, and I would never take this girl to a bar. And we would never kiss. Hey-ho, now I know I'm going crazy.

The late afternoon sun had a mellow, exhausted heat, before the cooler evening air began to move. It was so good to be here alone, with only a grounds-man for company, picking up crisp packets and other twenty-first century detritus.

The incident with the ticket girl had unhinged me somehow, unlocked a hidden room in my memory. For some reason she'd made me think of Carys. I'm the first to admit that I've kept the pain and grief of losing my wife bottled up. Well and truly bottled, and sealed with a cork the size of Surrey. The pain of her leaving is still as raw as it was - maybe that's the penalty for bottling up. And I'm not ready to go there yet, but as I sat in these ruins I did replay some of my nobler moments since the divorce. Some proud, medal-winning moments in the history of love and romance.

It's true that a girl did come on to me in '99 when I was hopelessly wasted in Lanzarote. I'd booked a last minute flight that summer, far too old for the 18-30 packages, and feeling bitter about that. I had no money, even less self respect, and blamed Carys for stealing all my best years and leaving me the scraps.

But as I say, I'm not ready to go there.

I spent ten days in Lanzarote, drunk, smoking pot and taking stuff I should know better than to touch. Hey it didn't make for the holiday of a lifetime. And I eye-balled the babes on the beaches, their rounded handfuls of bronzed, sheened flesh bursting out of tight swimwear. I looked but couldn't touch, and felt I was turning into a real dirty old man. It was horrible.

The night before my return flight, a girl (drunk admittedly) tried to get off with me. We made it as far as the beach, but I was unable to complete the deal – for want of a better expression. So now I had fear of failure to add to my travel-kit. Fear that even if I was lucky enough to turn a girl on, I wouldn't be able to finish it.

After that I made any excuse to avoid intimacy. Ran the other way, made up urgent appointments, even pretended I was gay. All my bits are still in working order – if I'm working them, but the fear's still there. And I've always wondered – was I failing Carys in the bed department without realising – is that why she found the accountant?

Recently I've been trying a lot harder with women, attempting to talk to them before I make a move. But my success has been limited. Very limited. Maybe that's why Susannah is so appealing – she's unlikely to hurt me as she's dead.

The heat was ebbing so I ate the whole apple, core and all, and took my Mars wrapper to the grounds-man.

Then I wandered through the ruins, and rebuilt first century Capernaum in my head. There was no central town planning -

unlike Roman sites – but streets only a couple of metres wide, dwellings higgledy as families grew and added a store-room here, a wall there. They built with field-stones and mud, on foundations of basalt boulders.

Between the clusters of houses, streets and passages ran in curved and crooked lines. Sewage would have been thrown into the dusty streets, stinking all year in this climate. Each cluster of dwellings was built round a central courtyard, the cool heart of the home. It's most likely a family group lived in each cluster, so Peter, his brother Andrew and all their families would have lived together.

In each courtyard diggers like me have unearthed a tabun oven, fish-hooks strewn about, grinding stones, presses and net-weights. Simple undecorated oil-lamps and locally made pots and wine jars, nothing glass, nothing imported. Just plain, homely objects from a simple community.

Peter's house is one of the biggest. The third century CE Christians - unhelpfully from an archaeologist's point of view - built a church on top of it, but we can still see the original house. Almost square, the west wall still reaching a meter in height and over eight metres long, the courtyard L-shaped. There's evidence of upper rooms, a staircase, and a large ground floor living room that was too big for the usual structure of arches or inner walls supporting basalt beams. So this roof span must have had wooden beams covered with reeds. Not a very solid roof.

Before 70 CE the house had been plastered inside and was being used as an early Christian meeting place, the walls inscribed with crosses and a boat.

I tried to reckon up – if Peter was contemporary with Jesus he was born between 3 and 6 BCE, so Susannah could have been born..... I looked along the wall, and read the marker 'West 17'. 17 CE would be about right, so by 70 CE she'd be a mature woman of 53, maybe a key member of the first church here.

Date 29.06.03

To taylordenton.arch.instit@hebron.com
From boogyhen@onetel.co.uk

I'm starting to feel Susannah. She was born 17 CE and was slim – she reminds me of a lily in flower. I even turned down a date because of her. How sad is that? Are you OK? How's my shard?

Love Ben

Date 29.06.03
To boogyhen@onetel.co.uk
From taylordenton.arch.instit@hebron.com

Hi Ben, So you found out that Susannah means 'lily' in Hebrew.

The shard has been filmed, photographed and revered – but you're the only one who's touched it with bare hands. For twenty centuries.

Glad you turned down the date.

Love Taylor

Capernaum, Galilee
CE 31

I soon had evidence to support my theory that Jesus is bad news for families. One afternoon a huge crowd gathered at Zebedee's house to listen to Jesus teach. A group of Pharisees had come all the way from Jerusalem to hear him, and to pick holes in his arguments. They annoy me even more than Jesus himself - at least there's nothing superior and artificial about *him*.

I'd stayed at home to help Momma and Gran bake another stack of loaves for the visitors. Momma was singing softly indoors, and Gran was keeping an eye on the bread baking in the courtyard, stoking more fuel onto the pebbles in the bottom of the oven. I was just taking a new batch of dough to Gran when I noticed a woman and three men coming into our courtyard from the street. The woman was a widow, slightly built and dressed in black, from her veil to her toes.

She stepped forward, 'Excuse me, but we're looking for Jesus. We heard he is staying here.'

'That's right,' I said, sighing - these days you can't get anything done for dealing with his visitors, 'I'll take you to him.'

I looked at the woman again, assessing her quiet beauty, and feeling the pull of her eyes which were like two deep wells of sadness.

'I'm his mother, and these are his brothers,' she said.

'Have you just walked from Nazareth?' I asked her.

'My sons have walked, but I rode on one of our beasts.'

'I will fetch you wine and bread, you must be thirsty after the journey,' I said, running indoors. I felt troubled, certain Jesus' family wouldn't have come for him unless there was a problem at home. And his mother looked so sad.

When they had eaten and drunk enough to refresh them, I led Jesus' family across the adjoining courtyard past Grandpa Jonah's to Zebedee's house. I was grateful that for once the entrance wasn't blocked with tourists.

'Wait here please, and I'll ask Jesus to come out,' I said.

I blinked as I crossed the threshold from sunlight into the dark house, and I began to thread my way between the crowd of people who were covering every cubit of floor space. As usual, they were very quiet, straining to hear Jesus' words.

When I got to the front of the crowd, I touched the hem of his tunic and whispered, 'Excuse me Jesus, but your mother and brothers are outside looking for you. Could they have a word?'

I could have hit him in the mouth when he answered, 'Who are my mother and my brothers?' and motioning at the seated crowd, *'These* people are my mother and my brothers. This is my family.'

'But they've walked all the way from Nazareth to see you!' I said, 'and you won't give them the time of day. What if it's something important?'

'Nothing is more important than feeding these lambs,' he replied.

I was appalled, and felt stupid and foolish picking my way back through the people to his family outside.

I tried to find the right words, 'Jesus is really busy at the moment,' I said limply, 'maybe you could see him later, when he's finished teaching the people.' I looked at his mother's sad eyes, and added, 'I'm so sorry, he wants to see you, but everybody makes demands on him, healings, requests, you know…' my voice tailed away.

'Healings, my eye. He's a carpenter, not a prophet,' said one of his brothers, 'come on mother, we've wasted our time. Let's get back home, we shouldn't have left Jude alone for so long.'

'Could you tell Jesus,' his mother said to me, 'that we miss him in Nazareth. Tell him I understand, but I want him to return home to me once, before what must come to pass.'

'I'll tell him – but are you sure you won't wait?'

'No, these people need him,' she said, 'and there will be many who come after this time who yearn to hear the words that you hear. You're very blessed that he's with you.'

'Come on mother, he's not worth bothering with,' said the tallest brother.

I watched the little party make their way back to the Nazareth road. One of the brothers un-tethered a donkey from the shade of an olive tree. He lifted his mother onto its back as if she were as light as an empty pannier. They didn't look back, but I watched them padding softly uphill, his mother so small and still young. I will never forget that image of three robed men walking away, and a woman saddled on a donkey.

So now I know - Jesus doesn't respect family values, and he doesn't even care about his own family. I've been right to call him a home-wrecker. I know his father is dead, and that makes it even worse. As a widow, his mother deserves his complete support - every good Jewish man knows that.

One evening, a week or so later, Dad spent the entire day with Jesus in the hilly country to the west of Galilee. He came home very late that night and said from now on he'll be calling himself, not Simon, but Peter - the rock. 'It's the name Jesus has given me. He's appointed twelve of us to be his messengers – he said the Greek word "apostle" is the best way of describing it, so that's what he's calling us.'

'What's it going to involve?' asked Momma.

'It means we're his team - we'll co-ordinate his movements and arrange time and space for him to be alone. We'll just be with him, and help him say and do what he's got to say and do.'

'How long does he need you for?'

'A month, a couple of years, who knows? Until all the people of the promised land have heard his message, I guess. Andrew, James and John are included in the team of twelve – so we'll be four short on the boats.'

'Four short!' Momma burst out, 'You're the four who run it – apart from you we've only got the hired hands!'

For the first time, Momma was exasperated, 'How will we feed ourselves Simon? How will I manage?'

'We'll manage – Susannah will run the pickling and potting, she's more than capable, and Zebedee will take care of the men and the boats, and the export business. We'll get by.'

'But he's always in Jerusalem. We may get by Simon, but at the cost of this family's happiness!'

'I never expected you to react like this,' Dad shouted, and swept up his cloak, 'I'm going out.'

'You've only just come in,' said Momma, once he was out of ear-shot. Then she crumpled into a heap on the hearth, like a little lost girl. I swept the flag-stones clean, stacked the bowls of meat and beans that Dad hadn't touched, and snuffed out the fire, 'Come on Momma, everything will seem better in the morning,' I said.

But the next day was even worse. Dad was working on the lake and he didn't come home. I spent all day in the potting house, packing the fish into terracotta jars - and marking the lids with our seal, with its little picture of a boat, a fish and a reed. After I had pressed the imprint of the seal into the lid, I scratched a mark to say whether the jar held smoked fish, or dried, salted or pickled. I worked right through the day and tried to make up for Dad's absence by doubling my usual efforts.

The sun was already setting when I returned to Momma in the house. Joseph was home from school and studying the papyrus given to him by the teachers at the synagogue. I could tell he was trying to keep out of Momma's way.

She had lit every oil lamp in the house, and was sweeping and moving pots and mats as if she was half frantic. As soon as I walked into the main room, she started to cry, 'Susannah, I don't know what to do - I've lost a drachma.'

'It's not the end of the world Momma, they're worth less than half a shekel, even without Dad working, we can afford to lose one drachma.'

'No, you don't understand – it's a drachma from my wedding head-dress – I have to find it. I know it's a sign, why else would it happen today? You know the disgrace for a woman who loses part of her bridal gown – it's fore-telling the end of my marriage.'

Momma never stopped sweeping and searching, and I

got down on my knees and helped her to look between the flagstones. Her bridal head-dress was laid out on the wooden table, so lovely with its colourful embroidery and tassels. There in the centre, hung the row of nine perfectly matched silver coins, and one space like a gap in a row of teeth. All around the floor Momma had opened chests and jars, turning the house upside down in her frenzied search.

'It means that I've lost Simon,' she repeated over and over.

While we were still searching, Jesus came into the house. He took the papyrus from Joseph, rolled it up firmly, and bopped him on the head with it, 'You should be helping Momma, little man.'

'But sweeping is women's work,' Joseph said.

'Finding the lost is every man's work, there is no higher calling,' said Jesus, and he got right down on his knees and helped Momma search for her lost coin.

'Have you looked inside the meal jars?' Jesus asked her.

'I've looked everywhere.'

'Look again!' he said.

To humour him, Momma stood up and walked wearily to the red jars where she keeps meal and flour. She lifted a lid.

'It's here! I've found it!' she shrieked, running to Jesus and kissing him on one, then the other cheek. 'It was here all the time! Run Joseph, fetch Grandma Tabitha and Aunt Deborah. We'll open a new wine-skin to celebrate. I've found my wedding coin!'

Momma held up the perfect silver coin with its little hole which would fix it to her head-dress.

Jesus just smiled and smiled and said, 'Great is the

rejoicing in heaven when one of the lost is found.'

Now, whenever I hear him tell the parable of the lost coin to the crowds, I smile to myself and remember it was our story.

There are times when the constant pressure of the crowds is too much even for Jesus. Dad and Uncle Andrew try hard to give him time alone, and time with the other men he's calling his apostles.

One morning Dad woke me up even earlier than usual and asked me to go with them across the lake. He and Jesus think alike about Galilee, because in a boat you can escape from Herod and Philip's territories by water to the Greek Decapolis. Dad often laughs to Jesus, 'We can play cat and mouse with Herod Antipas when he comes after us – the water's our friend.'

The eastern side of Galilee is wild and inhospitable, and I've only been there a handful of times before. Dad had decided to make for Gergesa which you can see from Capernaum. The hills on that side are steep and rocky, and the ground always looks burnt up and scored with gashes – the cuts left by the gullies which race down to the lake in the rainy season.

Beyond the Gergesene hills is wild desert country, the Greek Decapolis, peopled mostly by nomadic goat-herds – I've never been up there and people say it's a land of witches and devilry. Gergesa can look really lovely from a distance though, when the evening sun turns the heights to gold and purple, a patchwork of light and deep shadow.

Fourteen of us squeezed into the boat before dawn, and I sat with Jesus and Judas Iscariot in the aft deck. I like Judas, 'the man of Kerioth', he's the only southerner among the apostles. I like his sophistication and intelligence, so shrewd and thoughtful in comparison with us passionate Galileans. Jesus has asked him to be the group's organiser, and he has such potential for leadership. Judas never stops challenging Jesus whenever they're together.

All the way across the lake that morning, he nattered to Jesus about the coming of the Messiah, and the importance of getting rid of the Romans. That's his favourite subject – he's absolutely convinced the Messiah of Israel will rise up with a mighty army and sort the occupying powers out for good. It doesn't matter who you mention, Judas wants rid of them all - Greeks, Herod, the Romans and the Jewish authorities. He's yearning for a time of peace and prosperity for God's people, and he's utterly sincere. As Dad and the others rowed, Judas was lecturing on his idea to set up an army, using Jesus' healing power to mobilise a force that will turn our land around. I could follow a man of action like that, he is inspiring.

We landed at first light, and I made my way up the shore with Jesus while the men made a safe mooring. I felt my skin prickle all over because we were so near to the Gergesa tombs. This is a place of defilement, fear and darkness.

Suddenly, in the eerie half-light, I thought I saw a shadowy, hairy creature coming out of the tombs, half-man, half-beast. I moved very close to Jesus and my breathing became shallow and quick.

'Don't be afraid Susannah, I'm with you,' he said, putting his arm around me.

'What is it – who is it? And what's that horrible scraping, clanging noise?' I asked.

Before Jesus could answer, the creature let out a blood-curdling scream. It was too much for me, I clutched at Jesus' sleeve and clung to him.

Then I began to make out words in the screaming, 'What do you want with me? Son of the Most High God, Don't torture me!' and his scream plunged from a shrill call to a deep throaty growl. The creature was yelping and dancing like a rabbit on hot bricks, he had lengths of broken chains hanging from his ankles and wrists.

Dad and the others came running from the boat, 'Susannah - keep away from him, get behind me,' called Dad, but I felt safe close to Jesus.

As the creature came nearer, Jesus stood perfectly still, then raised his hand and called, 'What is your name?'

'Legion – because there are many of us, leave us alone, Son of God!' and the creature started to laugh with a crazy, wild laugh.

'Evil spirit, come out of this man!' called Jesus.

The creature's screaming and flailing intensified, and I saw froth bubbling from its mouth.

'Come *out* of him!' Jesus commanded.

There was a rushing of air, my cloak flapped around my legs and a coldness went through me. Wind ripped through the tombs and then suddenly, we heard a baying and honking above our heads. I looked up and saw a herd of pigs on the cliff above the shore. They were screeching and dancing, just like the wild man. What happened next was disgusting and I hate the very memory of it. We dislike pigs at the best of times, because they're unclean, but I can't bear any creature to suffer. The entire herd of pigs, hundreds of them, started to leap and run towards the lake. From their feeding ground on the hills, they stumbled and tumbled and fell from the cliffs, all the time braying and screeching, as they plummeted into the water. It was horrible. I turned away in tears at the sight, and Jesus put his arm around me, stroking my shoulder.

'Satan, you spoiler of my Father's creation,' he said, 'you shall not have the victory.'

Then I felt someone else tugging at Jesus' robe, 'Thank you, thank you, you've saved me sir!' It was the horrible hairy mad-man.

I yelped and leapt away before I fully understood he wasn't mad any more. His eyes were clear and bright and he was speaking intelligible Greek. Jesus hugged him – dirt, hair, sweat and all.

'You're free now, give thanks to God for what He has done,' Jesus replied in Greek.

'Oh sir, promise me the evil spirits will never come back.'

'You're free of them, have no more fear.'

'But I'm a Greek, before the evil came over me, I used to be a swine-herd, raising pork for the Decapolis. So why has your God - the God of the Jews, heard my prayer?'

'My God is God of all the world. Return to your people and keep from sinning.'

The man scurried away, jumping and whooping for joy.

We had gone to Gergesa for some peace and quiet, and it hadn't started well. And now a group of swine-herds who must have been tending the pigs, shouted down to us in Greek. I didn't understand all of it, but I assume it was pretty abusive. They had just lost their entire livelihood.

Dad decided it would be a good moment to take the

boat further up-shore towards the Jordan delta, where the best fish are caught.

I lay in the bottom of the boat for the rest of the day, while Jesus took the twelve ashore and spoke to them in private. I wanted an explanation of the power I'd seen, and my head was full of questions. All day long I thought of the hairy mad-man with running sores, and scars on his legs from the broken manacles, and who Jesus had brought back to life. I wondered what the swine-herd will say to his fellow Greeks - I feel sure that healing a Gentile will get Jesus into trouble.

But most of all, I thought about the sensation of Jesus holding me, and of the absolute security I had felt. It was a bit like one of Momma's hugs while Dad is out on the lake in a storm, but Jesus' hug was bigger and stronger. He kind of hugged me on the inside as well as the outside.

'But I hate him, I hate him, I hate him,' I called up at the sky, knowing that all I wanted was for him to hold me again. Then for no reason at all, the tears came - running down my face and into my ears, which is what always happens if I cry when I'm lying down.

'I want him to go away,' I sobbed, 'because he frightens me. But I couldn't bear it if he left.' The sun carried on beating down, and the swifts screeched and circled above, and something melted inside me, as I admitted to myself that I need him.

Not long afterwards, I said to Dad, 'It's funny but I'd miss Jesus now if he went away, I like the excitement.'

'Well, you'll have to get used to it, because he's going home to Nazareth.'

My heart missed a beat, 'Going for good?'

'We don't know, he's taking James and John with him

67

and wants to celebrate Purim with his mother.'

'She'll be glad to see him,' I said, remembering her sorrowful eyes.

That night I prayed to Yahweh that Jesus would come back to us again.

Capernaum, Galilee
29th June 2003

The apple and Mars Bar didn't do much for my raging hunger, and haven't done a whole lot more for my brain – because all the time I've been examining the ruins of Susannah's childhood home, I've been getting more and more dissatisfied with my love life past and present.

I'm convinced Susannah wasn't married – don't ask me why, but I reckon she never found the right guy. I was born too late.

And that's got me thinking about Carys again, we should never have married. We first met in a place just like this – a hot summer excavation. I was almost 23 and she was a lot younger, enough to make me feel guilty. I'd noticed her of course, along with all the other pre-university volunteers, noticed her petite figure and posh voice, and enjoyed practising my passion for photography when she was around. But apart from that, I kept my distance, afraid my mates would call me a cradle snatcher.

And I wouldn't have approached her. Unlike Susannah, I had no feeling of rightness, connection with Carys. She was just an attractive teenager.

But like most of the major events of my life, it all started because of the beer. We were sitting round the camp one night, on the edge of the desert near Abu Simbel, about a dozen of us who had decided to sleep out to keep cool. Me, Ned Walters (I wonder what happened to him?) and a herd of the female students. And I was fooling about, which was my usual style in those days, my only style in fact. We were having a drinking game, and the kid son of the site director was beating us all hands down – probably because he was ten beers behind the rest of us. And Carys kept laughing at every joke I cracked. Really laughing, throwing her head back and boring her eyes into me, making me feel like a fully paid-up comic. The stars were winking, diamond pinpricks on a huge velvet canopy, and life felt so bloody good.

The others went to bed and she stayed for one last beer, so

I was a sitting target. When she leaned against me and giggled, it was the easiest thing in the world to slip my arm round her waist. And when she lifted her mouth to my face, it was even easier to run my fingers through her baby-soft cropped hair and let her kiss me. There's something about desert nights that would make me reckless, even without a belly-full of beer.

She'd probably deny it, but it was Carys who proposed to me rather than the other way round.

We were in Amsterdam the following February, and it was colder than a polar bear's pantry. We'd been seeing each other on and off since the summer, and she'd escaped after her mock A' levels to spend an illicit weekend with me. Carys' parents weren't my biggest fans and I can't say I blamed them. Even at that age I looked hairy and unconventional, hardly the promising young graduate with a future.

It was sleeting as Carys took my hand and pulled me through the market into a steamy coffee-shop. She bought two hot chocolates with mountains of cream on top and daubed a dollop on my unshaven chin, 'I love you Ben Henshaw,' she said, her brown eyes glinting with light.

'Hey, that sounds serious.'

'Oh but it is!' she replied, with the utter sincerity of youth and wealth, 'Does it annoy you that I've said it?'

I remember feeling nervy. Didn't want to hurt her feelings, I hate hurting anyone. 'No of course not. It's just, a bit ..... sudden?' I looked at her questioningly.

'We've been together six months, I don't call that sudden,' she said. Her elfin face was troubled now.

'And you're right, I'm just not good at the serious stuff, and hey, I guess I love you too.' It was what she wanted to hear. I'd never said the words in my life, and they felt disjointed.

'Oh Ben, do you, do you? I'm so happy.'

I glanced round the café awkwardly, this was really embarrassing.

At dinner that night (Carys insisted on paying for us to eat in a proper restaurant, and Amsterdam is *not* cheap), we drank two bottles of wine and she asked me, 'Ben, did you mean it earlier when you said you loved me?'

I looked at her across the table, sitting in a warm pool of cream candle-light and the wine worked its way to my brain, 'Yes Carys I did.'

'Then will you marry me?' she asked with childlike simplicity, 'if it's OK for me to ask.'

'Wow! That's a big question.'

'But I always ask when I want something, it's the only way. And you're so funny and intelligent – if I don't ask you now, someone else will.'

That really made me laugh, 'Yeah, like they're queuing up. You're a gem Carys, so naïve. Let's get married, if your Dad doesn't blow a fuse.'

'Daddy always gives in when I want something.'

And she was right. That night was the best we ever had, as we walked back to the hotel I felt truly happy and loved, admired even. Knowing I could do a whole lot worse than marry Carys. Ironic really, I spent the next twelve years trying to make it work, and she didn't.

There's no-one to blame for marrying her but myself.

Capernaum, Galilee
CE 31

Jesus stayed away for ten weeks, right through the rainy season before Purim. I counted every Sabbath and there were ten of them. At first the crowds still came just like before, then Dad put up a sign on the Damascus road, and one on the southern road to Jerusalem. They read, 'Jeesus of Nazruth haz lefft Capurneeum.' Dad was never a reader or writer.

The signs didn't stop people trying of course. For the first few weeks after Jesus left, the crowds still beat a path to our door and asked for him. It broke your heart to see the cripples, the blind and the poor. They'd pinned all their hopes on finding Jesus, and you felt like a robber for taking their hope away.

After a while, the crowds thinned out and life pretty much returned to normal. It was so good to see Dad back on the boats with Uncle Andrew, washing the trammel net after a night's fishing, unloading the catch into baskets in the harbour, and checking his precious throw nets for holes. But he didn't have the same lightness of spirit as before. Often I found him sitting on the shore at dusk, wrapped in his cloak, thinking.

Purim came and went, and I started to scan the skies every day, watching for the cranes to start flying across the lake on their way north, just as they do every year. You can set your calendar by them - immediately after every Purim they come. Dad says they're travelling north from Egypt. For thirty days they fly across the lake, at a great height, with the sun shining on their white feathers, making them look like mannah from heaven against the blue sky. Their wings beat slowly as they wheel in the air, thousands of birds at a time, circling for an hour or more. I always imagine they're contemplating dropping down to the lake for a drink and a rest, but they never, ever descend. Something makes up their minds, and the flock sets off north toward Mount Hermon. It's the first sign of spring, and every day more birds come, until you think that Egypt must be over-run with them. Then suddenly, they stop coming, and the skies are empty again.

The very day after the last flock of cranes flew over, Jesus came back to us.

I was walking towards the shore to call Joseph in for supper when he came. Dad was in the boat, a few yards from the shore, and Joseph was sitting on a rock annoying a black lizard with a twig.

Suddenly I heard Dad shriek, 'It's the Master!' and I saw him leap into the water from the side of the boat. He was wearing only a long cotton tunic and a girdle. He strode through the water towards a man on the beach.

Then I recognised him, 'Jesus!' My heart flipped over and I ran too.

Dad threw his arms round Jesus and slapped him on the back, 'Welcome, welcome home Master, it's so good to see you! I haven't settled to anything while you've been away. How was Nazareth, and how are James and John? Come home and eat with us.'

Jesus was smiling and laughing at Dad's eagerness, 'I saw the sign on the road, and knew you'd written it Peter. I've thought of you and prayed for you constantly. I'm sorry I've taken away your privacy, your normality,' and he looked at me as he said that bit.

I wanted to tell him I'm glad he's back, but the words

wouldn't come.

'Susannah,' he said with laughter in his eyes, 'my little vixen – the one who bites me to protect her family.'

I desperately don't want to be thought of as vicious, I want him to care about me, like he does for Dad.

Momma and Gran and I busied ourselves to prepare a really special supper to welcome Jesus home again. We made mutton stew with lentils, plates of grilled fish, orange and lemon cakes and our best wine. He's always a thankful guest, and appreciates the trouble we've gone to, not like Dad and Uncle Andrew and all the men in our family. Ever since the incident over the lost drachma, Jesus has been like a second son to Momma. She won't hear a bad word said about him.

After we'd eaten, Dad asked Jesus 'Tell us about Nazareth, everything.'

'Let's talk about Capernaum instead,' Jesus said, 'there's nothing good to say about Nazareth. As far as everybody in my home village is concerned, I'm just the carpenter's son - they can't accept my teaching, "Who does he think he is?" "Give us a break – he's only Jesus, Mary's son," they say. I'm not able to pray and heal people there, there isn't enough faith, and I lose faith myself. I missed you all, missed your love.'

'We missed you and James and John, we even missed the crowds – it was awful having to turn the sick people away,' said Dad.

'Why didn't you heal them yourself?' Jesus asked.

Dad threw his head back in a great laugh, 'Me heal them – what a joke!'

'You've heard and seen me healing people. My Father will hear you just as He hears me.'

'Are you crazy Jesus? You have a special power.'

'The power belongs to my Father in heaven, He answers me because I call out to Him with faith, that's all. I pray that you receive that same faith in time.'

The next day I found Joseph in the rabbit pen, trying to heal a rabbit's broken leg. He was squeezing up his face and shouting, 'Get up, your sins are forgiven, you can walk!' I watched him try three or four times, cursing and kicking up a cloud of dust every time it didn't work. He shouted, 'Jesus says get up!' Then, 'Oh suit yourself - your trouble is you haven't got enough faith.'

That afternoon Dad burst in unexpectedly, 'Jesus is sending me on a mission with the other eleven apostles.' He always comes out with shocking comments when Momma is too busy too argue. This time, she was washing tunics in the courtyard, lifting water from the cistern and beating them clean on the flagstones.

'I'll be away for some time.'

'Hhmmm,' said Momma absent-mindedly.

'He doesn't want us to take anything with us, just go from house to house relying on hospitality, telling people about the coming of God's Kingdom and the need to repent. Andrew will write to you for me. Often.'

'Don't put your dusty feet on the linen Simon,' said Momma. I stood in the shade of our door lintel and felt my spirits sink. Jesus was going away again.

Dad invited all eleven apostles to our home for a farewell supper on their last evening at home. Zebedee, Grandpa Jonah and Grandma Tabitha were invited too. During the afternoon, I set out all our mats and cushions in a huge double circle around the fire in the middle of our main room. I swept, set bowls and cups and laid clean reeds beneath every place. Then I brought in spring flowers from the fields to make the place pretty; white Rose of Sharon, the blood red scarlet anemone, pink flax, and blue iris. I'd thought of everything.

'It looks pretty as a wedding party,' said Momma when she came indoors.

We served enough food to keep a Roman legion on the march. Dad and James had too much wine and got noisy and boisterous, and Jesus was full of encouragement for everyone for their mission, 'Remember what I've told you, keep faith with each other, be slow to anger and quick to forgive.'

'Aren't you going with them Jesus?' Zebedee asked.

'No, I have work to do here.'

'Where are you staying while they're away? Come to us!' roared Zebedee, 'we'll be glad of you when we're two sons short!'

My heart was in my mouth as I waited for Jesus to answer.

'Thank you Zebedee, but this is my home - until the last days.'

He has said it, our home is his home, he's part of our family, and I'm never going to lose him.

Just at that moment, an oil lamp in one of the wall niches went out. I noticed the glow flicker, grow smaller and then snuff out altogether. No-one commented, but I noticed the lamp on the stand beside the main door was flickering too. In my pride at preparing the room I had forgotten to top up the lamps. They're always refilled at the same time, so I knew all of them must be running out of oil. The second lamp went out, and a third started to flicker.

'Susannah ~ the lamps are going out ~ didn't you fill them?' Dad said.

'I'm sorry, I tried to remember everything, sorry!' I said.

'What an insult to our guests ~ they can't drink in the dark. Quick, fetch a jar of oil!'

Feeling stupid and embarrassed, I went from lamp to lamp, pouring oil into the circular holes in the tops and re-lighting the hot wicks.

As I reached behind Jesus to refill the last lamp, he turned to me and said, 'Don't feel embarrassed, your lamps will spread the message of the Kingdom.'

* * *

I didn't feel any better, but appreciated his gentleness.

The next morning, we all went to see Dad off. Jesus walked with us as far as the main Damascus road. He had paired the men up to travel together, Dad and Uncle Andrew were heading for Tyre and Sidon, Judas and Philip to Cana, James and John to Samaria. None of them had a bag or a purse or staff, not even a change of tunic. Momma was really fretting about that. But Jesus said to her, 'Don't worry Momma, our Father provides for the fishes and the birds, He isn't going to let Peter starve. Trust Him!'

'Let me give him a few shekels though,' she begged.

Dad laughed and held out his hands to take the coins from Momma. Then he lifted his strong brown arm and tossed them as far as he could, into the lake. We watched them fall, like drops of silver rain, into the water.

Jesus threw his head back and laughed, 'And God go with you, walk in faith and feed my lambs!'

We watched the six pairs of men stride away from us, to all four corners of our land, the short and the tall, stout and slim. Some looked back and waved to us, but Dad and Judas never turned their heads once. I knew Dad was dying to get started.

Everything felt flat after they had gone, and Jesus took himself off to pray – I've never known a person do so much praying.

I went back to my work in the potting house, thinking with delight that since Jesus came back, Dad has completely forgotten about my betrothal. And now he's gone away, I'm needed at home. It feels wonderful.

I was singing while I sorted and weighed the dried fish. Suddenly I heard a shout. I covered my head and went out into the hot sun of the main street to hear what was the matter. Timothy, son of the Tanner was leaping along the flat roofs of the street, jumping from roof-top to roof-top in his excitement. He brushed past the women who were weaving and drying flax on their house-tops, and past Jesus who was praying on Gran's roof.

Timothy was shrieking, 'The Baptist is dead, John the Baptist is murdered by Herod!'

I heard a groan go up from the neighbours, and something like a moan from Jesus above me. Jesus called to the boy, 'Come and tell me what you've heard!'

I ran up our outside ladder to get nearer, and Timothy bounded back towards Jesus, 'Herod has murdered the Baptist! His wicked wife – Herodias the adulteress – demanded the head of the Baptist on a plate for her daughter. And Herod gave it – because he was full of lust for the princess. It's true – one of Herod's servants has just been to fetch some papyrus and he told my Dad all about it. The Baptist is murdered!' and he leaped away again to tell the rest of the village.

Jesus slumped down on the flat roof-top, 'Oh Father, save your people – end this wickedness!'

Capernaum, Galilee
29th June 2003

What a day! When my head couldn't take another thing, it happened.

Just as I was leaving the site, tired and famished, a small blue Fiat pulled up at the entrance.

The young ticket girl stepped out of the driver's door, wearing fresh clothes. A crisp shirt, pedal pushers, her dark, polished hair loose on olive shoulders. I assumed she had come back for an evening shift.

'Hi!' she called.

'Er hi!'

'Thought you might still be here. I've brought you supper.'

She seemed shy now, perhaps regretting her boldness.

I couldn't believe it – no-one has ever done anything thoughtful like this before – probably why I'm so scrawny – I've never been fed by a woman. (Carys fed herself lettuce and organic lentils, but she doesn't count.)

The girl stood, awkwardly, her car engine still running.

I knew I had to say something to break the tension, 'I was wondering, sounds mad, but I'm planning to spend the night outdoors, part of my research...' oh God - I realised it sounded like I was asking her to sleep with me under the stars. 'I don't mean that *you* should...it's part of my research, oh bloody hell,' I said and turned away.

She saved me by laughing. A giggle at first, then a real hearty chest laugh.

I turned and laughed back.

'Get in!' she smiled.

As the Fiat bounced along the lake-side track I asked, 'Maybe you could direct me – I need a place close to the lake, where the first century fields would have been, perhaps with a view across the water. Anywhere like that where I could sleep out. I'm not being very clear am I?'

'What are you researching?'

'First century life. Peter's family really.'

'What will you find by camping out?'

'I dunno. But I want to do it.'

'You're crazy!'

She parked and led me along an almost obsolete path. If her father saw us this wouldn't look good. She couldn't be more than eighteen.

She was very informative, and her English was remarkable. She spoke with a very soft, almost French accent. Sweet. 'This is the kind of land that was farmed until a hundred years ago. The soil's fertile but very stony close to the lake, and they had to eke out crops from it. Ploughing, sowing, harvesting. But they had their fishing too.'

I spotted a large flat rock, 'This will do. I can camp here.'

She had brought a picnic of fresh bread, goat's cheese, tomatoes, olives and water, still cold from her parents' chiller. Absolute bloody heaven.

I ate in silence and she hugged her knees and looked across the water.

Dusk came suddenly, and darkness dropped on us like a blanket. One by one, lights appeared in the opposite hills, reflected on the still waters.

The girl stood up and then sat again, very close to me on the rock, her side almost touching mine.

This was getting very dangerous.

I said, 'Hey, I don't know your name,' regretting it immediately, the words sounding like a chat-up line.

'Names don't matter,' she said and leaned her arm against mine, 'but it's Ruth.'

'Oh but they matter completely,' I stammered, leaning back on to my opposite elbow, putting space between us without looking rude, 'like today I found out that Susannah means lily in Hebrew.'

'So?' She went quiet. Then, 'Who's Susannah? Your girl-friend?'

'No I haven't got one.' Oh damn it. Damn it, I thought, you stupid bloody fool. 'Hadn't you better get back – it's dark,' I said, stating the obvious. It was then I realised that by lying back on my elbow I was now horizontal. It hadn't been intentional.

There was a stillness between us and a late swift flew low above, screeching into the new night. I hoped she wouldn't jump me, but I wanted her to. My heart was thumping. Usually when I'm in this situation I'm half-cut. It would be so easy to imagine she was Susannah.

With one simple move Ruth turned and leaned over me, her mouth centimetres from mine, 'Kiss me, please,' she said softly.

This was terrible. I bounded off the rock, on the verge of doing a Ben – apologise, grovel, waffle in embarrassment.

Then I felt a peace coming from nowhere and spoke, 'Ruth, I'm forty-one, you're almost a child. I've never said this to a girl before.' I stumbled for the right words, 'Please believe, your kindness touches me deep down, but it would be wrong for me to take advantage of this situation. Love matters. I'm going to walk you back to the car now, say goodnight, and always remember you.'

We walked back in silence. She looked awful and I felt like a sod.

As she unlocked her car, she raised her eyes and said, 'Sorry, what must you think of me?'

'Don't apologise. I think you're lovely, and you've been part of a very special day. Take care, be happy.'

I watched her tail-lights disappear and felt a dull ache in my groin.

Bloody, bloody hell. What's happening to my life?

But the beauty of tonight. The stars. I've never felt such calm, and I replayed every minute of the evening before I finally fell asleep to the sound of the lake waves purring at the shore edge. I couldn't wait to email Taylor.

Capernaum, Galilee
CE 31

Jesus has been really depressed after Herod killed the Baptist. I reckon he needs Dad and John to chat to, but they'll be away for weeks. He goes out early every morning and late every evening, to think and pray.

One night I decided to follow him. He took the shore path going south towards Magdala, and I walked a few paces behind, keeping my eyes fixed on his pale robed outline. It was a starry, clear night, but with no moon. When he stopped, I stopped, and while he walked, I crept as quietly as a lizard.

Eventually he sat down on a large flat lump of basalt, looking south-east across the lake, to the narrowest part where it comes to a point. I crouched down in the grasses and waited. I was sure he didn't know I was there.

'Ah dear,' he sighed out loud, 'what terrible things they say about her. Peter's daughter. Ah dear!'

My ears pricked and strained as I tried to hear more, but Jesus spoke into the breeze and his words blew away from me.

'And her potential was obvious. It's a pity.'

I couldn't bear it, 'What, what do they say about me?' I burst out from my hiding place in the reeds.

'Why were you following me?' he asked in a low voice.

'Tell me what they say about me, why is it a pity?'

'If you creep about in the dark, you may stumble on sharp edges and get hurt. Learn a lesson tonight and stay in the light where everyone sees clearly.'

'But I wanted to know where you go, and what you do when you go out.'

'So why didn't you ask me?'

'Because I didn't want you to think I was nosey.'

'Oh Susannah, there's no point trying to cover up what's staring me in the face. You love to know what's going on, and you have a man's courage in a girl's body. But what would the villagers say if they knew you were creeping about after me in the dark? You'll get a reputation. They would think your feelings are inappropriate.'

I was thankful for the darkness which hid the fire in my cheeks, 'Well I won't make the mistake of being interested in you again. I was only worried because you've been so quiet since the Baptist died. You ought to appreciate that I'm looking out for you,' I shouted angrily.

He was quiet for a terrifying moment. Then, 'My little friend,' he said, 'your love is more valuable to me than a precious jewel. It will break your heart, and it will save you. What I'm going to say tonight I'll never repeat, so listen and remember.'

He looked out across the lake and beckoned, 'Come and sit on the rock below me. I understand what's in your heart Susannah. You hate me yet you love me. You resent the havoc I've wreaked in your family, but you love the excitement and the challenge I bring. You wish you were a boy so you could be one of the apostles, but are glad you're a girl so you can love me.'

I was sure he must be able to hear my heart thumping in my throat.

'The love you have for me cannot be fulfilled, but equally, it will never be corrupted, and it will become a light which shines for the whole of Galilee to see. Look across the lake at Hippos - the city on the hill - its burning lamps and lights can be seen for miles in the night sky.'

I lifted my eyes to the far shore where the Greek city of Hippos stands on the rounded hill above the south-eastern horizon. You can't see the city in the day-time when the sun's haze blurs the distant view, but at night it shines out like a beacon.

'That is how your love will shine, like the city on a hill - it can't be hidden. And because of *my* love for *you*, I'm giving you a new name tonight. You know the meaning of Susannah don't you?'

'Um, it's lily,' I whimpered.

'So you will be my Lily of the Field, growing white and pure, beautiful but tender. Whenever I call you by this name, you will remember that I loved you first with my Father's love, and your heart was big enough to love me in return. You will suffer very much, but my Father will bring something beautiful out of that pain.'

We sat, he and I, hugging our knees and looking out across the ruffled water. I couldn't take it all in, and didn't fully understand, but I stopped feeling so guilty.

'And now I'll tell you what I think about the Baptist,' he said. 'My heart bleeds for what Herod has done. We must pray for his repentance, for Herodias and the princess. But I trust my Father completely, the Baptist's work is done, and the way is made ready. I'll never forget my baptism in the Jordan, and the look in John's eyes that day, as he saw right into my Father's Kingdom.'

'Why do you always say "My Father"? You know it's blasphemous - we mustn't address Yahweh like that, it's forbidden by the Law.'

'The Law is made to serve Man, not Man to serve the Law, and I haven't come to abolish the Law, but to fulfil it. The day is fast approaching when every man, woman and child may call Yahweh Father. He is making a new covenant with His people, one that will last for ever.'

Suddenly he clapped his hands to his knees, 'It's late - we must go home now.'

We walked back to Capernaum side by side, and Jesus had me rocking with laughter as he told me stories about Dad and Uncle Andrew – or The Ferryman as Jesus calls him. He can make his voice sound just like them, Dad with his loud raucous bark, and Uncle Andrew's soft apologetic murmur.

We said goodnight, and when I awoke next morning, there was a single, freshly-picked lily of the field at the bottom of my ladder.

From then on I've loved him - passionately, protectively, with the dependency of an infant, and the thankfulness of a friend.

The crowds come all the time, and Jesus spends the whole of every day teaching and healing. It's become my job to take him food and check he's all right. Sometimes he makes me laugh, by saying things to the crowds that are meant for me, like the times when he teaches them not to worry, 'Isn't life more important than food? Look at the pigeons and the sparrows – they don't sow or reap, but your heavenly Father feeds them. And why do you worry about clothes? Look at the Lilies of the field – they don't work or spin, but not even Solomon in all his glory is dressed like a single one of these.' My heart beats faster as he says it, as I know what's coming, every time he turns his head and winks at me cheekily.

He speaks endlessly about God's Kingdom, and about

being ready, about counting others as more important than yourself, and about love. Time after time when I've taken him wine and food, I squat down on the grass, captivated by his words, drawn by his care for the people.

And the healings go on and on. We came to expect them after a while, although the visitors are always blown away by them. I always feel he heals people out of compassion, but that it's a distraction from the main event - he only wants to teach, but the people want to be cured. It makes you happy to see them though, Egyptians, Greeks and Jews alike, and I know why Jesus can't resist their out-stretched arms and pleading eyes.

It's strange, but the healing that's moved me the most, is one I never even saw. It was requested by Rufus the Centurion – Herod's Roman official who polices Capernaum.

He came to find Jesus who was teaching in our house, his heavy leather tunic creaking as he walked, and it struck me straight away that he called Jesus 'Lord.' Everyone else calls him 'Master', 'Teacher', or just plain Jesus.

'Lord,' Rufus said, 'my servant is lying at home in terrible sickness, please would you help him?' He's big as an ox, but his face was full of pain.

'Take me to your house, and I'll heal him,' Jesus said, getting up straight away.

'No Lord, I don't deserve to have you under my roof. But just say the word, and I know my servant will be healed. I'm a man with authority, and when I tell one of my men to do something, he does it – so I know your word alone is enough.'

Jesus was staggered – he said he'd never seen faith like

that in the whole of Israel, 'So go home and it will be done, just as you believed it would be!'

A little while later, Rufus came back into our house, and he practically bounded over the heads of the people seated around Jesus, 'Thank you Lord, thank you for hearing a sinner like me! My servant was healed at the very moment you gave your order. I'm an ordinary man Lord, and often a bad one, but your goodness has touched me to the core.'

Rufus is a big burly bloke, with calf muscles as thick as urns, but tears were running down the lines in his face like rivulets. He knelt before Jesus, wrapping his arms around the master's knees and called for a thank-you gift of his best wine and fruit to be brought into the house for everyone.

I stared at the shocking sight – a Roman centurion prostrate before a Jew, and thought to myself that if the Kingdom of Heaven - which Jesus talks about so much - has people in it like Rufus the Centurion who's a Gentile, then I really want to go there.

Capernaum, Galilee
30th June 2003

I woke before the first light of dawn feeling truly happy. Strange to be happy after turning down the offer of a night of passion. Last night was the first time in my life that I've been with a girl and ended up feeling good about myself. It wasn't like that when I lost my virginity. Sixth form party, bottle of white cider, older sister of one of my mates. Enough said.

And it wasn't like it with Carys, not when we made love for the first time in Egypt, or walked up the aisle of her local church.

Or with the drunk girl in Lanzarote. Obviously.

I lay on my camp bed (the flat lump of basalt) and watched the dawn sky peel through layers of purple, peach and pale blue, and wondered why I'm feeling so good.

Maybe because last night I was in control of myself, because I was sober, or because Taylor is beginning to like me. She's the first adult woman who's shown concern or interest.

Once the sunrise sky-show was over, I picked up my mobile and drafted emails to Taylor that would explain what I feel. This was the first,

To taylordenton.arch.instit@hebron.com
From boogyhen@onetel.co.uk
It's blowing me away, but you actually seem interested in me. Are you? I've never had much success with relationships, but there's something about you that really feels right.
Ben.

Too downbeat, so I tried again.

To taylordenton.arch.instit@hebron.com
From boogyhen@onetel.co.uk
Taylor, I think you're great - intelligent, caring, lovely. Would you be up for dinner? With a view to more dinners, and even breakfasts? I don't want this chance to slip by, I've done that too often.

I think I'm falling for you. Ben.

My heart was flapping under my ribs like a caged bird. I pressed the 'clear' button and held it down. That was a close one.

Capernaum, Galilee
CE 31

While Dad was away, we had a crisis. In the middle of a spring afternoon, a sudden storm swooped down on the lake, and I knew Zebedee was out on a boat with his youngest son Mark and the hired hands, using a drag net.

We get storms all year, whenever the wind turns and comes from the west, gathering force as it comes down the valleys and gorges from the high country. The lake can change from calm to rage within moments. Our sailors are terrified of a west wind - often you see them resting on their oars to sense a storm from the western heights, on its way to the lake. Then the surface froths up like a boiling cauldron on a fire, swamping small boats with waves twice as tall as a man. There isn't time to make for the safety of shore.

That day's storm was a bad one. I wrapped myself in my thickest cloak and went down to the harbour with Momma. We called and called for Zebedee and held on to each other and the harbour wall, but the wind whipped our words away.

When the worst of the storm was over, Zebedee's boat limped in. They were all safe, even Mark who's only three years older than me, but the boat was low in the water, and in tatters. There were holes in the side planks, but the mast and mast-arm were snapped. It was going to need more than a hammer and a couple of nails to put it right, but Dad and the others were miles away. Zebedee got the boat pulled onto the shore while we all stood helpless, quietly surveying the damage.

'We could do with Peter and the others being here

now all right,' said Zebedee, 'now we're short of men *and* boats. This was our best.'

'I can fix it. I am a carpenter.'

It was Jesus who spoke. He had come silently alongside us. I looked at him askance.

But he was good as his word. Jesus spent most of the next few weeks in the harbour. Joseph and I loved to watch him work. He had all of Dad's tools out of the boat yard, and Elias the Carpenter lent him the pieces he needed to repair the boat. The weather was getting hotter every day as summer came, and Jesus worked outside, stripped down to his tunic, with his strong muscular arms browning in the sun. Joseph and I would pull up a couple of terracotta jars and sit on their up-turned bottoms to watch him.

First he sawed new planks of Aleppo pine and jujube – Dad always says that cedar from Lebanon makes the best boat frame – but we hadn't any of that. Then he squatted on the ground and planed the new planks, making a pile of aromatic wood chips that curled around his feet and stuck to his clothes.

He whistled while he worked, and his hands touched the planed wood with such gentleness, the way Momma used to stroke Joseph when he was a tiny baby. You could tell he loved the wood and loved to work it. He edge-joined the new planks and fixed them into place on the boat with hardwood pegs, nailing them to the boat frame with iron nails. When he had finished the new side planks, he started on the mast, choosing a straight trunk that would be strong enough to carry the square sail. Dad's boat was going to look as good as new.

'Your Dad was a carpenter wasn't he?' Joseph asked him.

92

'He was. He taught me everything I know. And I worked for him as a carpenter for almost twenty years - before Dad died and after. I made tools for all the farmers in Nazareth, and at the end of the year, at threshing time, my brothers went round all the farms to collect our pay in barley, wheat, sesame or olives. I made doors from the dwarf oaks of Bashan, and ploughs and hoes from hawthorn, oak and redbud. Every wood has a different character, God made each one for a perfect purpose.

In fact, I know a good story about a Carpenter.'

'Oh please tell us, Jesus - I love your stories,' said Joseph in his best begging voice.

Jesus ran his brown hand along the smooth new mast and looked out across the lake, its waters now peaceful and calm. He took a deep breath, and sat down, 'In Hebron there lived two carpenters, both experts in their trade. They had two little carpenters' shops, side by side in two archways in the same narrow street. They started work at the same time every morning, and shut up shop at sunset each night. But they never spoke to each other, and never interfered with each other's work. The only contact they had was early in the morning when the first carpenter looked at the other and grunted. The second carpenter replied with a nod. And that's the way it went on for forty-five years, until both men were bent double with age.

One of the carpenters made ploughs and hoes for the farmers, and doors, window frames and furniture for houses, so he had become very rich. The other carpenter mended things belonging to the poorest people in Hebron, who couldn't afford to pay him at all, so he was very poor.

One day, Herod put out a decree that all the tradesmen in Judaea were to make a beautiful and wonderful gift to celebrate the birth of his baby son. Every carpenter, jeweller and craftsman was to make the most perfect birthday present they could carve or build. Herod promised to reward the maker of the most perfect gift with a great bag of silver.

Both carpenters thought long and hard about what they would make for the baby prince. The first carpenter decided to create the most expensive and ornate wooden gift, and he worked in secret for many days, carving a perfect replica of Herod's palace for the baby. He made wooden figures to go inside it, and wooden steps, roofs and battlements. It was so beautiful, he was certain the reward would be his.

All the time the first carpenter was carving, chiselling and planing, the poor carpenter carried on mending broken chairs and hoes that poor people brought. He didn't have the heart to turn anyone away, so he had no time to begin making the gift for Herod's child.

Now which of these two men do you think was sensible, and which was foolish?'

'The rich one is the sensible one,' said Joseph, 'because he's determined to work hard and win the reward - the other carpenter hasn't got a head for business at all.'

'Well, all too soon, the day came when the craftsmen must take their gifts to Herod. Proudly, carefully the carpenter lifted his toy palace on to a cart and pushed it to the King. The other carpenter came too, but slipped without notice into the back of the crowd of tradesmen gathered before Herod.

One by one the artisans carried their gifts and laid

each at Herod's feet, and he examined them in turn. At last, it was time for the rich carpenter. There was a gasp as the crowd saw the intricate wooden palace being carried forward.

But Herod wasn't pleased at all, 'Fool,' he shouted at the carpenter, 'I hate my palace, it's too small and old - I don't want my son to be reminded of a building which displeases me.' And with one movement, he brought his heavy foot down on the top of the wooden model, and broke it all to pieces. The first carpenter wept as his precious labour of weeks was destroyed in a moment.

Imagine the terror of the second carpenter as he stepped forward to bring the very last gift of all.

'And what do you have for me?' boomed Herod impatiently.

'Sir - your Majesty, I wanted to make the most beautiful thing in the world for you, and was afraid because I knew I couldn't do it. The most beautiful thing in the world was made not by me, but by God himself, and it is this.' The second carpenter held out his hand to Herod, and in the middle of his palm he held an almond.

'See the carving upon it,' said the carpenter, 'it was done by God himself. And when the young prince has finished playing with this nut, he may plant it and a great tree will grow, that will give him gifts of fruit for the rest of his days.'

Herod threw his head back with a great deep laugh and said, 'Truly carpenter, you have spoken wisely. And I will reward your wisdom with a bag of silver, for no man can build as perfectly as the God of our fathers.'

'That's not fair!' burst out Joseph when Jesus stood up, 'your stories are never fair, they're upside-down stories.'

'What do you mean little man?'

'They never end the way I expect – they're the opposite of real life. You always say, "Happy are the poor, for theirs is the Kingdom of Heaven, and happy are the hungry and thirsty" – well they're not, are they? You talk about the way things ought to be, not the way they are, and then you catch me out with trick questions. But I still think it's wiser to be like the first carpenter and earn money and try to win.'

Jesus' eyes were smiling, but I could see he wasn't going to laugh at Joseph, 'You see more clearly with your ten-year-old eyes than most adults in Palestine. But God our Father looks at the world in a very different way than men. God judges people by what's inside their hearts, never mind how much money or power they have, or how well they know the Law. A man may be poor by the standards of the world, but if he has God's heart, he will inherit all the riches of God's Kingdom when this life comes to an end.'

'So Yahweh wants us all to be poor and miserable does he?'

'Tell me Joseph, what do Momma and Father want for you?'

'They want me to go into the fishing business and be happy and rich, and never have to worry where the next meal's coming from.'

'And why's that?'

'Because I'm their child and they love me.'

'Exactly.'

And the boat was finished. Jesus replaced the lamp that had washed over-board in the storm, and the cooking pot Dad always keeps on board.

Momma had tears in her eyes when Jesus brought her down to the harbour to inspect his work, 'Oh Jesus, it's as good as new! You're a wonder.'

'I've enjoyed every minute - it's a pleasure to do the job I was trained for, but now I have to finish the job I was born for.'

Zebedee and the hired hands pushed the boat into the water and Jesus blessed it. This is a special time and I realise it every day, now Jesus is with us, the sun's shining, and everything is right.

After the boat was launched I sat beside Jesus on the shore. 'You miss him don't you - Dad I mean.'

'Of course I miss him, he's my friend.'

Jesus looked out across the lake towards the eastern hills. He wasn't seeing anything, I reckoned he was picturing Dad's round, grainy face - the face I miss so much it makes me cry myself to sleep. I threw a chip of black basalt into the water.

'Come and walk with me,' he said suddenly, in that way he has - half a request, and half a command - how a Centurion would speak to a foot soldier who happened to be his nephew as well.

I led Jesus south along the lake shore towards Magdala, and we crossed inland along the shepherds' paths. It was hot and bright, and the sky seemed like a hot lid over the earth. One of Zebedee's slaves was setting up the plough in the family's terraced fields. They had begun the second wheat sowing - Zebedee says we're lucky living around the lake where the soil is good enough to feed us twice a year.

'Look at him, tell me what you see,' Jesus said.

'It's Marcus, setting up the plough.'

97

'Look with your heart my Lily of the field – describe it with your heart.'

I blinked at the dusty earth and the brown boy, knotting my light veil under itself at the back to stop it falling in front of my eyes. I stared at the dusty fertile soil with its smattering of black lava stones that are the bane of workers' lives round here.

'I see Marcus lifting the plough - the wooden plough - the single furrow wooden plough,' I looked at Jesus sideways to see whether he would smile at my insolence or be angry.

But he was staring at Marcus as though he were trying to see inside his head, 'Go on.'

'He's lifting the yoke on to the bigger, older ox first - he always does that - while the younger ox is still dreaming of tonight's fodder. Marcus is hot and he's wiping his brow. Now he's whistling to the young ox and bringing it from his tether.'

'Tell me more about the oxen. How do you know their ages?'

'Because Marcus always yokes a strong, old ox to a young, weak one.'

'Why would he do that? Why doesn't he work two strong beasts together?'

'You know all this Jesus - why are you making me tell you? Marcus knows the young ox has to learn from the stronger older one. He takes all the weight of the heavy yoke and because he's older and wiser, he leads the young animal straight. Look at his strong shoulders, and the way his muscles are working under the weight of the yoke. And look at the little ox too, he's dying to wander off and sniff out something to chew. But the faithful old ox is guiding him.'

'My yoke is easy and my burden is light,' Jesus said, looking at me.

'Yes, until the young ox has to pull a plough alone - then he'll get a shock feeling the real weight fall on his shoulders.'

'That will never happen Lily of the field, I never leave an ox alone at the plough. That's the way my Father ordered it.'

'You're crazy – why do you call yourself an ox? Now Marcus has seen another hired worker over the wall and is calling hello. He's looking back and trying to plough at the same time. It won't work. Look now Jesus! - the point of the plough is drifting, it's all out of line – Marcus will catch it when the sower comes along. The oxen need Marcus to keep them perfectly straight – Zebedee will say he isn't fit for service. He shouldn't have looked back. I hope he doesn't get a beating.'

Jesus sighed and rubbed his forehead, 'I have a yoke ahead that no-one can take from me, I must bear it alone and its weight will crush me.'

'No Jesus, you're the strong ox - that's what you said, so you'll never be crushed.'

'Now you're seeing with your heart, little one.'

'And I'll help you Jesus - I'll be your young partner ox. I'll be right beside you if you ever need me.'

'Don't make promises Susannah – you must *pray* to be given strength, but never promise it.'

'I hate the way you say dark things sometimes, why can't it always be summer, with Marcus ploughing and you and me sitting together? I hate looking into the future, the way Dad does when he reminds me about my betrothal. That's the best thing about Dad being away, his mind's on other things.'

'You will never marry.'

'Why? How do you know?'

'It's part of the price. But your love will be greater and deeper than any woman's love for a husband. It is written, *"For you who love my name, the sun of righteousness will shine out with healing in its rays – you will leap like a calf going out to pasture."'*

'That's better, I like that a lot better than you being a crushed ox.'

The very next day, Dad came home. As soon as the message reached our house that Dad and Uncle Andrew had been spotted on the Capernaum road, we all went crazy. Joseph ran all the way to the crossroads to meet him, while Momma and I threw a hasty meal together. It was the very hottest part of the day, and when we ran to the road, at first we could see nothing through the shimmering midday heat.

But Jesus must have seen further than us, because he ran along the road calling, 'Peter, Andrew!'

Then we could make Dad out - I've never seen him looking so hot and hairy - or thin. He saw Jesus and bounded forward, 'Master, Master, you won't believe it! – We've driven out demons and anointed people with oil, and guess what? We healed them!'

Jesus whooped with joy, a huge great throw-your-tunic-in-the-air kind of whoop. 'Well done Peter son of Jonah, my prayers are answered – well done!' and the three of them hugged and slapped each other on the backs, and Dad shouted his head off.

By the time Dad had hugged us all and told us at least fifty times about the demons, the oil and the healings, we were all as hungry as he was.

That was a wonderful meal in our house. I've never laughed so much, while Dad recounted their fear and their sore feet and the triumphs. 'It was weird, the first time we had a healing, we didn't believe it ourselves – I thought the bloke was having us on. He was blind, and after we'd anointed him with oil, he started leaping about and saying, "I can see, I can see!" and frankly, I didn't believe him. I thought it was his idea of a joke. I looked at Andrew and he looked at me, and we started to laugh. I was just waiting for the man to say, "Only joking – I wasn't blind at all!" But he didn't.'

Jesus laughed and laughed, and told Dad, 'Stop it – you're making my sides hurt.'

Dad ignored him, screwed up his eyes pretending to be blind, then opened them wide saying, 'Ah-ha, that fooled you! But we had another healing – how could it happen when we didn't believe it ourselves?'

'My Father is very gracious,' laughed Jesus, wiping his eyes.

'Well we believed it after that, all right. Making someone better is the best feeling in the world - especially the little children. But there was one time it went horribly wrong. We had moved on from Sidon to Tyre, and we were full of confidence. I was feeling pretty pleased with myself and people were calling us heroes. I'm ashamed to admit I believed them, and stopped thinking about your orders Jesus, I was planning to take a detour to Jerusalem. I thought I'd make quite an impression there.

I was still casting out demons in your name, but in my

own power. So, on this day, a huge crowd had gathered to hear us speak and watch us heal Matthias the Leper, but it didn't happen. I prayed out loud - and Andrew helped me - and at first when he wasn't healed, we weren't too worried. I knew I could do it. But even when I cast out Matthias' sins, and told him he was clean, and hollered and threw myself down on the ground and begged - he was still a leper.

What made it worse, Matthias was standing a way off, so that he wouldn't defile the crowd with his sores, and from his position on a rock set apart, he was very visible. One after another, people started to shout insults at me and call me a fraud, a trickster. I went on trying, which probably made things worse. So the people wandered away and they never heard what we needed to tell them about the coming of the Kingdom.

I was devastated. I don't mind admitting I went off by myself, sat by the sea and wept as I've never done before. I knew I'd let you down Master, and my head had swelled with pride. How come you never, ever show off? You're the one with the power - we only use your name, but you're not arrogant. I kept picturing you and the gentle way you have, pointing people towards God and away from yourself. Well, I was a broken man. Andrew managed to carry on after that, but I was too ashamed. I hung my head and kept to the back of the crowds.

But you're right Jesus, God is gracious to me, because one evening soon afterwards, I was walking beside the shore and bumped into a cripple – I actually tripped right over him. He was slumped beside the tax collector's booth, hoping for a coin to fall his way. It was late and there was no-one about, just me, him and the sea birds crying.

Then the worst possible thing happened – he recognised me, 'Hey you're the miracle man aren't you? Help me Teacher! I'm a poor cripple.'

I told him he'd got the wrong bloke.

'No, you were teaching in the synagogue only last week, and I couldn't get to you, please heal me teacher!'

'You've made a mistake – it was the taller, slimmer bloke, Andrew the Ferryman - you must have seen Andrew.'

'No it wasn't, you were both there, but it was you who healed the blind girl - I know it was you!'

'Well, that was last week, and this is now. I can't heal you.'

'Why not, aren't I good enough? I'm certainly sick enough – I've been this bad since I was born, and I've got no home, no family, no money. Please help me.'

'I can't.'

'Why not?'

'I've lost the power.'

'So ask this Jesus then, that's what you told us last week. You said Jesus' Father will do anything if we ask him in absolute faith. So where's your faith?'

I looked out at the sea, bathed in sunset colours, and realised this simple man was teaching me, rather than the other way round. I guess it will always be that way Jesus - when you're not there, we have to help each other.'

Jesus' intent face was shining with pleasure, 'Not always Peter, my Father will send the Holy Spirit to you when the time is right.'

'Well, I looked at this poor chap, with his useless legs and sad ugly face, and I actually cried for him. I didn't say anything much, but I felt a love for him pour into me, and I just asked you to help him Master. I put my hand on his shoulder, and he stood up. I was more shocked than I'd been at the first healing. Then he hopped, jumped and skipped around me, kissed me and danced away into the town. I sat there weeping for joy and praising God.

After that, Andrew and I agreed it was time to come home. And not only because we were longing for one of Momma's lamb suppers,' Dad said, hugging her waist with his strong, muscular arm.

You could have heard a head of corn drop in our room, we were so gripped.

And then each of us began to smile, and I began to cry. It was truly beautiful.

None of us have seen Jesus so happy before. He looked just like a proud father watching his son read from the Law for the first time.

I asked Gran about it at bed-time and she seemed to understand, 'Jesus feels like a grand-parent does, he's just happy to see your father coming of age, and knowing that now there's someone to pass on the teaching with him. I've always thought Jesus' life must be a lonely one.'

So the happy times have come again. Dad's home, Jesus is with us and the summer days are burning themselves out towards autumn. Every patch of earth is scorched brown and dry, all the bright flower colours of spring faded and gone.

Date 30.06.03

To taylordenton.arch.instit@hebron.com

From boogyhen@onetel.co.uk

I'm knackered. Last night I camped by the lake and turned down my first chance of a bonk in two years – please book me in at the Jerusalem rest-home for mad archaeologists. And she was lovely.

I need help - The gospel of Mark mentions Bethsaida-Julias and I want to go there – it's where Jesus fed the five thousand. (I'm hoping to find a few stale crusts as there's a shortage of bars round here.) Where do I start?

I never got round to asking you – are you happily married/divorced/single or with someone? None of my business but you asked me.

Love

Ben Suddenly-turned-lucky-and-threw-it-away Henshaw

Date 30.06.03

To boogyhen@onetel.co.uk

From taylordenton.arch.instit@hebron.com

Hi Ben,

Your email made my day – Professor Asaf asked me what I was laughing at.

Plenty of confusion about Beth.Julias – it is NOT to be confused with your site Bethsaida - though most people do.

Beth.Julias was named by Philip and lay north of the lake, where the Jordan used to flow in. Up from the modern es-Saki lagoon. In 1st C CE the Jordan delta was slightly east of present entry point.

Will your research bring you back to Jerusalem? I go on vacation 5th July for two weeks with a friend (male).

You're right – it's none of your business, but I'm almost single – the holiday should change that.

Love Taylor.

Date 30.06.03
To taylordenton.arch.instit@hebron.com
From boogyhen@onetel.co.uk
I hate him.
Ben.

Capernaum, Galilee
CE 31

Jesus is anxious to spend time alone with Dad and the other apostles - for the first time, he seems fretful.

I wonder whether it's the season making him feel that way, hot and impatient, but he keeps urging Dad, 'Time is precious Peter, I must be alone with you and James and John, there's so much I need to share with you.'

Dad is always laid back, 'There's time enough Jesus, remember what Solomon said, *'There's a time for everything, and a season for every activity under heaven, a time to be born and a time to die.'*

'And he also says, *'A time to be silent, and a time to speak.'* Now is the time for me to speak to you, before it's too late.'

The very next day, Jesus asked Dad to prepare the boat and take him across the lake to Bethsaida Julias with the apostles. He planned to start out very early, before dawn, so they could escape the crowds and spend a day talking and praying. It wasn't the best place to choose in my opinion. You can get to Bethsaida Julias on foot along the path which runs around the northern shore from Capernaum.

Although we'd promised Jesus to keep quiet about where he was, one of the pilgrims managed to prise it out of Joseph. He was just setting out for the synagogue for his school lessons and a man asked him, 'When will the Master return from Magdala?'

Joseph was well and truly hooked, and gabbled, 'He hasn't gone to Magdala today – he's at Bethsaida-Julias.' Then a shadow moved across his face, 'Oh no – I promised not to tell!'

That was all it took of course, the man must have told his party, and then the others simply followed. Within moments, people were streaming out of Capernaum along the northerly path and I knew it wouldn't take them long to cover the four miles to the inlet of the Jordan.

I was mad with Joseph, and screeched at him like a tom-cat. I didn't know what to do for the best, and ran to Zebedee's house to ask Mark for advice.

'I'll row out there with you, at least then we can warn Jesus,' Mark said.

And that's what we did, both of us rowing as fast as we could. A trail of people was already visible snaking from Capernaum around to Bethsaida-Julias. Some people were running.

My heart sank, and when we landed, we found Jesus on a piece of raised ground, already surrounded by a crowd.

I squatted down beside Dad, 'We tried to warn you - Joseph let the rabbit out of the bag.'

'Don't blame Joseph love, there were people here when we arrived, and Jesus' heart went out to them. You know what he's like - he said that from the boat they looked just like a flock of sheep without a shepherd. He's been talking to them ever since.'

I think this is the first day I listened to Jesus with the ears of an outsider. I put myself in the shoes of these travelling foreigners and imagined what it would be like to hear his words for the first time.

He was talking to them about sheep, 'The good shepherd doesn't drive the animals from behind, but walks ahead of his flock who follow willingly because they trust him. When an animal is injured, he carries it over his shoulder, near to his heart. His skin is burned almost black from the sun, and he leads his flock by road and over hills, towards new pasture.

'The animals know his voice, and when they sense danger they run to him for protection. When a lamb falls into a ditch, the good shepherd lifts it out with his crook and sets it back on the right path. He spends his whole life with the sheep, day and night, from birth until death.

'And when darkness falls, the good shepherd lays himself down in the doorway of the sheep-fold, making himself into the gate to protect his flock from wolves and thieves.'

While Jesus was talking, every one of us could hear the bleating of sheep and goats being led to pasture. Above the sound of Jesus' voice, and the lapping of the waves on the shore, we could hear a shepherd boy piping on the hills – a maddening tune without beginning or end, making stumbling progress up, up, and then tumbling down the scale. These days, such large numbers of animals are required for sacrifice that you can't go a mile without passing droves being led towards the temple in Jerusalem. They're so much a part of our life that I've never thought about them. Now Jesus was making me think.

'I am the Good Shepherd, who lays down his life for his flock - you know my voice, and I know you. And just as I know every one of my flock, my Father knows me. No-one may come to the Father unless he comes through me, I am the gateway into the Kingdom.

'I have other sheep who are not yet in this sheep pen, and I must bring them in also. They will listen to my

109

voice and there will be one flock and one shepherd. Beware the wolves and thieves, little ones.'

'What does he mean about laying down his life Dad?' I asked.

'That he's dedicating his life to teaching us I reckon, and how he's given up his job as a carpenter, all that.'

'But when he says things like that he makes me afraid of the future. While you were away he told me he has to bear a heavy yoke which will crush him.'

'Hey Susannah – he has God's special blessing and power upon him, there's no need to be afraid.' Dad sounded certain and I brushed away my fears.

When Jesus finished talking, the sun was low in the sky.

Dad pulled Jesus to one side, 'It's late Master - we should send the people away so they have time to walk to the village to find supper before dark. They didn't come prepared for a day out.'

It was true, people had rushed after Jesus without time to pack food. Children in the crowd were whining and crying, 'I'm hungry Momma, I'm hungry.'

Jesus turned to Dad swiftly, 'They're hungry, so give them something to eat.'

'It would take eight months of my wages to feed this lot,' replied Dad, 'there must be five thousand people here, counting the children.'

'Find out how much food they have between them,' Jesus said.

I laughed out loud when Dad and Uncle Andrew came back to Jesus. Between them they had a total of five flat loaves and two opsarion – a small pickled fish of the kind Momma would give us as a snack.

'That's your lot, shall we pass them round?' asked Dad sarcastically.

'Ask the people to sit down,' Jesus said.

Dad and the eleven others moved through the crowds and people formed seated groups on the hillside.

I was close beside Jesus.

He stood with his back to the crowd and lifted the little basket of fish and bread towards the setting sun, and I saw his outline bathed in light. It was as if the rays of the sun were coming out of his body.

'Thank you Father for the mighty work you are doing here for your people,' he said, 'and thank you that we have this bread to offer.'

It's hard to describe what happened next.

Jesus called to me, 'Bring me baskets Lily, and when you run out of baskets, bring cloaks.'

I was so busy asking people to pass their baskets and cloaks forward, that at first I didn't notice what was happening. Every basket I passed him was empty, and when he passed it back, each was full to the brim with fish and bread. Dad and Uncle Andrew, Philip, Thomas and all of them were helping. Every time Jesus touched a basket or a folded cloak, it was filled with food. One by one people started to laugh and whoop with joy as they saw what he was doing.

It took us a long, long time to pass out the food, and sweat was pouring from Jesus' head and neck. There was enough for everyone, even at the furthest edge of the crowd we could see people tossing loaves into the air and shouting, 'Halleluiah – it's a miracle!' Eventually, when everyone was fed, Jesus himself sat down to eat. I watched him lift his tired arms and put small mouthfuls of the tasty fish into his mouth. He was scanning the sea of satisfied moonlit faces with a look of pure compassion.

A lump rose in my chest and burned until tears spilled onto my cheeks - tears of tiredness after the long day, and of pity and love for this man who has changed my life. Once I started crying, I couldn't stop.

'Hey my little Lily, don't weep - everyone else is happy,' he said.

'You just can't stop yourself can you?' I replied, 'You came here to have some well-earned peace and quiet, and my stupid brother ruins it all, then you have to teach the people and feed them, and it all costs you, I see how much it costs. I want somebody to give to *you* for a change.'

'First the price must be paid, then the giving can begin,' he said, and there were tears in his eyes too. 'I'm very tired, thank you for caring.'

Right at that moment I'd have laid down and let a chariot run over me for him, nothing else in the whole world mattered.

Bethsaida-Julias, Galilee
1st July 2003

There's nothing at Bethsaida-Julias. Nothing to see, no archaeology, so I'm not even sure where the town was.

Since yesterday I feel really low and have decided I may as well give up on this whole search. The idea isn't even funny any more, especially as I won't have Taylor to share it with.

I wish she'd mentioned the holiday guy sooner. My stupidity amazes me, but I'd let her emails build my hopes up, especially the one when she said she was glad I turned down the date.

And she said I had the perfect body. Now I know that didn't mean anything, but I'd begun to see my body in a new light. I really regret sending the last email, it was so un-cool. I never admit I fancy a girl unless I'm drunk. Idiot.

As if a stunner like her would ever look at me - a Digger who's only mildly interesting because I found something unique.

Now even the thought of the shard is stale. Big deal - I dug it up, but what does that change, who does it help? All it's done is turn me crazy. If there was anywhere else to go, I'd leave, but the thought of digging at Et-Tel again is even less appealing than tracking Susannah.

I was so low last night I walked round looking for the blue Fiat, (not that I would have done anything if I'd found it), and made myself feel worse than ever. I've lost the peace that came over me when I spoke to Ruth.

We're born, we die, we muck up the bit in-between. What's it all about?

All I managed to find here was a mound that might have been big enough to seat 5,000 Jews when Jesus fed them. I wonder whether Susannah was there?

The sun is so hot. So hot. I need to sleep.

* * *

I must have drifted off. When I woke just now I felt different, calmer. And I had the weirdest dream - that I was sitting on this mound and it was covered with thousands of bleating sheep.

Then I noticed my Susannah standing amongst them,

wearing her creamy robe decorated in yellow beneath her throat. Just like a lily.

She called to me, 'You will find me in Jerusalem, you will find peace in Jerusalem.' And as she spoke, she turned into Taylor.

So I'm going to Jerusalem – which isn't a novelty - I was there only the other day. But the unusual part is I'm planning to walk. From Bethsaida-Julias to Jerusalem on foot – about 85 miles.

I've checked my wallet, and haven't spent anything since I left Tiberias, so I'll be OK for cash. It's 4 miles to Capernaum, where I can buy some food, another 7 miles to Tiberias for a shower and a launderette. That leaves only 74.

I could do it in a week, even in this heat.

And I don't need Taylor's approval or advice. At least I've got a plan.

Date 01.07.03
To boogyhen@onetel.co.uk
From taylordenton.arch.instit@hebron.com
Hi Ben, Your emails are the highlight of my day. Have you recovered from your night of passion that never was? Where next? I really envy your bravery – it would take somebody very special to get me off my butt for an unplanned journey after them – if it ever happens to me, I'll know it's for real.

I've been reading the gospels to find you info on Simon Peter – I should have sent more than Mark, but as Peter dictated this gospel, I thought it was the best place to start.

Take care
Love Taylor

Date 02.07.03
To boogyhen@onetel.co.uk
From taylordenton.arch.instit@hebron.com

Hi Ben
Are you still there?
Love T

Sender Taylor 02.07.03
Where R U? I am worried. Hav I offended U? TB. luv T

Capernaum, Galilee
2nd July 2003

I arrived in Capernaum early last night and found a bar where I proceeded to get totally wasted. The first four beers went down in fifteen minutes. My memory cuts out after my eleventh, but I woke at the side of the road this morning, feeling like I died two thousand years ago – or more.

I only hope I didn't get nasty, and wasn't thrown out by the owner. I'm completely filthy and am on my way to the showers and local launderette. Beer didn't help – I still feel crap.

* * *

While I got myself clean, laundered and civilised, I decided I must start eating properly or I'll be truly scrawny, especially as my Digger muscle bulk is fading already. I've been proud of my arms and shoulders since 1986, and don't want to turn into a complete Wendy. So I began a programme of press-ups and sit-ups to make me feel better about my body.

This afternoon I sat beside the main road and thought about Susannah – re-focussed on my dream girl before I start my journey.

It would have been common practice for 1st century CE Jews to walk to Jerusalem for Passover or make temple sacrifices, and they would have avoided the wild road through Samaria that was populated by brigands. Instead they would have used the road close to the Jordan, so that's my plan.

I read on in Mark and realised that although Jesus used Capernaum as his base, he spent a lot of time travelling the surrounding area preaching with the apostles. I reckoned

Susannah wouldn't have been able to travel with the men, and she may have spent a deal of time watching the roads in and out of the village, waiting for her Dad.

Just like I spent countless times as a kid, sitting at the bottom of our cul-de-sac looking for my Mum. I was sure she would come back to us, and didn't want to miss the moment when her red mini would drive up the road. I hated Dad when he called me in and told me to forget about her.

Part of me is still waiting.

Capernaum, Galilee
CE 32

I'm so angry, the whole of my breast is tight with a burning hot rage. I've tried to calm myself and remember the good times of last summer, but my anger keeps rising and brimming out of me. Momma and Joseph can't speak without me flying into a frenzy.

I've tried to keep the business going and manage the potting alone, Mark and Zebedee have taught me the rudiments of fishing, but I haven't the strength to use the nets. Uncle Zebedee says I may be the only girl who has ever worked on the boats in Galilee, and that I'm useful aboard, but it's crazy trying to manage like this. We haven't enough to pay the tax collector next time. And I'm worried.

Jesus left with Dad and the others as soon as the early rains began after last harvest, and six new moons have passed since then. It's now Purim, and a full year since Jesus returned to us from Nazareth.

And Dad's father, Grandpa Jonah died while Dad was away. His final words were enough to move a cold Pharisee, he whispered, 'Tell Simon I love him, tell him to listen to Jesus, and that I have gone to the God of our fathers to wait for him.'

No doubt Dad and the others are having a fine old time in Tyre and Sidon and the ten towns of Galilee, healing the blind and lame, while my heart breaks.

Jesus did send me a papyrus from Caesarea Philippi, and I fed on that for many days, his first precious written words to me,

'MY LILY OF THE FIELD, MANY HAVE HEARD MY FATHER'S WORD AND HAVE BEEN HEALED. SEND WORD TO US AT SIDON. DO NOT BE IDLE, WE SHALL RETURN BY PURIM, YOUR FATHER IS ANXIOUS ABOUT YOU. I PRAY FOR YOU CONTINUALLY. J'

If they don't return soon, I shall run away to Jerusalem and marry the son of the temple guard. How can they expect me to live without a husband? I have the heart of a woman and the needs of a mother because I am in my fifteenth year.

* * *

I'm so happy. Yesterday while I was working in the potting house with my back to the door, the light suddenly darkened behind me, and I felt two strong arms seize me round the waist.

'My Lily!'

I shrieked to wake the dead from a tomb, 'JESUS!!'

He whirled me round and round until I begged him to stop, and cried with joy, because I couldn't help it.

And then they were all in our courtyard, Dad, Andrew, John, James, Judas - it was just like being in Heaven. I haven't stopped smiling since.

I was bursting and called to Dad, 'I'll run and fetch our friends.'

'No Susannah, not this time. Jesus wants us to keep quiet, we're not telling anyone he's here.'

'Why not?'

'Because he needs time to teach us.'

'Won't it be a bit obvious Jesus is here now the twelve of you are back?'

'It won't be for long daughter, enjoy this time.'

So we hid ourselves in the house, and had a private supper.

Momma, Gran and I sang as we prepared to serve the thirteen men and Joseph.

Food seemed to come from nowhere – Momma must have had a stash of opsarion, chicken, olives and lentils – because we certainly haven't been getting them.

The men were tired from their long days of journeying, and we didn't know how to begin asking about all they've seen and done, so the group was strangely quiet. Jesus was very thoughtful, while James and John were having a heated debate under their breath.

Suddenly Jesus said the oddest thing, 'The Son of Man will be handed over to the people, and they will kill him. But after three days he will rise from the dead.'

'Pardon?' I asked, 'where did that come from?'

'Susannah, hush your tongue,' Momma retorted.

'No Sarah, let her speak,' Jesus went on, 'her mind is quicker than any of the twelve. I am speaking of what must happen Lily, remember the heavy yoke.'

'Oh please don't bring that up again, tell us a story instead.'

'There will be no more stories in the last days.'

I felt rattled, 'Stop speaking in riddles. Who is the Son of Man? And when are the last days?

'I am He, and the time is now.'

'Don't Jesus, no-one could ever put you to death – the people love you, they adore you,' I protested.

Suddenly his temper flared, and he turned on James and John behind him, 'What are you two arguing about now?' he shouted. 'You've been at it all day.'

My two cousins fell silent at once.

'Tell me!' Jesus said, it was an absolute command.

James and John annoy me. They're both moaners, and complain when they should be doing. They love each other as brothers, but fight like two mangy dogs over a bone. Now they looked really guilty and uncomfortable.

John began, 'James was saying…'

Jesus interrupted, 'I want to know what *you* were saying, James can speak for himself.'

'I'd rather not say.'

'James?' Jesus asked.

'And I'd rather not say either.'

'Then I'll say for you,' Jesus said icily. Then he turned very gently and said, 'Come to me Joseph, my lad,' holding out his broad hand to my little brother.

Joseph stepped forward and Jesus held him around his waist.

'Who is my second in command Joseph?'

'Er, you don't have one do you? Is it Dad?' Joseph stammered awkwardly.

'So I'll ask you another way, when the Kingdom comes, who will sit at my right hand?'

'You honestly haven't told me, so I don't know,' Joseph said, looking worried. 'And I thought God the Father was going to be sitting at your right hand – but I must have got it wrong. Unless it's Elijah. Sorry,' Joseph said, casting his eyes to the ground.

'You are a clever, clever boy,' Jesus smiled, then turned on the men, 'You worthless rabble, unless you become like this child you will never enter my Father's Kingdom. Since we left Nain, James and John have been arguing about which of you is the greatest – and I tell you now, whoever wants to be the first, must put himself last. You must be servants to every man, woman and child, just as I am to you. And whoever wants to share my glory in the Kingdom must drink from the same cup of suffering that is coming to me. You don't understand what you are asking for.'

He pulled Joseph tighter to himself, 'Whichever one of you loves and serves children like this one will come into the Kingdom. Shame on you all!'

To say there was an unpleasant atmosphere was understating it.

John broke the silence, 'Master, forgive us, and please don't talk about dying, or about leaving us, we can't bear it. I'm sorry Master.'

Jesus stood, I had never seen him looking this mad, 'Momma, excuse me, I'm going out,' he said.

When he left I felt as though the heart had gone out of our home.

Jesus didn't come back all night. I know because I waited up for him. After trimming the lamps, and saying goodnight to the men as they left in twos and threes for their beds across the courtyard, I knew I wouldn't be able to sleep. Dad had hustled Momma up the ladder – anxious to hurry into bed for their first night together for six moons. I could hear Momma laughing upstairs like a girl.

I put out the fire in the courtyard oven, then covered the open fire with palms to keep the stones hot all night ready for Momma's morning cooking.

It was the same ritual I've followed a hundred times, just as Momma, Gran, and her mother had done a thousand times before her, and that comforted the fear in my heart. I've never seen Jesus angry like tonight, and was chilled to the bone by his talk of the last days.

So I went out, forbidden as I am, into the second watch of the Capernaum night. No good Jews are abroad in the middle hours of darkness, but I knew Jesus was out there somewhere.

There was a party going on at Levi the tax collector's home, a very wild and drunken one by the sound of it. Jesus has been to Levi's house several times, provoking Dad to have almighty rows with him about mixing with the unclean.

Everywhere else in the village was utterly dark and quiet, every beast and good Jew asleep in stable and home. I walked to the very edge of the harbour, beyond the last house, but daren't go any further, because I was afraid of walking past the rickety shacks.

There's no danger here in daylight, but I know what goes on at night. Behind the soft tasselled doors, among pools of ochre candle-light, with scented oils reaching through the still night air.

So I sat on the very end-stone of the harbour wall, and looked across the lake, wondering where Jesus had gone.

What I heard next disgusted me. Quietly at first, then as loud as a rutting ox, I heard the groans of a fat man copulating. Enough to turn me from marriage for ever. And I knew this noise was coming from no marital bed.

I couldn't help myself - some ugly force pulled me away from the water towards the bothys. It was easy to see into the first hut, its tasselled curtain not thick enough for cover. The interior was tiny, with space for no more than a bowl and a mattress. Hanging on the wall was the unmistakable pure white linen and blue stole of a teacher of the law. And in the middle of the mattress was a humping figure I recognised at once, Jonas the Pharisee, the very one who had first scorned Jesus for healing the paralysed man.

'You hypocrite!' I said under my breath, as my stomach turned sour with revulsion.

But my shock and disgust were nothing compared to my feelings a moment later. I could hear voices coming out of the next-door bothy and felt compelled to see who was there, dreading what I may see there.

So I crept like a stalking cat to the open doorway. This tassel screen was thicker than the first, but revealed enough to satisfy my sickening curiosity.

There, leaning on the mattress against the dirty palm walls, with his arm around Miriam of Sepphoris, was none other than Jesus! My Jesus!

I let out a choked sob and stood fixed in place, no part of me able to move but my blinking eyes.

Miriam was half dressed in a soiled red tunic, open to the waist, her hair loose around her shoulders, eyes blackened with kohl. Her head was leaning against Jesus' neck, and with his right hand he was stroking her arm tenderly.

Suddenly it occurred to me that he isn't married, he's never spoken of marriage or betrothal, and so here he was, using a prostitute to feed his secret lust, the urge that makes him no different from any other man or beast in Galilee.

'No,' I whimpered, 'no, no!' and ran headlong into the dark, beyond the shacks and away from Capernaum. Tears were blinding my eyes and I tripped over my robe.

I screamed at the night, 'No! God of Abraham, don't let this be happening!'

Then I was aware of footsteps behind me, bounding quicker and nearer.

'Go away from me!' I yelled, 'I hate you.'

'Stop,' came a woman's voice. It wasn't Jesus running after me at all.

I turned like a vixen protecting her cubs, 'You she-bitch, you devil from hell - Miriam of Sepphoris. Don't come near me!'

In the darkness Miriam's uncovered breasts were white as sepulchres.

'Sit down and be quiet!' she commanded me.

I was utterly empty, and dropped to the ground.

'Don't judge him. How dare you?' she asked huskily. 'I love him, I love Jesus with all my heart.'

'Don't speak his name, you whore of Babylon, you're not worthy to touch the hem of his cloak,' I spat the words at her.

'I'm as worthy as any sinner – his love saved me, like it will save many.'

'He doesn't love you, he *can't* love someone like you,' I was sobbing now. 'It's me he loves.'

Then she did what I least expected. Miriam squatted beside me on the stony ground and put her arms around me, 'Of course he loves me, because the greater the sin, the more he cares.'

I could smell the richness of her perfume, and feel the silken skin of her breasts. As I cried I wondered how many men had lost themselves in this softness.

'This is the second night he's come to me,' she said.

'Don't. Don't tell me,' I pleaded.

Miriam held me closer and stroked my unveiled head. 'The first night he burst in when I was working, and beat my customer from the door, his business not finished. That time Jesus didn't stay long, but told me to stop sinning and that his Father loves me. Of course I couldn't accept or believe that.

"How will I live?" I asked him then, "I can't work for anyone now?"

He said he would pray for me.

While he was away I tried to change, to find paid work, but no-one would hire me, even in the fields. So I slipped back into the old ways, because heaven knows there's enough demand for my trade, but I hated myself for what I was doing. I thought of Jesus every day. And now he's come back, and visited me again. This time he arrived just as Jonas the Pharisee had finished, but he made no comment. He hasn't blamed me or been angry, just repeated my name over and over, 'Miriam, Miriam, my little sister.'

'Then he talked and hugged me, telling a tale of a guttersnipe who became a Queen. And he prayed for me.'

'Did he...did you...have you.....?' I stammered.

Jesus' voice broke into our darkness, 'Do not ask Lily. That is not for you to ask or know.'

I could see the lightness of his cloak as he knelt before us both, the thorn bushes dark behind his pale silhouette.

'Miriam, Susannah, you are two daughters of my Father, and you are beautiful in heaven's sight. What I have shared with you Miriam is for the ears of no-one except women from your past. But Susannah, your story is for all Galilee to hear. Speak boldly of life, love and joy. When I am gone, tell out my story.'

Now Miriam and I called out as one, 'You can't leave, don't leave us Lord!'

Miriam wept and clung to him, 'There's no man like you Master, no man who treats a woman with respect and fairness, there will never be another Jew like you.'

'So love is all the more precious, because our time is short,' Jesus said. 'Let's go home Susannah. And Miriam - remember what we spoke of - I shall send for you tomorrow.'

'Goodnight Master,' she whispered, and knelt to kiss his robe before the darkness swallowed her.

As we walked back to the village Jesus held my small hand.

'Are you going to be with Miriam tomorrow then?' I asked.

'In the morning Momma will ask you to find a hired girl to help with the cooking and cleaning. You will tell her that you know the right girl. And Miriam will work for our family.'

'But Jesus, she can't - she's a common whore.'

He stopped at once and dropped my hand, 'Don't ever, ever say that again Susannah. Miriam is no different to you, NO DIFFERENT in any way. She's a forgiven sinner, just like you, Simon Peter or anyone. It will weigh heavily for any man or woman who condemns her.'

Next day it happened just as Jesus said.

At breakfast Momma complained, 'I can't go on any longer without help round the house, we're practically feeding a legion, and my mother's too frail for all this work.'

I piped up, 'I know someone Momma, Jesus introduced her. She's from Sepphoris and needs work.'

'Well what are you waiting for child? Run and find her.'

As I rounded the first street corner, I bumped into Miriam. She was washed and dressed simply in plain beige linen, head veiled and her face fresh of make-up.

She smiled at me with the joy of meeting a true friend, and I know she has become part of our family.

Later, Jesus found us together at the bread oven, 'My two angels!' he laughed, 'A lily and a sheaf of ripe corn, great is the rejoicing in heaven today.'

We didn't understand what he meant about heaven, but basked in his approval.

Date 03.07.03
To boogyhen@onetel.co.uk
From taylordenton.arch.instit@hebron.com
Ben – I'm worried sick about you. Are you OK? There are
so many news reports of suicide bombers that I've half
convinced myself you were in the wrong place at the wrong
time. Please, please email. It's only two days 'til I go on vacation
and I can't set off unless I know you're OK.

Big over-reaction from a researcher to ex-digger, but I care.

Love and prayers Taylor

Date 03.07.03
To taylordenton.arch.instit@hebron.com
From boogyhen@onetel.co.uk
I'm fine, no need to worry about me. Have a great holiday –
I'm having a top time – good crack, plenty of talent, catch up
with you some time.

Ben

As soon as I saw 'email sent' on my handset I regretted it.
Even for me, this note was superficial and insincere, but I'm
still angry with her. And why should I flatter her ego when she's
about to spend two weeks with some super-stud?

Date 03.07.03
To boogyhen@onetel.co.uk
From taylordenton.arch.instit@hebron.com
Dear Ben, I get the message. Keep safe, take care, you're
a hell of a guy. With or without the shard.

Best wishes Taylor

Tiberias is hot and overcrowded – although I've been away
for less than ten days, I'd already begun to enjoy the slower
pace out of town. The sound of car horns and smell of city

pollution are an insult to my senses, and they dim the purity of the lake somehow.

But maybe I'm blaming the place for what's happened to me here today, which is unfair.

It's all because I checked my mail box first thing this morning – I only bother to come about once a month, as I never have much mail. But today there were two letters - both about as welcome as a drugs Czar at a rave.

Number one – a charming letter from mother-dearest, who's currently on holiday in Switzerland with the boyfriend.

Forget any pre-conceived ideas you may have about motherly love, they don't apply here. I was brought up by my Dad, and I love the guy, he did an OK job.

But the woman who calls herself my mother isn't worth the time of day. Since leaving us, she's enjoyed the life of Reilly - she never married the guy she went off with, he probably wasn't bad enough, but her career and love-life have gone from strength to strength. Currently she's heading up some division of rural health for the United Nations. The Ministry of Cruelty to Children would be more her line.

Her letter requires a translation:-

'Dearest Ben

Having a wonderful time here with Mario, who sends his love *(he pretends to accept you so why do you treat him so badly?)* and we both hope to hear from you soon. *(You're a complete pain in the butt and are totally unreliable but I want you to call.)*

Keeping busy at work, though the Iraqi conflict has made life more difficult for my entire team *(I am a very important person and you should revere me more),* and it is a relief to know we are doing some good, *(you see I am a worthy person – shame you don't appreciate me).*

How is Dad? *(pity he can't mention me in the same cool, together kind of way)* and how is the dig? I was telling friends at dinner all about you the other night *(you're a complete embarrassment, but I get mileage out of pretending you're a consultant on Time Team)* and we are hoping to visit you before summer is out *(I say this every year and never do it)'.*

There is more, but I'll spare you the laughs.

Number two – a short note from Carys. Who hasn't contacted me in three years.

Holly Cottage, Maresford

26 May 2003

'Ben,

How are you? We're fine, and enjoying the burst of summer weather in Kent. Hope Et-Tel is yielding some fruit.

Sorry to contact you unexpectedly, but we really must resolve the issue over Tnymaes – I'm expecting a baby in the autumn, and we will need my share of the equity by then.

You may find it easier to email me, address below, and I'm sure we can sort this without recourse to the interference of solicitors.

Sincere best wishes,

Carys.'

As I read this, my stomach felt as though it had been smashed with a barbed club.

So she's pregnant, at thirty-five, and all she ever said to me about children being the pits of the earth was a lie. The truth is that having *my* child would have been the pits. Anyone else's is fine.

Now she's going after half of the one thing I kept in the divorce, my tiny cottage in the Welsh woods. Un-bloody-believable.

And she's threatening me with legal action if I don't co-operate. All very politely put of course, because that's the kind of well-brought-up girl she is.

I've been pretty emotional the past few days, but this takes the goddam biscuit. I read the note four times, then tore it into thin strips and burned them with my lighter, including the piece with her email address. And I might as well admit it, I stumbled to the harbour and wept. Really wept. Choking salt sobs to melt any on-lookers heart.

We always said Tnymaes wouldn't be sold. It's all I've ever owned, and not even worth much. A tiny stone hut near Tywyn at the foot of Bird Rock, one of the best places on earth. When I found the cottage it was derelict and Dad lent me eighteen hundred quid to take it on.

The summer day when I set eyes on the ruin is as clear as yesterday in my mind. I was youth hostelling and bird-watching – don't laugh, they were happy times, and on the way back to the hostel I diverted to swim in the river that runs around the base of Bird Rock. I found the hut built up against an outcrop in a little wood, and reckoned it was once a shepherd's cottage. It had part of a roof, and the remains of two simple stone rooms, with a bread oven in the blackened fireplace.

The farmer fell over himself to sell, and I spent the first two years after graduation rebuilding and renovating. I was waiting for my first paid work in archaeology, and temping as a milkman, barman, whatever I could get to pay for the cottage.

When I'd finished, my love for the place was unreasonable and total. I dug out a bit of a garden, planted teasels and foxgloves, and furnished the inside with old furniture trawled from agricultural auctions and house-clearance sales.

The two rooms were snug and neat, a kitchen parlour with bedroom behind, Little House in the Big Woods meets Huckleberry Finn. My little bit of heaven.

Carys loved it, and after we married she introduced the Laura Ashley element, and planted fruit bushes and beans. Organic of course.

When we made love in front of the fire she would cry, and say that if I died she would live here for ever because the place was an extension of me. Ben's Den she called it.

Even at the divorce, she agreed Tnymaes could be excluded from the negotiations, and contented herself with half my trust fund (set up by mother-dearest), half my pension (meagre but mine), the car and the full five grand from our savings account. But she left Tnymaes alone. Probably because it wasn't worth much in 1997. And because I rolled over and saved her any legal fees by giving her everything else. I just wanted it to be over.

So I kept Tnymaes and it's been my haven ever since. It had never felt like Carys' home, and the fruit bushes died years ago – my teasels choked them out.

Now I've realised I can't set one foot in front of the other towards Jerusalem with these issues lurching out at me from the past - where they belong, and where I've tried to keep them in locked drawers marked EMOTIONAL DANGER - DO NOT OPEN.

As I looked across the waters I could feel something bubble up in my chest, not anger exactly, more like indigestion, a physical pain of some kind. Then I pictured Carys' stony expressions, and remembered all I've given her of myself. And the bubble rose up and popped in my throat, becoming pure, distilled anger.

The only way I could imagine dealing with this was to reply. Not a Ben letter – in Ben-speak. That would have gone something like 'Dear Carys, so pleased you're pregnant, my love to you and Jerry – do let me know what you would like as a gift for the baby. I will put Tnymaes on the market right away and you may have all the equity. Lots of love Ben.'

I started with a letter to Switzerland.
'Dear Mum,

This is the first time I've written to you from a place of honesty. When you left us in 1970 I was just a kid, and couldn't tell you how I felt. Whenever you contact me now, some of that pain comes back and bites me on the leg.

I will try to show an interest in Mario in future – but the bottom line is – I'm jealous of him and all the love you've given him rather than me. Since the age of 8, I have longed for your hugs and attention.

I know you'll be pleased to hear that I've dug up one of the most significant finds of the last century – an early Christian ostrakon that could be from Simon Peter the Apostle. It's caused quite a stir – but I have taken time off to escape from the publicity. I could tell you some bull about researching the historical background, but the truth is my head is shot to pieces and I don't know who I am or where I'm going.

Now I'm asking you to do something for me – my first request in 41 years. If this letter arrives in time, please meet me in Jerusalem, at the Caliph bar, Betzalel, July 15th at noon.

I would appreciate seeing you alone, but understand if you want to bring Mario. In the hope of a better relationship in future,
Ben.

That was the easy one, surprisingly, amazingly easy, it felt so good to tell the truth. As I wrote, Mum kind of shrank and became less of an icon of destruction, more a human being who had made big mistakes. That was a new and lovely feeling. I was actually enjoying myself.

I fiddled with my biro and tore a new leaf out of my notepad,

'Carys,
Your letter is an insult and is below the belt even for you.
Try to take an objective view of yourself – you left me for a guy you'd been sleeping with for two years, and never said sorry.
You took all my money and more than all my self respect.
Though I begged you to have a child for five years, you forced me to drop the dream because of your dislike of kids.
And now it suits you to come after me for more cash.
The answer is no. Take me to court, threaten me with the firey pits of hell and the answer is the same.
I loved you too much for too long, and now I am letting go.
Enjoy the bed you made. Go lie on it.
Ben.

Wow, that felt good! On re-reading the replies I could hardly believe the words were mine, so I put them in the mail before I lost my bottle, and redirected my post to Jerusalem – care of the University.

With half the day gone, I filled my rucksack with provisions, and set out on the road south. I felt completely liberated, free of the chains that have bound me to women all my life, knowing neither Mum or Carys can get in touch with me until I reach Jerusalem, and Taylor is doing her own thing on vacation. So it will be me and the road.

Suddenly the realisation hit home, although I've always considered myself to be a free spirit, I've actually been as free as a drug smuggler in a Thai jail. Tied, bound and gagged by the need for a love that has never come my way.

Love, love. That's it, what I have searched, thirsted and yearned for. Sure, Dad loved me, but he was a man, and I needed Mum too. So I fell in love with Carys who was the first girl who looked at *me* needily. I mistook her hunger for love, and gave her everything, my loyalty, money and commitment.

Without understanding this, all I'd ever wanted was for her to fill the void left by losing Mum, pity Carys has to be the least loving girl in the northern hemisphere. Self-contained, opinionated, hungry for attention, but not loving. Even though we were married, she never let me in.

Stubbornly, I've continued to love and need her for twenty-odd years, still hoping she could mend the hurt in me. And I've never healed, which is probably why I can't relate to women, I'm either in awe of them, or - if I'm drunk enough to lose my insecurity - I use them for sex.

As I never believe a woman can be interested in me, I fail to read the signs or try to understand them. What a mess to get into.

As I stepped along the lakeside road, I took a few deep dredges of Galilean air into my lungs, and let the seriousness of these revelations sink in. It helps me to know that Susannah, Peter and Jesus lived and loved right here, centuries before. I had a sudden compulsion to open Taylor's little gospel for some kind of re-assurance, and my eyes fell on the words, 'Have faith in God, have no doubts in your mind, then whatever it is you pray for in faith, God will give it to you.'

I reckoned this meant I could ask for a Ferrari, but as I'd have significant doubts God would respond positively, that was ruled out.

As a kind of insurance policy, in case there is some life force out there, I asked for peace. It wasn't a prayer – more a stab in the dark, 'God, if you're really there, could I have some peace in my life?'

No answer of course, but I would have been shocked if there had been.

The five or six miles from Tiberias to the southern tip of the lake went all too quickly. Part of me didn't want to leave Susannah's home, but I was drawn on by the assumption she would have travelled to Jerusalem many times, and also by the dream when she promised I would find her there.

From the southern delta with the Jordan, I looked back at the blue and windless lake, every tree defined in the crystal atmosphere, the snow-dusted ridge of Hermon rising as a backdrop in the north. Beautiful, utterly good - no wonder Jesus made this place his home.

It was hard to leave, but I have to find Susannah's shadowy footprints, and follow them.

Capernaum, Galilee
CE 32

Perhaps we're all becoming tense, but there's been a bad atmosphere between the men since they returned with Jesus. Not just that first night, but all the time, a kind of underlying bubbling, like the bottom of a pot on the fire, just before the water starts to boil.

Usually I love this time of year, with the richness of the citrus harvest and the end of winter rains, feeling the earth become warm under my feet. But not this year.

Dad has been fractious and moody, and though he's tried to regain his peace of mind by returning to the boats, nothing has helped. Several mornings this month, I've sat on the shore to receive the catch and take breakfast home to Momma, and Dad has rowed in, angry and frustrated.

'I get no pleasure from this life any more,' he moans, making it sound as though it's all my fault. 'I've lost the joy. Sometimes I wish Jesus had never come.'

'You don't mean that.'

'Yes I do.'

There's no point arguing with him when he's in that mood.

Yesterday he was worse than ever, and by nightfall he'd shut himself in the potting house with a new wineskin. Full I might add.

When I put my head round the door I had no idea he was there, but he saw me and it was too late. He was slurring, and his eyes were moist and unfocussed.

'Aren't you juss the lucky one?' he sneered at me, 'scaping betrothal, stayin' here and livin' the life of a.....

136

man.'

'Don't start Dad, I won't argue with you when you have a wineskin for company.'

'I'll drink what I like, do what I like, I'm your father,' he slurred.

'Unfortunately.'

That was it, of course - as ever I couldn't help biting back, and regretted the word as soon as I spoke, 'Sorry Dad, sorry.'

'You ssssnake, no-daughter-of-mine,' Dad tried to grab me but tripped and fell across the stone jars, cursing and embarrassing me. I was glad we were alone, especially when he started to cry.

So I took the wineskin away and fetched a jug of cool well water, and mopped his face while he supped long draughts.

'What have I become, where am I going?' he snivelled.

'Dad you're going to Jerusalem with Jesus.'

'But I want my old life back again...'

'None of us can have the old life, but we wouldn't want it now, not after the taste of life with the Master. You know that really.'

'Sssshh, Shall I tell you a secret daughter?' he was still slurring.

'No Dad, better not.'

'But Judas won't mind.'

'Judas?'

'He's got a plan, a big plan,' Dad was making unsteady sweeping gestures with his arms as he spoke, 'to stop Jesus talking about dying. We know it's what he wants – it will be part of the end days. Judas has gathered a gang of supporters, Zealots,' Dad was slumped over me now, and unstoppable, 'and they're going to make Jesus their military leader. He's going to lead an army to overthrow the Romans and return our nation to the land of milk and honey of our fathers' days. It will be God's Kingdom on earth. God's Kingdom Susannah, God's Kingdom. Yes. There will be such bloodshed and change. Change!' He was yelling triumphantly.

'Dad, Jesus doesn't want bloodshed. He wants love.'

'Ah but he doesn't understand our people yet, he will though, he will. It's all going to happen in Jerusalem, Judas will proclaim him King, the Jewish authorities will welcome Jesus because he'll do public miracles and prove who he is.'

'And who do you think he is?'

'God's anointed leader for our people. Our king.'

'Dad you know better than that – we've got to face up to it – who is he?'

Completely unexpectedly Dad started weeping again, and clinging to me like a little child, 'He's …he…. he's the one.'

I waited.

'He's the Christ.'

'Dad!' I whispered, 'that's wonderful.'

I was silent as I let the power of Dad's realisation sink in, and he looked at me with big watery eyes.

Lifting my hands to his shoulders, I squeezed him, 'So now you've seen it, don't talk about an army and militia or bloodshed any more. It won't happen, so try and talk Judas out of it, because the worst thing you could do is proclaim Jesus King in Jerusalem – can you honestly imagine the Jewish authorities welcoming that? Put it out of your mind Dad, they mustn't go upsetting the Romans.

Let Jesus do the leading.'

'You're such a daughter!' Dad enthused, 'where did you learn to be so like a son?'

I laughed now and tousled his thick wiry hair.

'Get up Dad, wash yourself and go to bed, sleep is what you need. And don't touch the wine again, it makes you thick and ugly, I don't like to see you this way.'

I helped Dad across the street and he leaned on my small shoulders as we wended our way home. He was so heavy and strong that I could hardly bear his unsteady weight. We found Jesus sitting by the embers of the courtyard fire, and he realised immediately that Dad was three parts skinned. He smiled, 'Bed Simon Peter, you will need a clear head for the next stage of our journey.'

Dad stumbled across the yard toward Momma and comfort.

'He's depressed,' I confided to Jesus, into the night silence broken only by the incessant grating of cicadas.

'I know. Come with me Lily!' Jesus said suddenly.

'Where?'

'To Jerusalem for the Passover.'

'Yes, I'd love to, but will Momma allow it?'

He ignored my question, 'Are you brave enough for what you will see there?'

'Of course, I'm fifteen years old, I'm a woman.'

'Pray with me my Lily.' He tugged at the hem of my tunic, his eyes pleading in the firelight.

I knelt beside him on the rush matting. There was a pause.

Then I stammered in panic, 'Are you waiting for *me* to pray for *you*?'

'Of course, please pray my love.'

'Can we pray here … aloud? Away from the synagogue?'

'My Father is everywhere, not just in the synagogue.'

'How shall I pray?'

'Just call on him as Father.'

I screwed up my face and hoped I would be spared punishment for blasphemy, 'Er Almighty one, God of Abraham, mighty, powerful ……. spare your wrath…' It was hopeless.

Jesus said, 'Pray like this little one, Dad in heaven,'

I half opened my eyes and squinted at Jesus. He had just used our everyday word for Daddy, to speak to Almighty God.

But he continued praying as if it's completely normal to address Yahweh that way. The law tells us not even to speak his name. I closed my eyes again and listened.

'Glory be to your holy name. Hear us as we pray in faith. Give Susannah the courage of a lion of Judah, and the softness of a flower. Protect us from evil on the road to Jerusalem, keep our hearts pure for you, and our minds true to your commandments.

Father, give me the strength to face what must come, and faith to believe you will bring joy out of my pain and suffering. Amen.'

I felt bold now I had heard Jesus pray, and added, 'Amen Father, and make me brave enough to help Jesus bear the yoke. Help me to be there for him, and love him. Amen.'

Next morning Dad must have regretted he'd drunk so much wine, because Jesus woke everyone before first cock-crow. When I came down my ladder I found the main room full of men, sandals and fresh tunics. They were preparing for a journey. Again.

But unlike the other times, Jesus wasn't joyful or excited, just withdrawn.

Dad was eating fistfuls of unleavened bread and gulping leben, complaining the weather was giving him headaches. Everything felt out of joint to me, even Momma was out of spirits.

And to crown it all, we had some unwelcome visitors - a huddle of Pharisees, up early and bent on causing trouble. Gran had shown them into the courtyard and we all bowed our heads to them in a show of respect, including Judas.

The three men treated Jesus with a slimy sarcasm, 'Master, forgive us for troubling you at this hour,' they sneered, bowing their heads. All the time they spoke I noticed them look at one another with knowing sideways glances.

The shortest man seemed to be the spokesperson, 'Master, we know you are a teacher, and well versed in the law,' the other two figures smiled at each other, 'and that you are guiding the people on weighty matters. We come to you to settle a very difficult question, one that has plagued our wise minds.'

I saw the fat Pharisee wink at his thin friend and I glanced at Jesus to see if he had spotted it. His eyes met mine with a weary expression, as though one more stupid question was going to make him lose his temper. But I knew he would dig deep in the bottomless well of patience he has for people, even contemptible ones.

The short Pharisee went on, 'What is the correct interpretation of the law Master, should a man be permitted to divorce his wife?'

Dad and the men weren't remotely interested, this was about the thousandth such question we'd had in the last twelve moons, and they went back into the house.

I could see from the glint in the Pharisee's eyes that he didn't actually want to know the answer either, he was just trying to catch Jesus out, and make him say the loving but wrong thing.

Jesus was rubbing the palm of his left hand with his right thumb, and I knew he wouldn't be caught out this time. He was tired of these parasites, who aren't interested in what he has come here for.

He answered with a question, 'Tell me, what does Moses say about divorce in the law?'

Of course they were able to answer this, and all three piped up together, like navy-clad triplets, 'Moses allowed divorce…as long as the man wrote on the divorce papers…and if his wife does not please him.'

Jesus squatted down on his heels and breathed out heavily, the Pharisees - looking mighty pleased that he was indulging them - flicked the flags clean with their little linen cloths. Then they squatted too and blinked at him, like three lizards in waiting.

Jesus began to speak, 'My Dad was a carpenter, but he loved birds, they gave him hours of pleasure long after he had put the tools of his trade away at night. He kept doves, and reared them for sale to the villagers, to be used for sacrifice, and as time went by he made a deal of money, and our storerooms were full of birds.

One of the things my Dad liked most about doves is the devotion of the male to the female bird, they never take another mate if their partner dies.

There was one particular hen that was most special to

my Dad, because he had reared her by hand with drops of milk taken from our own flock. He had found her abandoned in a nest and rescued her at a few days old. Unlike all our other doves, this one had a blemish on her breast and one wing, the colour of dry blood. So she could never be used for sacrifice and was imperfect to all eyes but his.

Within a short time, his favourite young cock bird had chosen the stained hen for his mate. Dad was angry, in case their young would have stained feathers and be no use for market. So he tried everything to separate them, he kept the hen in a wooden box, but the cock sat beside it and coo-ed for her release. Then Dad hid her in the rabbit pen, but the cock brought grains of corn and dropped them through the reed screen for her to eat.

Eventually the cock stopped feeding and lost weight, and my Dad relented. When he set the birds together again, their joy was complete and they never left each other's side. They raised three broods a year for their lifetimes, and not one of their young had a single blemish. So I ask, why do you think the Lord God made doves faithful?'

'Because he made creatures to be joined in marriage.'

'So don't separate them.'

This wasn't what they wanted to hear, 'But master, many men have wives who do not please them.'

'God made man and woman, male and female, to become two halves of one whole. That is all you need to know about God's law. Stop ignoring His commands so you can follow your own teachings.' And he rose to his feet and swept them out of our home with his arm, like three irritating insects.

And before I had time to think, he was calling for the twelve, 'Time to be on the road to Jerusalem - Simon, Andrew, come on.'

Miriam had only just heard I was going to Jerusalem with the men, and she suddenly burst from the inner room, 'Momma says you're leaving with Jesus! Susannah, I'll miss you so much - remember everything, come home soon, and tell me all that happens on the road and in the city.'

She held me tightly - ever since she came to us, Miriam's hugs have been better than anyone's because she holds me with all of her body.

As I let her go, her cheeks were wet with tears, and my heart ached for her, 'Miriam, my eyes will see for both of us, and I'll protect him. Promise.'

'I know,' she replied, kissing my cheek.

Just then Mark appeared through the street door, and boasted to me across the yard, 'Come here cousin, I'm in charge of you!' I knew Mark had been included in the party as my chaperone, he was the only reason Momma had allowed me to travel with the men. Mark doesn't get distracted like Dad and the others, he's reliable, faithful, dependable. Without the two of us, life would be harder still for Momma, but our friends would share their food with her now the boats are idle. Jesus had promised all would be well, and we know his promise is as good as law.

I kissed Momma and reassured her best as I could, 'There's no need to worry when I'm with Jesus, no harm can come to us,' and in turn she reminded me, 'You must speak to Zebedee in the city and he will arrange for you to meet the son of the temple guard. Remind your father when you arrive. Tell Zebedee to send me word, and make sure Simon Peter speaks of the bride price.'

Then Dad gave her a great bear hug, and we were away, disappearing into the silent streets. The first streak of dawn was marking the sky, and we made no sound except our new sandals padding on the baked streets and pathways along the shore.

I looked back at Capernaum many times, and in the half-light I could pick out the whiteness of the houses for a long time, and I knew that Momma, Miriam and Joseph would wait for us.

Jordan, Galilee
4th July 2003

By noon the heat was so intense I couldn't walk any further. So I sat and dug my old map from the recesses of my backpack. It's old but in perfect condition, because I've got a thing about maps, folding them right, keeping them flat, and not writing on them. (Carys marked her friend's house in Milton Keynes on my OS map and I had to throw it away. We had a big row about it – she couldn't understand why I thought it was ruined.) I opened the map carefully, smoothed it and laid it on my knees.

The Jordan valley is part of a huge geographical fault beginning in Syria and running south through the Dead Sea, on to the Red Sea and Africa. The river Jordan rises on the western slopes of Mount Hermon and drops quickly to enter the lake, falling even faster when it leaves on its journey south, where it drops 650 feet in a winding course of 65 miles.

The riverside path is known as the way of the Jordan – it's centuries old and follows the meandering serpentine of green water through part open country, part wooded groves of tamarisk, willow and poplar, with outcrops of sandy rock jutting beneath branches.

My first experience of the way of the Jordan is sadly out of joint with the 1839 lithographs in my little reference book. Since David Roberts visited Israel, the Jordan has been heavily diverted for irrigation, and no longer flows as a wide, strong current, more of a trickle.

We don't know where Jesus was baptised, and the river isn't the same now, it would have been wide and shallow enough for hoards of pilgrims to wade in together two thousand years ago. As I walked it struck me as a dying river, dark, cloying somehow. But it's historic and that'll have to satisfy me. David Roberts was a lucky bloke, but I'll have to use my imagination.

At one point on today's journey the river path opened up into a flat landscape and I had a good view across the plain, where a couple of roads crossed. Their surface was white with powdered limestone dust, every car here leaves a billowing trail, as it snakes across the surface of the earth.

Crossing the plain from east to west, I saw a camel caravan of about twenty animals, with a couple of donkeys at the rear who kicked up the floury dust in clouds. But unlike them, nothing came from the soft feet of the camels as they padded silently as shadows. A sight like this wouldn't have caused a stir in Susannah's day, but it impressed the hell out of me.

It was so hot in the open, the heat a nervous tension enclosing the world. I was compelled to stop and watch the caravan go by, and pulled my hat tighter over my eyes – my crows' feet beyond repair now. Two thousand years ago, Galilee was crossed by military highways and camel trails, a figure in the distance could have been an imperial messenger riding to Caesarea with tidings of the Emperor's death, or a dreaded tax gatherer working for Herod.

Susannah would have seen camel caravans of Phoenician merchants, marching Roman cohorts, litters of the rich, strolling players and even gladiators. Although she was part of a small Jewish community, she would have met sun-browned Egyptians, Negroes, small dark Iberians and tall fair Greeks. The world kind of walked past her door.

It was easy to find a sheltered spot to camp beside the river, and I calculated I'd covered fifteen miles in the first day. Not bad in 42 degrees of Israeli summer.

I switched on my phone to check for messages, rolled a cigarette and lay back to smoke it, looking at the stars through the canopy of olive and willow leaves above, savouring every drag. My peace was smashed by the harsh ringing tone of The Buffoon on my mobile.

I fumbled for the handset in surprise, 'Hello!'

'Hello, Ben?'

'Yes.'

'It's Taylor – sorry to bother you, but I'll be leaving for the airport tomorrow, and I just wanted to say good luck – and be careful, things are tricky in the city at the moment.'

'Thanks. How are you?'

'I'm OK,' She paused, 'I miss hearing from you.'

'But you've got your holiday romance to look forward to.'

'Oh Ben, I wish I'd never mentioned him.'

'But it's true.'

'It's complicated.'

'I see.'

I knew I'd taken the call up a blind alley - we had nowhere else to go. I'm a donkey, why can't I communicate with women? Maybe if I said that, she would stay on the line.

'Taylor…'

'Yes.'

'Nothing.'

Silence.

I tried again, 'I had a letter from my ex. She's pregnant.'

'Is that good news?'

'She always hated kids.'

'Maybe she grew up.'

I regretted telling Taylor – I wanted sympathy, not a philosophy. 'Well enjoy your holiday,' I said, rounding off the call.

'I'll try, but…..'

'Yes.'

'Nothing, try not to worry about your ex. She's a fool.'

I waited.

'For leaving you, I mean. Cheerio.' And she hung up.

I had a feeling of butterflies in my stomach – the sort I used to get before a footie match at school. Excitement, nervousness. She had complimented me and it felt lovely, even though I knew I'd acted like an idiot on the phone. I justified myself because Taylor is about to jet off to the Med with a guy I'm sure is the coca cola man. Tanned, muscular, half naked, irresistible in an office, never mind on a beach. That way madness lies, let me shun that.

So I thought about Taylor's body instead, and imagined what her tan would look like in a white bikini.

Then for some terrible reason Carys' body came into my mind, and I tried to fight the image, calling aloud into the night, 'No, no, don't.' My words bobbed away on the current unheard, riding downstream with the dark waters.

But the image of Carys was before me, just as I've fought seeing her a thousand times in the last six years.

Summer, the middle of a working day. I let myself in, walked into our bedroom, windows wide open, to find Carys' naked body sprawled across the bed. Our bed. Her eyes closed in spent contentment. With a sickening realisation I knew she wasn't waiting for me. She called lazily, 'Jerry, come back to bed.'

I stood fixed to the stripped floorboards.

A man emerged from our en-suite, naked, thin, pale. He saw me and yelled.

Then Carys screamed, and grabbed the sheet to cover herself, from me, her husband.

And I, who had more right than either of them to scream, was utterly silent, watching their frenzied attempt to grab clothes and dress, as if I was in a trance. I remember walking downstairs, devoid of feeling, and putting the kettle on. No idea why I did that, no idea at all. When Carys came downstairs, I was sitting at the pine kitchen table with a full mug of tea. Numb, dead inside.

Carys was hyper, 'Ben, this wasn't how I planned it.... We must talk....' She was in a frenzy of nervous activity.

Jerry thundered down the stairs and tried to introduce himself I recall, dishevelled, his tie not right, a briefcase and car keys in hand. 'Ben, sorry, er, Jeremy Flack, er cheerio.'

He looked puny and weaselly. I remember wishing he were some sort of Greek God - it would have been easier somehow.

Then they kissed goodbye, as if they were married and he were leaving for the office. Which he was.

And as soon as he was out of the door Carys turned on me like a she-wolf, 'What the hell were you doing coming home at this time of day? Why don't you bloody-well say something...if you had shown more interest in me I wouldn't be in this position! It's all your fault!'

So I hit her. I'm ashamed, and try never to think about it, but I stood up, and slapped her across the face with the flat of

149

my hand.

Then Carys really screamed, threatened to phone the police, and beat me out of the house, by hitting my arms and torso, and lobbing my car keys out of the front door. I held my arms up to protect my face, and allowed her to manipulate me over the threshold. She slammed the front door and I heard her bolt it from the inside.

My whole world was inside the building. When you're in shock you think the oddest things, I remember wondering how on earth I would retrieve my passport, ID and photograph of my baby brother who died. As if she would destroy them all.

Everything still worked, my legs, hands, brain. But nothing was connected any more, and for days I had no sensation, no feelings at all. I didn't even get drunk at first. Just spent hours and hours sitting in the car a few metres down the road from our front door. Or outside Carys' office. I wasn't following her exactly, I simply didn't know what else to do.

We met a week later to talk things through - her expression, not mine. She picked the wine bar, the time and subject matter.

We hadn't met since the bombshell had dropped. I arrived at the bar first and watched her come in, looking pale, her brown hair scraped back into a neat ponytail, suited, professional. She was carrying papers, and her diary.

'Ben, thanks for coming.'

I still couldn't speak.

'We need to sort things out,' I hoped she meant repair things. 'Arrange for you to collect your stuff. It's lucky we don't own the house – so it'll be easy to sort. A joint mortgage would have made things so much more complicated. What are your plans?'

'Plans?' I said bleakly.

'Have you found somewhere to live?'

I blinked in confusion – I had been sleeping in the car for a week.

'I've sorted your clothes into boxes, but there's all the rest to go through.'

'But I'm not leaving.'

'Ben don't be ridiculous, you can't kick *me* out. It wouldn't be fair.'

I blinked again. Fair. Plans, I couldn't make any sense of these sharp words, falling from her honeyed lips like drops of poison.

'How long Carys?'

'What do you mean?'

'Jerry - how long?'

'A while.' She looked at the floor, 'a couple of years.'

'Two years!' A dam of emotion began to break over me, this was terrible. 'Since before Paris, before *Paris*? No, say it's not true, Carys please!'

'Ben, don't be like this, you know things have been awful for ages. We just grew apart.'

'Of course we bloody-well grew apart once you were screwing Jerry!'

'It wasn't him, it's been much longer than that, you don't give me what I need. You never grew up did you Ben? You're sarcastic, immature and unable to show love. Life's one big joke to you, with your childish phrases and nights on the beer. But I needed more, I needed conversation, communication. Jerry gives me that.'

'You never said.'

'Well I'm saying now.'

I stared at her as if she were a stranger, scrutinising her grey eyes, seeing the harshness I'd always mistaken for intelligence. And the thin-ness of her lips, mean-looking, determined. But her body was still slim and shapely and I wanted to take her, right there, as I hadn't done for months. The pain of all her rejections felt more acute than it had ever done, the small movements in bed as she slid away from me and put a few inches of flat sheet between us. Every, 'I'm tired Ben, don't,' seared into me afresh.

Then I saw an image of our street, twenty-three black bin bags, four boxes. A hired van. The end of a life. And Carys driving away to work so she wouldn't have to watch.

The image faded as her car turned the bend, and I opened my eyes to the Galilean sky. The pain in my chest was as bad as any coronary scare – I was choked, and screamed out loud, with the six-year-long ache of it.

The scream began as her name, 'Carys', but turned into a deep-throated cry; primeval and gut-wrenching. And then came the tears, sobs, a great river of pain. I was crying 'Jesus, Jesus Christ!' starting as a blasphemy, but becoming a plea, 'Help me Jesus, help me!' feeling the well of grief that I had feared for so long, letting it take over and melt my very soul.

I was prostrate on the riverbank, my mouth flat to the ground, nostrils filled with the smell of rich earth. My shoulders heaved and fell as I wept.

Suddenly a woman's voice spoke from nowhere, 'It will be all right.'

I lifted my head and looked for the speaker, thankful for the darkness which would hide my face.

The young woman stepped forward from the shore path, and I noticed a gentleness about her movement, and that she was wearing a light coloured shawl.

Silently she motioned to the ground beside me and sat down.

My sobs were quieter at last, more relief than grief. Why was I crying now, six years after it all happened, so long after the divorce papers were signed and shoved in a drawer?

I lifted my head toward my silent companion, searching her face for consolation.

Without warning she giggled, then threw her head back and laughed so that her shawl fell from her head. In the shadows I couldn't make out her face, but I sensed such vitality in her, such capacity for love.

'Hello, I'm Ben,' I sniffed.

'The youngest tribe, the favoured son, Benjamin. Lovely name. Goodnight Benjamin, may the Lord bless you and make his face shine upon you. Until we meet again.'

She touched my arm and was gone in an instant, back to a group of shadowy figures, and for a moment I caught the sound of men talking. One guy in particular seemed to be looking my way. I felt soothed by the woman's presence, and fell asleep soon afterwards.

I woke only once in the night, and noticed the girl's friend was still looking my way. I couldn't see the others, but he was sitting, still and calm, and it felt good that I wasn't alone.

Jordan, Galilee
CE 32

In the two Sabbaths since we left home I've come to life, and we're further from Capernaum than I've ever been. Dad's full of high spirits, the gloom that descended on the men at home has vanished. Mark and I speak together of the adventures on the road – we're being followed by a crowd of people, Egyptians, Greeks, even Samaritans. Often Jesus has to take Dad aside with the twelve to speak late into the evening. It's the only time they have to be alone.

Since leaving the lake, we've kept to the way of the Jordan, and I can never be tired of the changing scenery – the river thunders over boulders in places, dropping through wide gulleys, and opens across great plains in others. Some days the waters are wide enough for hundreds of people to wade and play under the hot skies, at other times we're enclosed in wooded valleys. The dark river laughs, chatters and moves, yet it's the same water that smoothes itself under the sky in our lake of home.

There have been many healings and miracles, but Jesus is more preoccupied now than before. The men are bullish and full of excitement about him arriving in Jerusalem. Dad and Judas are the most excitable, and keep saying, 'When you're recognised by the High Priest everything will start to change...We've been waiting five hundred years for this Master, the prophecies are about to be fulfilled.'

But I feel fear in my heart, though I haven't spoken of it aloud. Something isn't right, I feel Jesus is being hunted toward Jerusalem, and the city won't be a friend to him.

I've had very little time with Jesus, but there have been some special moments that I'll share with Gran and Miriam when I return.

For the first two nights after leaving Momma, we were still alone, because the crowds hadn't caught up with us. Although we passed many travellers along the way, and Jesus stopped to talk to everyone who asked, we camped alone. As usual, the Master hadn't let us bring any food, not a morsel, and despite Dad's joking requests for mannah from heaven, we make do with what we can find. Mark nets rabbits, Uncle Andrew catches river fish – some with his bare hands, and I find berries and herbs.

Judas and James always light the fire, and the men cook any way they like – Gran would be astonished, no pots or jars, just hands and charred meat. It's wonderful, I feel like a man on a wild journey across new lands.

Jesus keeps smiling at me, and never criticises me for wearing my tunic shorter, or going without my veil. Dad honestly hasn't noticed, he's just full of excitement about the Master being hailed King of the Jews in Jerusalem.

On one of those first nights as we sat after supper, Jesus was especially quiet. The last embers of our small fire were glowing softly, the flames quite spent.

Dad stirred the centre with a reed, and just for an instant the heat quickened and burst into life again. Then he spoke in a different tone than I've ever heard him use before, 'Jesus, there's something I must say to you. When you first came to Galilee I resented you and wanted you out of our hair. I'm really sorry about that now.'

Jesus lifted his face toward Dad and smiled gently in the fire-light, 'I know Simon-Peter.'

Dad went on, 'Life before you came was pretty simple,

hard but predictable. I knew my trade, and loved my home. I've never expected much, and had all a man could want, a good wife, and a son to follow me. Never gave much thought to people outside the family, nor to God if I'm honest, I just attended the synagogue and followed the law when it suited me.

But you took me out of my safe harbour, and pushed me into the storm, making me think about things I've never even considered. I resented your probing eyes, and searing honesty, but I was just a simple fisherman with a stubborn head. You know I'm not a learned man, and I'm hasty in my words...'

The men laughed at him fondly, '*You* hasty brother! Surely not,' said Uncle Andrew.

'But Jesus, I need you to know that I love you, more than any brother or friend. It feels vital to say it now, in case the moment never comes again.'

The glow of the fire lit up every furrow of Dad's sun-browned face, and I felt a surge of love bubble up for him. Jesus reached across James and laid his hand on Dad's burly forearm. 'Thank you Peter, and you're right – if you had not said this tonight, you would never have had the chance.'

'What do you mean?' asked Judas abruptly.

'You all know we're heading for Jerusalem,' Jesus went on, 'and I will never return this way again with you.'

A wave of shock and anxiety rippled through our group. I felt a choking pain in my ribs, 'Jesus, don't say it,' I begged.

'In Jerusalem the teachers of the law will say the Son of Man must die, the people will spit on him, whip and put him to death. But on the third day he will rise again.'

Dad asked, 'Who is the Son of Man?'

I whispered, 'Dad don't, he's talking about himself,' my voice quite gone. 'It's the ox with the crushing yoke isn't it?' I asked Jesus, tears brimming in my eyes.

He put his arm around me, but Dad leapt up and waved his arms in the night air, shouting, 'No Jesus, I won't hear you speaking like this! I've had enough of you dying and rising again. So don't say it!'

Jesus stood to his full height and fixed Dad with a terrible stare, as if he saw seven demons inside him. 'Get away from me!' he roared at Dad, shocking us all with the strength of his anger.

Dad yelped, 'I'm sorry, I didn't mean….'

'Get behind me devil from hell, don't tempt me again to think like a man. You don't see with God's eyes, and you try to turn me from what is important.'

Dad reminded me of Joseph after he's had a smack - he was full of remorse and embarrassment. He snatched up his cloak and staggered uphill away from the path, and I knew he would shed many tears before we saw him again. I feel so sorry for Dad, he's impetuous and passionate, but full of love and regret. And although he was still angry, Jesus stared after him needily.

During the rumpus, Judas had started talking animatedly to the men, and they were moving aside from Jesus to conspire. I know Judas so well, bless him, he always reacts by planning to raise up an army and crown Jesus as King of the Jews. He has a passionate heart, combined with ruthless ambition.

Jesus was restlessly chipping one stone with another, and staring repeatedly in the direction Dad had gone.

Suddenly he stopped chipping, and looked towards the

157

Jordan, like a fox sniffing the air for a scent. He was completely motionless. 'Lily, one of my lambs needs us. Look close to the water and go to him with love.'

I squinted towards the Jordan and could make out a bundle of clothing that might contain a body.

The man was prostrate and weeping, wearing odd, short clothes, and I wondered if he were poor, travelling to find work.

After I had spoken a few words of comfort I prayed for him quietly in my head, and laid my hand on him as I have seen Jesus do a hundred times. Then I went back to Jesus.

'Thank you little one,' he said, 'you have done a great thing tonight for my Father in heaven.'

Jericho, Galilee
CE 32

We left the river path and headed away from the water in the wide plain of Jordan toward Jericho. The heat was merciless, and the wilderness parched. I knew it wasn't far to the city - visible on the horizon as a green oasis ahead. But Dad told me it looks far nearer than it is, and we had another night and a day of journeying to reach the city.

The nearer it became, the more my eyes widened. The road drops down and down into the city of Palms, Joshua's Jericho, until it seems you are at the bottom of the world. Dad has told us tales of this place since we were big enough to sit at the table, tales of Elisha's fountain that still flows, jars and jars of it every day, so the people of Jericho are never without clean drinking water. The city's lower than anywhere in the Promised Land, and is a sight to restore the weariest eyes.

Dad says it must be as good as the hanging gardens of Babylon, trees dropping with fruit, a lush garden city of palms and dates. Herod has a built his brand new winter palace here, gleaming in the sun, the marble walls keeping sickness out and opulence in.

But wherever there's wealth, the poor gather, and they come here in great numbers to beg from the rich who spend the winters in the air that's milder than Jerusalem. Before we met Jesus I had no sympathy for beggars, they sickened me with their deformities and cries for help. Jericho's full of them, especially close to the palace and around the fountain spring.

We spent the day in the city, but Jesus was anxious to

move on before night-fall, and by now we have a huge crowd following us. The numbers swelled throughout the day while Jesus preached at Elisha's spring.

As we left the western city gate we had to pass the huddle of beggars outside the walls. They were all calling out for coins but one man was screaming, yelling at the top of his voice. Although everyone knew Jesus' name, this man was screaming to him, 'Son of David!' Not many people call him that.

I could hear his shrieks over the sound of the crowd, and all the other beggars yelled back at him to pipe down.

The beggar increased his shouting all the more, 'Jesus, son of David, have pity on me a blind beggar!'

'Quiet Bartimaeus, Jesus doesn't want to hear you,' yelled a lame man.

But Jesus stopped in his tracks, 'Ssshh, be still, someone needs me.'

The crowd was so thick that Jesus couldn't reach Bartimaeus, and he asked Uncle Andrew to fetch him. Andrew called out, 'Bartimaeus, take heart, the Master is calling for you.'

The blind beggar leaped to his feet and jumped in the air, tossing away his cloak in eagerness. That impressed me as it was probably all he owned in the world, and yet in comparison to seeing Jesus it didn't count for a fig.

The Master made a space among the people and ushered Bartimaeus to his side, 'What do you want me to do for you?'

'Rabbuni, please make me see again, heal my eyes as they were before, then I can return to the fields and won't need to beg any more.'

Jesus turned to the throng and said, 'See this man, his

faith is great, learn from his example.' And turning to Bartimaeus he said simply, 'Go, your faith has saved you, and you will see again.'

As he laid his hand on the beggar's head, I watched the milkiness clear from his eyes. They became clear as two green pools. It was another miracle.

Bartimaeus twirled round and round and examined the backs of his hands with fascination, kissed Jesus, and laughed for joy.

'Now go back to the fields, you are free,' Jesus said.

'Oh no Master, I'll follow you, wherever you're going,' Bartimaeus replied, 'as long as I have eyes to see.'

Jesus hugged him and smiled - it was the first time I've seen a reaction like that – most people rush away when they're healed. They want to tell their family, show their friends, they can't help focussing on the bodily healing, while Jesus is actually offering healing to the heart. I can see this now, but it was a slow process – I didn't understand any of it when he first healed Mad Daniel.

That evening we were all thirsty, and Jesus pointed to the white stone wall that lines the edge of the road, and called to me, 'Lily, if you cross this stony terrace and go through the olive trees to the bottom of the valley, you will see a well for the shepherds and camel drovers. Take your pitcher, drink deep from the well, then fetch us some water.'

I was pleased to be doing something for him, and glad to be the only girl for once – because that means there's no-one else to fetch him water.

So I clambered over the stone wall and dropped through the olive grove. Just as he said, I found a pool of shade, and beneath it a stone basin with a tethered camel standing nearby. I tied my pitcher to the rope and dropped it down to the cool water below. Filling it only part way, I lifted it to my lips, savouring the long cold gulps, just for me.

When I had re-filled the pitcher to the top, I paused and looked towards the road. Our little party had swelled to three hundred followers, but Jesus was always leading the way while people took turns to walk with him.

Most of the group were sitting down in the evening light, and I noticed a trail of girls with pitchers, following my lead to the hidden well.

As I returned, Jesus was speaking to the huddle around him, 'The harvest is ripe, look at the fields, they are white for the harvest,' he said, gesturing toward the horizon.

Timothy the tanner piped up, 'But Lord, it isn't harvest time, we've only just had Purim and Passover's not here yet.'

'Unclean, unclean,' joked Dad as soon as the tanner spoke, and everyone within ear-shot whooped with laughter. Jesus has made such a fuss of the tanner at home and had so many arguments with the priests who say tanners are permanently impure from handling dead skin and flesh. Jesus won't hear of it – he says only hypocrites are impure.

The tanner was laughing too as Jesus answered him, 'But I am not speaking of the barley or flax harvest. Look with your heart.'

His words took me back to the day we watched the oxen together, and tears came in spite of myself. I pressed through the huddle and passed the full pitcher to Jesus who said, 'Ah, Lily's here, she will explain, she is used to seeing with her heart.'

I brushed my wet cheeks with the back of my hand and lifted my eyes to the road ahead. Far off, under the setting spring sun, a whiteness caught my attention. It took a moment before I could make it out, then I realised, 'Yes Jesus, I see.'

'Tell us,' he encouraged me.

'Far in the distance I can see a group of travellers, and the whiteness of their garments is gleaming in the sunshine. They may be Samaritans, perhaps journeying from Jericho to Sychar in the hill country. When Jesus speaks about harvest he doesn't mean grain, he means the Father's harvest of souls. Comparing these figures to heads of ripe wheat is just Jesus' way of saying we all need to hear about the Kingdom of Heaven, and to be ready for it. There are so many people and there's so little time.'

Jesus was beaming with delight, 'That's it Susannah, that's it!'

Timothy was gripped now, 'Master, tell me how I can become clean and enter the Kingdom of Heaven.'

'You're not unclean because of your trade, only what is inside can make you unclean ~ bad thoughts or an evil heart.'

'But in Capernaum I heard you say it's very difficult to enter the Kingdom ~ in fact you said it's easier for a camel to pass through the eye of a needle!'

Dad called out, 'And that's tough, even with one of my biggest net needles!' The crowd laughed again.

'I was speaking to a rich man then,' Jesus said, 'not to you. And I wasn't referring to a net needle.'

'Riddles, riddles, always riddles,' Dad said, and he

wasn't laughing any more, 'Time to give us some room, and give Jesus peace so he can drink. Move back now.'

The crowd grumbled as Dad moved through, herding them until people thinned out and started to set up camp.

After a few moments, Jesus beckoned me away from the men and we walked a little apart, 'Lily, it is time.' His voice was low and serious. 'You have already seen into my Father's Kingdom, because he has given you special eyes. The apostles miss so much, and have even more to learn - there is no easy way for them to understand. You will be spared some of their pain my Lily, because you have already seen the truth. But your suffering will be terrible.

We will not have another moment alone, so drink in these words, I no longer need to speak in riddles to you.

Go ahead of me to Jerusalem where you will stay with Zebedee and cousin Mark. Mary of Magdala will join you there. I am going to Bethany with the men, and you will wait for me in the city.

What must happen in Jerusalem will break your spirit, and many who love me will deny me.

Pray for me, do not cease praying from now until after the second Sabbath. I am chilled to the bone with fear of what must happen to me, but I know the Father has me in his hands. Believe me Susannah, there is no other way but this. I have sweated blood and prayed for any other way, but there is none.

I am the Son of Man, and the Son of Man must pay the price for all the world. My yoke is not made of wood, although I must bear that too, the yoke the Father will place on me is the sin of every man, woman and child who has ever lived. I will carry it so they do not have to, then anyone who believes in me and repents for their sin will be like the younger ox, spared from the weight of it. The Father will accept them because of my suffering. His will be done, but I am so afraid.'

As he spoke, a coldness crept inside my chest and head, icy as water of Galilee in winter. We had walked a distance from the group, and they were far from earshot.

Suddenly Jesus broke down and wept. Not tears as I had seen before, but huge shaking sobs. He clung to me in desperation, putting his full weight on my shoulders, and burying his face in my veil, 'Help me, help me,' he pleaded, 'I need you but I have to bear this alone.'

This was the hardest thing I've ever done, and if there has been any part of the child left in me, it grew up in that moment. I fought for words from my tight, aching chest, 'Jesus, I will be with you, I don't understand what must happen, but I'll follow and watch and pray. Whatever you're afraid of is in God's hands, and he's your Father.'

Jesus continued to weep, reminding me of Barnabas the Levite when he lost his only child to fever.

I knew for the first time I must be strong for us both, 'I may be a weak woman, but I will fight for you like a lion of Judah.'

Jesus raised his head from my cloak and said, 'I entrust you to my Father. Go now Lily, do not look back, and don't stop praying.'

Jericho
8th July 2003

I've had a few days to think about things since the dam burst. Emotion is a weird experience – it connects parts of the past that have nothing to do with each other. But I guess thinking has made the journey pass, and in this heat that's a blessing.

The scenery has transformed since I left the Jordan and climbed inland toward Jericho. I'm not sure whether I'm in the ancient territory of Judah, or Samaria – it's one or the other, but the terrain reminds me of the TV series 'Jesus of Nazareth' I saw years ago. Thankfully without the constant orchestral music for dramatic effect.

I've passed Bedouin tents with genuine Old Testament chickens pecking outside, and climbed through grey olive groves where ancient trees cling between rocky outcrops. Nothing is very green here, uncurling fig leaves are as close as it gets, with a few slender spear-shaped cypresses, but the colours are mostly flinty, white and umber.

I made my way to Elisha's spring, and sat by the murky, weed-covered pool of water that collects on the hills far above Jericho, and travels through underground springs until it spews out here.

Even though it's not a particularly romantic place now, there are palm trees, and it's very ancient. Once a desert oasis, now a tourist attraction.

I saw a church named after Zaccheus (he's not in my gospel so I can't help you there), and plenty about the walls of Jericho that tumbled down. They've found the archaeological evidence now, though for years opinion has raged on the dates. I can't get away from my profession out here.

And I can't get away from beggars either. It doesn't matter whether you're in Tangiers or Bishops Stortford, they're everywhere. Beggars make me cringe. I don't know how to react to the hassle, feeling guilty whether I look the other way, or toss them money.

And most of them have about as much in the world as I have, and drink roughly the same amount. They always see me coming, Mr Ben S. (for Soft-touch) Henshaw.

But there was one guy outside Zaccheus' Sycamore tree who got to me. He didn't say anything, just sat there looking elderly and frail. Sat beside a wooden bowl, tracing a pattern on the dusty ground at his feet. It seemed like the modern world had passed him by, and for some reason he moved me. Instead of being an annoyance, he tugged my conscience, and I felt a kind of bond. So I flicked all the change from my pocket into his bowl. And he looked up at me with such gratitude and unspoken joy, his face melting into a smile..

I don't know if I made his day, but he certainly made mine.

As I've walked away from the city, (looking really sad now with an old tee shirt tied round my face Arab-style), I've thought.

About the beggar's lovely wrinkled face, and Carys' words in the wine bar the day we said goodbye.

Six years after she said the words, I've been un-picking them. First, that I never grew up. True, I still think childish thoughts, and shy from responsibility, but I've longed for a family of my own, so the potential must be there.

Next, I'm sarcastic, and see life as one big joke. Yeah, my sense of humour is pretty dry, but life has never been even remotely funny in my experience. Painful, a disappointment maybe, but never likely to raise a laugh.

And unable to show love. That's fair comment, but how would I know how to give something I've never received? And that's where my baby brother comes in. Little Joe, almost seven years my junior and dead before I could know him.

He only lived for nine months. In the winter of 1969, we had an almighty fall of snow, and I held him up to the sash window in my room and showed him the whiteness across the city. I can see him now, a dark-haired, delicate little thing, lifting his chubby arms to the window, thrilled with his first sight of snow. In the morning Mum told me he was gone, she never did say where. At first I didn't realise he was dead, and expected him to come back. Whenever I mentioned him they told me to hush up.

It was twelve months later when Mum did a runner, that I finally plucked up courage to ask Dad, 'Has Mum gone to stay with little Joe?'

He looked completely bemused, 'He's dead Ben. You know that.'

'You never said.'

'We didn't want to upset you.'

My eight year old brain was stupefied at his lack of logic, 'It upsets me that I didn't know he's dead. I want to go to the funeral.'

Dad's face was grey and ravaged, 'It's too late Ben, we buried little Joe last winter.'

I remember running out of the house and up our street, and just carrying on running until my legs were burning with muscle exhaustion. I didn't see where I was running, but when they found me I was right over the other side of town. I couldn't cry or grieve, my anger at Mum and Dad overwhelmed all other feelings.

So I learned young, you love your Mum – she leaves, you love your baby brother – he dies.

And that's pretty much how it's been until a couple of nights ago when that gentle young woman sat with me. She had no need to do that, I could have been an axe murderer, a pretty upset one admittedly. There was something about her, and I don't mean in a sexual way, something loving and centred and strong.

I'm definitely not centred. That was proved during my half dozen counselling sessions after Carys left. As I represented only one half of the marriage it wasn't going to bring her back, but the sweet little woman who patiently passed me un-necessary Kleenex identified that I am have repressed anger, fear of intimacy, and no centring.

I thought that was a load of bull at the time, but now I'm beginning to wonder. It's galling to admit she was right, but I never express anger – or any emotion much. If anything bad happens I get drunk, and next day I still feel bad, plus I have a massive hang-over. The thought of letting all the anger out is just too scary.

And the last fortnight has proved I do fear getting close. I've run a mile from Taylor for fear of getting hurt - reminding myself of the little brown lizards that are ten a penny round here. They lie out in the baking sun, the quick beating of their throats visible to the naked eye. Then, just as you get in reach, they're gone, swift as a whiplash, so fast your eye can't follow. That's what I do, whenever I see commitment or rejection coming – whenever I might become vulnerable to pain.

And I want what that young woman had. Her surety of who she was, not running or chasing as I do, just as I'm doing right now in fact, by pursuing Susannah. This tendency in me has been made worse by my profession which has taught me to go after the unreachable, dig 'til you drop. And hey, I dug for twenty years, but now I've dropped.

So as I left Jericho on the western highway I made a resolution, that I'm going to stop running, stop hiding.

I'm going to face my demons in Jerusalem – mother dearest being one of them, and I'll stand my ground. Hopefully.

Part Two

Jerusalem

Jerusalem
11th July 2003

I'm seeing the great city with brand new eyes. Jerusalem, Ir-Shalom, the city of peace, is one of the saddest cities on earth, a battle-ground where a two thousand years war still rages. Pushed and pulled as the beating heart of the world's three biggest religions, it's ravaged by man as much as it's revered.

I approached this morning on the road from Bethany – the way Jesus entered the city for his last Passover. Away to the left the ground falls away into the Jordan valley, and the streak of blue beyond is the Dead Sea. It's a barren country, with twisted volcanic hills, and the Mountains of Moab at the horizon, brown streaked with violet shadows. A desert place forever dedicated to the God of Abraham. All along the way I heard the drone of bees and rasp of grasshoppers, until city car engines drowned them out.

Modern Jerusalem is sprawling, hilly, and totally dominated by the golden Dome of the Rock, the epi-centre of Muslim worship. How ironic that the city where Christ died is overshadowed by another faith.

As I dropped toward the city across the Mount of Olives, I tried to imagine away all that's modern, and peel back time as the city shrank in my imagination. I let go of everything outside the old walls, took away the TV aerials, high-rise blocks and minarets, and left the flat-roofed beige houses in narrow streets, with clumps of olive trees between.

They say Jesus entered Jerusalem through the Golden Gate, the traditional route of the Messiah in Jewish prophecy, but it's been sealed by the Muslims since the twelfth century. Good job the Messiah hasn't turned up since.

So I chose to enter the walled city through St Stephen's Gate instead. Inside the old city, some streets are paved and traders haggle in tiny dark shops hung with hessian tarpaulins. This was the Jerusalem that would have assaulted Susannah's senses with its smells, strange sounds and foreign accents.

173

Tonight is Friday, the start of the Sabbath, and I wanted to experience the event which at my rough calculation must have happened 52 times a year for 6,000 years. That's quite a few. So I shopped for beer, fruit, bread and salami in the afternoon, and took up watch in the Jewish quarter of the old city. Long before sunset, women were scrubbing their yards and streets white, and young and old were hurrying home. Indoors they would be cleaning cooking utensils, lighting Sabbath lamps and preparing to read from the law, just as the men do every Sabbath eve. I saw small boys in Sabbath clothes and was fascinated by the sight of strict orthodox Jews in their long black top-coats, beards and black hats.

Once the sun had set there was nothing much to see, every Jew indoors praying and keeping quiet, so I walked the short distance to the western wall.

Standing before the holy wall I felt unutterably sad for the Jews, God's chosen race who are more to be pitied than any other people. In the last two thousand years they've lost their land, and their main chance.

The wailing wall seems to symbolise their plight, it's the only part of their holy temple left, since the Romans blitzed it in 70 CE. Thinking this boring piece of outer wall wasn't worth trashing, the Romans left it standing. So this piece is the last scrap of the holiest Jewish site on earth, a shard of Herod's temple, built over Solomon's temple, built over the rocky altar where Abraham tried to sacrifice Isaac.

To cap it all, once the Jews had lost their temple, the Muslims moved in and nicked the site of the rock, building their mosque on top.

So all the Jews can do is stand at the wall and wail to their God, stuffing prayer papers between the stones.

I felt bereft for them, an entire people who have lost their purpose, not noticing the New Testament had come along and superseded the Old.

To lighten my mood, I had a beer (only one) at the bar where Taylor took me to lunch, and then checked into the cheapest inn on the outskirts of the new city where I can base myself until July 15th. If Mother bothers to turn up.

Jerusalem
CE 32

All my life I've been fascinated by the great city of the Jews – wanting to see it, but terrified of marrying into it. Now I'm really going there, and not a hint of betrothal.

I said goodbye to Jesus and Dad at camp in the morning and they gave Mark his instructions, 'Go straight to Zebedee's house in the upper city. There will be thousands of pilgrims and you must be careful not to lose your way, or lose Susannah,' Dad said. 'She's only a girl, but she's mighty useful to me.'

'We'll be fine Uncle Peter, I know my way,' Mark replied.

Then I had to part from Jesus, and this time was worse than any of our previous goodbyes.

'My Lily,' he said, holding out his hands. As always, he was completely focussed on me, he's like that with everyone he heals or speaks to. With Jesus you know you're everything to him, and that he will hold you in his heart.

I tried to say 'Goodbye,' but the word got lost in a choke.

'Be strong, I have conquered the world,' he said, kissing me softly on the top of my head.

'At last!' cheered Judas, punching the air with his fist. 'That's the spirit Master.'

Mark led the way, and I fought every instinct to look back at the crowd containing the man I love most in the world. As we walked, Mark was jabbering about Passover and Zebedee's fish business, and I didn't listen to a single word, just thought about my conversation with Jesus the night I followed him along the lake path, when he had said I would never marry.

Right now it struck me that he was right, I can't be married because no other man will ever be all in all to me.

And I made a resolve, that I'll make sure no harm comes to him in Jerusalem.

It was half a day's journey from our camp to the city, and for the last Roman mile, we could see the wonders unfold between the hills ahead.

At this distance I had my very first sight of the holiest place on earth - our great temple - and could even see smoke rising from the inner altar. I devoured every detail, its brown, turreted walls, flat roofs rising in tiers, and at the western side, the inner temple. A blaze of sunlight reflected from the inner sanctuary which is higher than any other part, faced with cream marble and overlaid in parts with pure gold. Once, before the exile, this spot housed the ark of the covenant, and Moses' tablets of the law. The sight and emotion took my breath away, I stopped in my tracks, hands to my mouth.

'Beautiful isn't it?' Mark asked.

I held my breath in awe, then fell to my knees on the dusty path. 'God's temple, the place where God dwells on earth, before my own eyes,' I said. It was too much to take in. Such wonder, such holiness.

The entire temple is built on a massive platform of rock, flattening the hill beneath.

On the very top of the Holy of Holies are gold spikes which Mark says keep the birds away so they can't defile it. Herod began to rebuild the temple only fifteen years before Dad was born, and it still looks brand new. It has a harsh, inhospitable appearance somehow, compared to the old city which is coloured like a lion's skin. Its tawny yellows, dark browns and pale golds contrast with the flat new brown of Herod's walls.

But just like Jericho, Roman eyes watch over Jewish life in the very heart of the city, because they have built the fortress of Antonia right beside the northern temple walls, its white towers an unbearable insult to all Jews. In the bright afternoon light, I saw the flash of Roman breastplates on the ramparts, a reminder that we're being watched and hounded even here. No wonder Judas wants Jesus to lead an army to overthrow the Romans, and I don't blame him for wanting rid of them.

The city is surrounded by deep valleys on three sides, and Mark led me down the Mount of Olives to the Spring Gate, flanked with crenellated towers. I kept tripping over stones in my eagerness, too spellbound to take my eyes from the views.

Mark guided me through the lower city, and Dad was right to warn us about getting lost, because every alley and street is thronging with visitors for Passover. I've seen simple Galileans like us, prosperous Jews from Alexandria, white-robed priests and Levites, Sadducees, Pharisees with their broad fringed garments and phylacteries on their brows, and countless Roman soldiers in helmets and chestnut coloured tunics with spears. They're everywhere, making sure there's no trouble, though their presence is more likely to cause a riot than stop one.

Heralds are abroad proclaiming the forthcoming Passover, bridges have been repaired, and even the sepulchres have been whitened. Pure on the outside, full of dead bones within.

Zebedee's office is in the upper city above his fish shop.

He's very wealthy, and married Salome who's even wealthier, and says she's related to Jesus' mother. I was afraid of meeting her as we've hardly spent any time together, and she's so different from the other women in our family.

Unlike Dad, Zebedee has a head for business, and he saw a chance to make good money from the lakeside fishing trade, by establishing a contract to supply fish to the High Priest's palace. My cousin John is a qualified temple priest, so Zebedee has done really well for his family. Although he hasn't spent much time there since Jesus came.

Even if Mark hadn't been with me I could have asked any stranger and found the way to the fish shop of Zebedee – it's so well known. It's in the smartest part of town - Mark has promised to show me the poorer quarters as long as I don't tell Dad - and although it's smaller than our home in Capernaum, it's far grander.

Even the entrance corridor is plastered over the bricks, and they have a mikve ritual bath which we don't need as we have the lake, 'God's mikve' Dad calls it.

Salome rushed down from the inner rooms to welcome us, and I needn't have worried - she was lovely to us both.

'Susannah, my darling,' she coo'ed, 'I'm so pleased you've had a safe journey, and Mark, no longer my little son, a man already.' She kissed him on the mouth tenderly and I could see how much he adores his beautiful mother.

I was no more than ten when I last saw my aunt, and now I notice such a quiet beauty in her. She's tall and slender as a reed, with black hair that shines like darkest olives in oil. And her tunic is made of the finest linen, richly embroidered and tied with a green girdle. As she welcomed us, the bangles on her wrists jangled prettily, and she must have noticed me looking at them because she slipped one from her wrist with a smile, 'Susannah, a welcome gift, and celebration of your womanhood. Come inside.'

Never in my life have I owned anything like this golden bangle, marked with crescent moons, and it will never leave my wrist. I followed Salome into the house, breathing in her scent, and promising myself that I shall become like her, beautiful, alluring and grown up.

The days that followed have been a blur of happiness and noise. The city is never quiet even at the third watch of the night, with always a dog barking, men staggering home the worse for wine, or a Roman guard clattering by. I have helped Salome in the preparations for Passover which is only a Sabbath away, and we had word from Bethany that Dad is on his way to Jerusalem.

I've been finding my way around the city and begging my aunt to send me on errands. This morning she allowed me to go for fruit and milk, and I bounded out of the house toward the lower city, as excited as a new lamb at pasture.

The streets are narrow and dark, descending in a series of narrow steps which hug the contours of the natural hills beneath, and not far from Zebedee's house, booths line the steep sides, each street packed with people of all ages and races.

As I thread my way slowly through the maze of streets, occasionally a donkey's head knocks my shoulder, or a sack of millet presses against my face. I watch and wait in fascination for the obstruction ahead to clear.

Sometimes the sun, slanting down from above, falls on a pile of oranges and melons, cucumbers and artichokes, or upon a round person sitting beside a mound of Syrian silk. The lanes are striped by sunlight, through tarpaulins of skin and fabric, sewn together in a patchwork of dark and lighter squares. Sunlight pierces through them like water spurting through a punctured wineskin. Workers sit cross-legged making mats and shoes, or beating ploughshares. And in the midst of this frenzy, old men have set stoves in the street, topped with boiling pots that never seem to be knocked over. Every step is a new adventure, every sound strange to my ears. But I'm never afraid, for I know God is in the temple, and that he is Jesus' own Father.

Sometimes I pass an open gate giving me a glimpse into a cool paved courtyard lined with Roman columns, and a lemon tree in the centre. All the buildings are jumbled close together, and bound by the city wall which clasps Jerusalem in its brown stone arms. When the crowd becomes too oppressive, I divert to a city gate, where framed in the graceful arch I drink in the landscape of air, mountains and hill-sides. That's when I know that however much Jerusalem draws and fascinates me, I must return to the lake, and freedom.

Salome knows every errand will take me half the day, and she doesn't worry. Momma would be furious if she knew what I am seeing and doing alone. It's wonderful.

But today I was gone so long my aunt had to send Mark to find me. I was standing at the Horse Gate looking towards the Bethany road, wondering when Jesus would arrive, when a new sound erupted. It seemed to be coming from the Golden Gate just north of my vantage point. For a moment I thought I could hear the name 'Jesus!' being shouted, so I hitched up my tunic and hurried toward the noise of the crowd and musical instruments.

As I reached the temple, the crowd had become so thick I could barely move, and I knew it would be impossible to get in through the Huldah Gates from the city below. It was further, but I decided to retrace my steps to Horse Gate, run round the outside of the temple wall and follow the crowd from behind.

A huge throng was climbing the steps into the temple through the Golden Gate, many people carrying olive branches, or palms. Girls were dancing with tambourines, young boys played flutes, and a few men even trumpeted rams horn shofars. Now I couldn't mistake the cries of 'Hosannah! Blessed is he who comes in the name of the Lord!'

Tagging to the crowd I asked a young girl who was carrying a palm, 'What's happening? Is it a festival procession?'

'No sister, we're with Jesus – he's coming to be proclaimed King of the Jews. He's already reached the temple.' And she started to clamour and chant with the rest.

I had a sick feeling in the pit of my stomach – what was happening, how could this be real? Why were they calling Jesus a King?

It was easier to push my way through the people from this side of the crowd, and I nipped between bigger and sweatier bodies until I had climbed the steps into the outer temple courts.

There was plenty of space here, where the Court of the Gentiles opens up, and the crowd wasn't as thick inside as out. Suddenly I spotted Bartimaeus, who used to be blind, standing near the steps waving a palm frond twice as big as him. His seeing eyes were full of joy.

I followed his gaze and saw Jesus, raised slightly higher than the people, because he was sitting on a colt, its back covered with a richly coloured cloak.

My heart turned over inside my stomach, partly from excitement, partly from fear, and I ran hard towards him. Dad saw me coming, called my name, and I knocked into Thaddeus and Thomas Didymus, two of the twelve.

'What's going on?' I demanded.

'Susannah! Well met!' Thomas laughed.

'Why are they calling Jesus King? What are you doing?'

'I'm not really sure, you know I don't like to rush into things, but Judas and your Dad seem to think the time is right. And Jesus arranged it all – he sent me to fetch the colt to carry him into the city.'

'But the Scribes and Pharisees will go crazy. He'll be in danger.'

I had already noticed a huddle of them gathering at the doors to the inner temple courts, and didn't like the way they were brooding. Everything felt different and wrong, suddenly my Jesus was public property, and he looked so vulnerable sitting on such a foolish beast as the gentle donkey. The temple guards were patrolling the Court of the Gentiles, watching Jesus and looking edgy.

I was completely unprepared for what happened next. While I watched, the colt kicked and butted, angry with the crowd. As it kicked, it turned toward Solomon's porch on the eastern wall.

Jesus was now facing the porticoes, lined with tables, baskets of money, doves and tethered lambs. Immediately a shadow passed across his face, like the lake before a storm.

He leaped down from the donkey, 'What do you think you're doing?' he yelled to the men in the colonnades. Snatching the cloak from his back, he threw it to the ground and strode to the porticoes, 'What is this? How *dare* you make my Father's house into a robbers' den?'

He bounded to the tables, piled high with sacrifices for sale, and started to throw them over. Each table was solid and heavy laden, but he had a warrior's strength, seizing the edge of each with a violent roar, and tipping it over in fury, 'This is a house of prayer, not a bandits' market!'

The money changers and sellers were absolutely terrified, a few tried to grab their pots of shekels, but most just fled.

When every table was down, Jesus set all the animals free, untying the lambs and opening the doves' cages. The lambs bleated and ran about stupidly, but the doves took to the skies and soared.

I sank to the ground and put my head in my hands, unable to help, control or stop this. The anger of the Pharisees, huddling menacingly now, the fury of Jesus, as white birds circled around and around our heads.

Whatever has begun is unstoppable now.

Jerusalem
12th July 2003

The heat is terrible. They're saying this is the hottest summer for thirty years, and the thermometer keeps rising. I've never known such merciless, oppressive skies, and boy am I glad I'm not in the trench.

I've been trying to find the shadiest sites today, and started in the Kidron valley which was outside the first century city wall. Like most Jewish pilgrims of his time, Jesus would have bathed in one of the ritual mikveh baths in the Gihon spring when he arrived, and he probably felt better afterwards if it was hot as this.

I've been using a plan of the old city, trying to transpose the names and places on to the modern map. And it's a tough job. But today I had a bolt of inspiration. I was tracking the city gates and came across the old name 'Needle Gate' on the ancient plan. Something jogged my memory – I had read something about the eye of a needle in my little gospel.

I sat down in the shade of the alley and pulled it out. Flicked through the grubby pages. And found it, which really chuffed me, in chapter 10. Jesus said it was easier for a camel to pass through the eye of a needle than for a rich man to enter the Kingdom of God. That's when I had my inspiration. Since I arrived in Jerusalem, I've seen loads of mules and ponies laden with saddle bags, baskets and dangerously wobbly panniers. Vendors pile them several feet high. Sometimes, when a street or gate is too narrow, they have to unload the whole pile before they can get through.

So I've made my own discovery – when Jesus talked about camels and needles, he was talking about this Needle Gate in the city. If the rich man wanted to get to heaven, he would have to unload his saddle-bags of money and leave them behind. That way the money wouldn't be a hindrance to getting right with Jesus' Dad. So rich men can get to heaven after all! If there is a heaven of course.

I felt like yelling 'Eureka!' and wanted to tell everyone in the street. And especially Susannah.

That's when I realised I'm going to have to find some facts about Jerusalem to try and plot the place as Susannah would have known it, so I dusted off my ID and blagged my way backstage at the Bible Lands museum. It's a pity Dad never sent me to Sunday school when I was a nipper, because then I might have more of a clue about Christian sites. As it is I've only got the gospel of Mark to go on, and I AM NOT BUYING a Bible. Even for research purposes. But the guy at the museum was very helpful.

I spent a while looking at first century finds in sterile, air-conditioned cabinets, pressing my nose to the glass like every other tourist. More shards – no ostrakon to match mine of course - but lamps, needles, tools. Each cabinet the graveyard of diggers' heart-stopping discoveries.

Just one item tugged my heart, a small bangle, very corroded but confirmed as 1st C CE, marked with little crescent moons in relief. The blurb said it was found in the Garden of Gethsemane excavations. Dropped among the olive trees, and lost for two thousand years.

Best of all, the curator let me sit in his air-conditioned office to leaf through reports of archaeological surveys.

Admittedly his museum is pretty biased, but I'm beginning to be stunned by the sheer weight of archaeological evidence backing up the gospel narratives.

The diggers have a tough time of it in Jerusalem because all the major sites had almighty Byzantine churches plonked on top by builder-crusaders, so it's not easy to get access to the archaeology.

But I was very impressed by the summary of studies done at the Pool of Bethesda. Mark doesn't mention this place, but apparently John describes it, which is always helpful for an archaeologist. It was known as the sheep pool, probably for washing sheep before sacrifice, its two pools were fed by rain water and underground springs. When full, the upper pool would have overflowed into the lower, causing the water to stir and eddy. The sick used to hang out by the pools believing that when the water stirred they could be healed if they jumped into the reddish mineral-tinged water.

For years experts thought John's story of the cure of the sick man at the Pool of Bethesda was moonshine, because none of the known sites had the five porticoes mentioned by John. But recent excavations have uncovered two large rock-hewn pools at the traditional site. And guess how many porticoes they found? Neat.

When I couldn't find any more excuses to sit in the cool museum office, I took a walk to see the pool for myself. And it's impressive. The height from the edge to the bottom just emphasises the effect, the water now below a stack of buildings piled above two thousand year old archaeology.

For some unfathomable reason, the sight of the pillars really moved me, and challenged my certainty about the universe. They're so solid, so real, so there. If John wrote about this place, does that make Jesus real? And if he healed people, does that make him the Son of God?

Because let's face it, how can there be a God when the world's in such a mess? If I created it, I wouldn't allow all the suffering – so what kind of a God is he?

I've always realised we're not here by accident, the chimpanzees with the type-writer argument is nonsense. Although Carys was an agnostic, she spouted facts like; every human cell needs a precise chain of 200,000 amino acids and they've computed that the minimum time required to get all 200,000 together by chance would be 293 times the maximum age of the earth. She had a book on the chance theory of creation, which concluded it's as likely as a tornado blowing through a junkyard that contains all the parts of a 747, accidentally assembling them into a plane, and leaving it ready for take-off.

I guess if you're a stubborn enough anti-creationist, you can say the chance is still there.

It was too hot for philosophy, so I went to the university to check my mail. Just for a minute as I pushed open the door of the Archaeology Institute, my heart missed a beat. Only two weeks ago I came here to see my shard, and met Taylor. Inside this building is her desk, her lab-coat, her professional life. And now she's sitting on the deck of some yacht in the Med, sipping Pimms and making passionate love to the guy from the coca-cola ad. Bastard.

Professor Asaf's secretary recognised me and treated me with respect, still a shock, 'Mr Henshaw, lovely to see you again, the Professor will be very annoyed with me if I don't keep you here until he returns from lunch. Do take a seat and I'll fetch your mail.'

She brought me an ice cool water, despite me looking like a nomad on a bad day, my filthy skin coated with a greasy layer of sweat. I vowed to go straight to the launderette, and then shower.

Holding out my hand for the bundle of envelopes, I spotted a final pay advice from et-Tel. So another £845 has hit my account. I smiled to myself at the pointlessness of my life, I'm 41 and I've got less than a grand to my name. What a credit to the British schooling system, and to my profession. But then I remembered, somewhere within these walls is a find that's absolutely priceless, and it's because of me. That makes up for a quite a lot.

Two tax demands forwarded from the UK, a franked cream envelope, and a postcard. The view was uninteresting – the usual turquoise sea and white beach, but the flip-side said,

'Hi Ben

First time I've ever written 'wish you were here' and meant it.

T.'

I ran my forefinger across the words, letting myself imagine her smooth hand as it had dragged across the paper, forming the precious words. Where was the coca-cola man? Had he seen her write it? I hoped so.

I slit the cream envelope idly, not hoping for anything.

Inside I found a single sheet of headed notepaper.

Togg, Tavistock & Leverett.
Solicitors.

Oh bloody, bloody hell, this is all I need. A letter from the ex-wife demanding the immediate sale of Tnymaes, and requesting confirmation that it's being put on the market. She hasn't wasted any time, I only posted her letter in Tiberias.

As I folded the papers to shove them in my back pocket I noticed another small envelope on the floor, and recognised Carys' small backward sloping hand at once. I swore under my breath, picked it up and pulled out several folded sheets.

'Ben,
Yesterday I instructed my solicitor to send you a demand for the sale of your cottage. However, on reflection, I've re-read your letter and reckon you deserve an answer. You asked me to take an objective view of myself, and I have spent the last two days trying to do that. Maybe it's such a shock because this is the first time you have challenged me since I told you about Jerry.

'Told me!' I said aloud, thinking back to the way I had discovered his existence.

'It may be a bit late to say this, but I really loved you. Not when we first met – then I remember thinking you were grubby and hilarious, but within a fortnight I'd fallen for you. That was the best summer of my life, when I believed for six weeks that I could be an archaeologist, and met my soul-mate. You made me laugh, and made me grow up – you know I'd been ruined by Mummy and Dad and always had my own way.

You were so independent and adult in my eyes, and you didn't seem to need love. So of course I hungered for your attention and wanted to make you notice me.

This is all a bit rambling, sorry, but I often think of those first few weeks, the beach picnics, and nights under the stars. You were my first – as I'm sure you always knew, but there, I've said it.

And I truly wanted to marry you, that's why I asked you, and

189

of course, you fell in line and we did it, and I hope we never regretted it. We had such happy times at Ben's Den, and for long after the wedding didn't we?

I never intended to have an affair – but we hadn't been getting on and you'd become so morose. I just couldn't reach you any more. When I tried to talk, you cracked an inappropriate joke, and that made me mad. And we stopped making love as often.

Then Jerry came along and paid me compliments and made me feel like his little princess.'

I cringed at this, I'd forgotten her way of speaking, but at least she was telling me why. I devoured the next page,

'It nearly killed me when you found out, and by the way it happened. That's why I was such a beast about the divorce, because I felt so awfully guilty.

Jerry is just an ordinary type of person, we've settled down into a normality that you and I never had, and that's why I've decided to have a family, before it's too late. Mummy has mentioned grand-children so often, and you know, most people do have a baby. Please understand it isn't because I didn't love you, but you never seemed the fatherly kind to me. And I didn't feel motherly. We both changed.

And I do want to say sorry, so here it is, for Jerry, for the affair, for the divorce etc. It would be nice to be friends before the baby is born, although we won't be best chums. Obviously.

So on reflection, as I say, I won't be asking for anything from the sale of the cottage, please forget my last letter. And I'll let you know when the baby is born.

You are a very special person and I hope you find happiness. I know it wasn't my gift to give you, but I hope you find her.

Love Carys.'

I lifted my eyes from the paper and stared blankly at the opposite wall. This was totally unexpected, nothing less than a bombshell. On four sides of Basildon Bond, Carys had said more to me than in twelve years of marriage. Incredible.

She had loved me. She had been a virgin. It's true that I'd

withdrawn from her - that's my safety net. Because the more vulnerable I feel, the more afraid I become. I remembered my walk through the Jordan and my realisation – if I love someone, they leave.

So I had stopped showing Carys love, but she had still left, which wasn't supposed to happen. This was confusing.

I put my head in my dirty hands and allowed myself to toy with the idea that maybe my baby brother didn't die because I loved him, maybe that's not why Mum left either. As a kid I suffered rejection and assumed I was to blame.

My adult experience, spelled out by Carys now, is that closing down and withdrawing love isn't the answer. So maybe I need to rethink.

It's weird, but as I stared ahead, I actually felt my love for Carys loosen, and fall from me. Yes she was cute, yes I had cherished her, but she wasn't my missing half. Instead she's a daughter of middle-England, and will be much happier making jam for Jerry's tea than she would have been with me.

I am free. Her explanation has finally set me free.

Mark found me eventually. I had tried to retrace my steps to Zebedee's house, but in confusion I'd missed the way. In the end I collapsed in a heap beside Potter's Gate and didn't move. It was almost sun-down when he came.

'Susannah, Mother is *so* worried about you. Where have you been?'

I looked up at him silently.

'You've been crying - you look awful.'

That did it, and I burst out, 'Oh Mark, Jesus has been here and it was horrible. He tipped up all the money-lenders' tables - I've never seen him so angry, and the Pharisees are going to get him. I know they will.'

'That's not what I've heard cousin. People are rejoicing that Jesus has come as king, he rode into the city in triumph – the authorities can't stop him because the people are on his side. Everything's going to be wonderful. Think what he can do with his healing power now.'

I let Mark steer me home through the poor quarter, which had lost all its appeal, all I saw here was squalor and need. I ached to be in Galilee with Jesus sitting by our fire. Like a hot stone dropping to the bottom of the pot, I knew with utter certainty that it will never happen again. Not ever.

Salome forgave me in return for my promise not to stay out so long again.

'I hear the men have gone back to Bethany with Jesus,' she said, 'they're staying with Martha and Mary until Passover.' Then she beckoned and ushered me into the inner room whispering, 'I don't know how to say this, but we've got a visitor. I've been trying to be polite, she's in the next room, but I don't think she's quite, you know - respectable.' Salome pulled an uncomfortable face, 'She says she knows you.'

'I'll speak to her,' I promised, though all I wanted was my mattress and sleep.

I stepped next door and saw a figure clad in dirty red and huddled on the cushions. Although I couldn't see her face, I'd recognise her hair anywhere, 'Mary!' I cried, 'how wonderful to see you!'

Mary lifted her head and jumped up as she heard me, 'Susannah – I'm *so* pleased you're here. Jesus told me to come and meet you.'

Salome stood in the doorway looking uneasy, 'And you are?'

'I'm sorry Aunt, this is Mary of Magdala, one of Jesus' closest friends, and part of our family. Miriam brought her to us, and she loves Jesus.'

'I see,' said Salome, as if she saw plenty, but nothing she liked the look of.

Then an image of the shacks down by our harbour wall flashed into my mind, and I understood what Salome was thinking. There was no point being anything but honest, 'Aunt,' I began, 'Mary used to be a prostitute.'

Salome stepped back a fraction and took hold of the door lintel.

Mary butted in, 'No Susannah, let me. May I sit down?' she asked.

'Of course,' Salome said, but she remained standing.

'When Susannah first met me, I was in a bad state. Very bad. I've lived all my life in Magdala, where my father works in the dye business. There's no excuse for what I'm telling you, because although we needed the money, I could have worked with the cooper making barrels, or at the dye works or pottery kilns. But when I was very young I lost my betrothed and never got over him. So I turned wild, and slept with a man, and then my self respect was gone. It was one or two men at first, then a host of them, I learned quickly that a prostitute is never short of customers.

Now and again I visited the girls like me at Capernaum, and recently Miriam told me about Jesus. She's given up her trade because of him. You can imagine how cynical I was until I met him.'

'I haven't seen him,' Salome said.

'He's the Lord!' Mary went on, her face lighting up. 'Since we met I've given up the old life completely, and he's set me free from the past. I came to the city intending to buy new clothes to replace these red rags, but then I saw a precious ointment and used all my money to buy it. I'm going to anoint Jesus with it, a gift from the last of my sin money.'

Salome's expression had softened to pity, and she dropped to the cushions beside Mary.

'I can't wait to meet him, and you're welcome here sister, may God bless you for your love.' Her face broke into a smile, 'Wait a moment, I have an idea.'

Mary grinned at me and we hugged while Salome was gone. She returned with an armful of fabrics, and flopped them onto the cushions. 'Tunics,' she said, all spare, Zebedee gives me far too much money and I have no need for all these,' and she lifted the edges of the cloth with her beautiful hands.

'Salome!' Mary breathed, 'These are exquisite!'

'They're yours,' she replied, 'how about this pale blue? It would be so good with your dark eyes.'

And we began to sift the fabrics, choosing fine embroidered tunics and soft cloaks for Mary. Then we dressed her in the prettiest, and Salome brushed her long chestnut hair until it shone.

Mary kept saying over and over, 'I wish he was here, I wish he could see me like this.'

'He will,' Salome said, 'and I think he'll be delighted.'

Next evening Zebedee, James and John came home for supper. They had left Dad and the others in Bethany. Though Salome was overjoyed to see them, and her sons were as pleased to see Mary again, the meal wasn't a particularly happy one.

James was more cheerful than his brother. 'The pace is quickening,' James told us, 'and it won't be long until Jesus is given the authority he deserves. Judas has been talking to some of the Pharisees and they're really interested in meeting Jesus. He hasn't told the Master about it yet, but he will when the time is right.'

'That's my worry,' John interrupted. 'Why is he so anxious to keep it from the Master? It isn't right to do things behind closed doors, I don't feel happy about all this. The chief priests, scribes and elders won't leave him alone. They want to trick him into something they can pin on him, preferably blasphemy. Today they tried the Roman taxes trick.'

'Pardon?' Salome asked.

'You know, is it right for Jews to pay taxes to the Romans?'

'And is it?'

'They can't catch him out like that, Jesus is searingly honest and quick – he just looked at a denarius and asked them whose head was on it. Then he told them to pay Caesar what belongs to Caesar, and give to God what belongs to God.'

'That's amazing. How did he think of that?' Salome asked.

'He doesn't think of it mother, he just sees the truth and speaks it.'

'I'd like to meet him. Very much.'

'Then they tried him on divorce, and the greatest commandment, but they can't fault him. Nicodemus showed up well and agreed that bunt offerings and sacrifice aren't important to God.'

'John!' Salome burst out, 'don't say that in this house!'

'No mother, they're not - what if a man has a cruel and brutal heart against God or his brother, but goes to the temple every day to offer sacrifices? That doesn't please God. He cares about what's inside the heart.'

Salome lifted her slender hand and pressed it to her white forehead. 'Everything is rocking, the old ways are passing away even as we speak,' she said. 'What will become of us all?'

I spoke up for the first time, 'Come with us tomorrow Aunt, come and meet him. He'll answer all your fears.'

In the morning the men led us to the temple along Herod's wide paved streets, and a large crowd had gathered to hear Jesus speak in the Court of the Gentiles. My stomach felt like a pot of butterflies as we moved towards him, knowing he hadn't seen us, absorbed in feeding his flock.

We moved to the front and waited for the right moment

to speak, and I watched him as an outsider would. He was sitting on the steps to the inner courtyard, one foot on a higher step than the other, an elbow on his knee. His robe was pale, edged with Galilean blue, and he had pushed it back so everyone could see his eyes.

Even from five fathom's distance the colour of them was startling, the blue of spring irises. But it isn't the eyes that make him beautiful, not even his tamed strength. It's the outpouring of himself, the love that brims out of him and runs over.

He was telling the crowd a story, and I couldn't wait. 'Jesus?' I called timidly.

He looked up, scanned the faces quickly, until our eyes connected. Then he let out a great laugh, and stood, 'Susannah! And Mary!' The crowd waited patiently, just like sheep.

We rushed to him then, and he whirled us round, 'But how beautiful you look Mary, your tunic is perfect.'

She was too happy to speak.

'You must meet the mother of James and John Lord,' I said, bouncing up and down impatiently.

'Master,' Salome said gently, as she stepped forward and knelt before him.

I was struck by her loveliness, and his humility.

I didn't hear what they spoke of, but Jesus smiled broadly.

Then he invited us to sit down and hear his story. The elders were hovering by the inner courtyard doors, and he invited them to come closer. They looked extremely uncomfortable, as if they would rather be anywhere than here. Their sycophantic smiles didn't fool me.

I looked around at the four rows of columns, each so

wide it would take three men to encircle, and the triple-aisled porticoes beneath, empty now of traders and coins. The only ornaments were the carved ceilings Herod had intended. So Jesus had made a difference already, and for a moment I wondered whether the authorities really might accept him. I closed my eyes and let the sound of his familiar voice wash over me, and for some reason it made me feel unspeakably sad.

We had missed the beginning of the story, and it was something about a vineyard. All Jesus' parables are about ordinary things - farming, family or inheritance.

'So the tenants said, "This is the son of the owner, come on, let's kill him, then all his wealth will be ours." So they did it, murdered the son, and threw him out of the vineyard.

So what do you think the owner should do?' Jesus asked the crowd.

The Pharisees and elders were whispering together, and didn't look happy.

'Get rid of the tenants!' suggested an old man.

Jesus looked down at the ground and nodded slowly, 'He will come and evict the tenants from his vineyard, and grant the lease to new tenants. Although the first tenants have been there for years, that won't save their skin.

Listen Israel, listen Jerusalem, my heart bleeds for you, but it is not too late. If you do not tend the vineyard, it will be taken from you and given to others who are outside the promised land.

Look at these great stones, if you do wrong now, not one of them will be left standing. Not a piece of marble the size of your fist will remain. The owner of this temple will not be appeased if you reject His son.'

Then, 'Enough,' shouted one of the Scribes, 'speak no more tales of blasphemy.'

One of the Sadducees tapped the Scribe's shoulder, 'Careful, brother, tread warily. He has the ear of the people. We must choose our moment.'

Jesus shook his head disdainfully, 'The moment will be of my Father's choosing, not yours, hypocrites!' and he spat on the ground below their fine robes. I had never seen him spit before. They visibly recoiled, then retreated to the safety of the inner temple.

It was the strangest reaction, but Jesus looked up at me, and winked.

He must have seen the horror in my face, and put his finger to his lips.

Dad was in fine spirits, he hugged Salome, then me, and asked 'What do you think of our great temple Susannah?'

'Beautiful,' I said.

Jesus smiled at me, 'Come inside my Father's house Lily,' taking my hand in his left and Mary's in his right, leading us all forwards.

I was so glad I hadn't dared enter the inner temple before, because now I was climbing the fourteen steps to the gate hand in hand with Jesus. My heart was beating fast as he led me through the embossed bronze gate into the Court of the Women, laid out as an open cross under the cloudless sky. I held my breath in wonder. The Beautiful Gate was ahead of us, inlaid with silver and burnished gold, the whiteness of new marble everywhere. All our eyes were fixed on the entrance to the Court of Israel and the Court of Priests beyond, where no women may enter.

Dad and Uncle Andrew strode ahead and were admitted, but Jesus stayed with me, Mary and Salome. As the guards opened the Beautiful Gate, the pungent smell of burnt offerings intensified and made the air headier. I was less than eighty furlongs from the Holy of Holies, the house of God on earth.

Just for a moment I saw the screen behind the Court of Israel, and my heart thumped.

Suddenly I was aware that Jesus was staring not into the inner sanctuary, but at me. I met his gaze, and asked him, 'What's the matter?'

'You really love my Father Lily. That is all I ever need to know. Looking at your face here makes it worth it.' He seized my arm anxiously, 'I don't want you to watch what must happen.' He looked and sounded panicky, 'Remember that I said it. Remember!'

'Mmm,' I replied dreamily. 'You know, I don't think it matters that the Ark of the Covenant isn't here any more. Because God still is.'

As we came out into the bright sunshine of the Court of the Gentiles, the crowd pressed around Jesus again, crying, 'Speak to us Master.'

I heard one or two calling, 'He's the Messiah,' and others hushed them immediately, 'Don't say that in front of the priests.'

Jesus looked tired, 'Beware of the Priests and Pharisees. I'll wait for the men in the shade,' he said, and waded through the people towards the porticoes.

'What did you mean beware the Priests Rabbuni?'

'Heal my sister Master, she has sores on her leg.'

'Tell us another story Sir!'

Jesus looked like a hunted animal. 'Peace, all of you. He sat down outside the treasury and put his face in his hands. I knew he was praying.

After a while he raised his head, 'Now, little ones, sit down, I will speak to you.'

A Levite pushed his sister forward, 'Look at her sores Master,' and he lifted the hem of her tunic.

I have a strong stomach, but the sight made me shudder. Her leg was being eaten away by disease.

'Oh Father,' Jesus said, and to the girl, 'Do you love God?'

'Yes Master, she replied, covering her leg in shame, 'but I love my mother most because she's sick and needs my help.'

'Then go and show her your leg. It is healed. Your faith has saved you.'

The girl clapped her hands and turned to leave, she trusted Jesus without looking at her leg, but her brother wasn't satisfied, he just had to pull up her tunic and see for himself. The cloth was still stained but the flesh beneath was perfect as new-born skin. The crowd let out their breath in unison.

Jesus waited for them to settle. One or two were whining quietly now, 'Truly he is the Messiah, Hosannah in the highest heaven!'

All the while a trickle of people were coming past us to drop coins in the temple treasury box, and I couldn't help staring. A Scribe came by in his long robes and made a big show of lifting his coin heavenwards as he prepared to give it. At first I thought it was a silver denarius, then I saw the flash of gold. So it was an aureus, worth twenty-five times as much. I felt impressed and inadequate.

Some Jews put in Roman pennies, and a Pharisee came by with a whole bag of coins, saying aloud, 'Thank you God of Abraham that I have so much to offer,' and he emptied the bag noisily. This wasn't a good place for Jesus to try and speak.

An old woman, dressed in dirty black widow's habit, was waiting in the porch for a gap in the queue to the treasury. She was clutching two lepta, the smallest Jewish coin. It's worthless now, we only get an eighth of a Roman penny for it – Dad has strong views on the devaluation of our currency.

Every time she stepped forward to give, someone else pushed past her and tipped a couple of denarii into the box. Jesus was fascinated, and couldn't take his eyes off the widow.

Then he turned to the crowd, 'How much is a denarius worth?' he asked us all.

'Sixteen Roman pennies,' yelled a small boy.

'And what is it worth to God?'

The boy looked blank.

'Let me ask you another way little man. Come forward,' Jesus smiled. 'What is your name?'

'Elihu sir.'

'Well Elihu, if a man has a thousand denarii at home, and gives one away, what is that one worth?'

'A thousandth!' Elihu said proudly.

'But if a widow has only two lepta and gives it all away, what is that worth?'

'That would be stupid sir, to give away all your money, especially if you only had two lepta.'

'Well done Elihu, but it is never stupid to give God your all. That's what I meant when I said beware the

Scribes and the Pharisees, demanding you bow to them in the marketplace, and praying aloud for all to hear. They devour the last lepta of the poor. Heavy will be the price for them. They ought to enjoy their wealth on earth for it is the only reward they will have.'

There was another sharp intake of breath from the crowd, and several people looked over their shoulders to see if the temple priests were listening.

But there was no mistaking that the old widow had heard, and as we left the temple courts Jesus prayed a blessing on her and she remained beneath the porticoes, weeping.

Jerusalem
13th July 2003

Since yesterday I've had a new lease of life. Carys' letter has been a tonic. And I've decided, it's so damn hot that outdoor sightseeing is impossible until dusk, so I've made a plan. Today I'm researching in the Jerusalem Public Library, which is huge, cool and quiet.

It's years since I shut myself away in a library – York 1984 in fact when I finally realised I had three weeks until finals. I never left the Uni library and scraped a 2:2 somehow.

The good news is there's an internet room here, and I was early enough to get a screen. My search started out pretty random, I couldn't resist looking at Hellenistic and Roman pots to try and match the one that became my shard. Think I found the type, round, flattish, interesting to me anyway.

But I actually came here to research first century CE Jerusalem. And I've fallen in love with the Herodian temple. Wish I'd been involved on the digs here. They've followed the line of the remaining western (wailing) wall, and dug a tunnel enclosing a 300 metre length of Herod's pavement in the outer temple court. I'll go there later.

There's no end of squabbling about the Temple Mount, the site of the temple, and radical orthodox Jews continually threaten to destroy the Muslim shrines in the hope of rebuilding their temple. Some of them won't even walk on the Mount, for fear of stepping on and defiling the site of the old altar.

I've been putting together a sketch of the Herodian temple, where Susannah may have heard Jesus preach. It was a bit like a rectangular onion, layers within layers, containing the heart of Jewish faith. Built on terraces, each inner layer was higher than the last. The outer Court of the Gentiles was huge and contained an inner temple about 150 metres long which you entered from the eastern side. Outermost and east of the inner temple was the Court of the Women, where the Levites stood to sing.

I was getting so carried away I actually drew a few pin-men

and wrote 'Levite Choir' underneath. Wonder what they sounded like?

The west door of this court led into the small Court of Israel through the Beautiful Gate, and beyond a screen was the Court of the Priests. Both courts were open to the sky. Men were freely admitted to the Court of Israel to observe services, receive benediction and prostrate themselves, and once a year into the inner Priests' Court too.

Once entering the Court of Priests you didn't turn your back on the central temple within, but moved anti-clockwise and went out through the opposite gate. Here the central altar glowed red with burnt offerings on a fire kept alive day and night, beside a slaughtering place with rows of rings for tying animals for sacrifice. The stench of blood, incense and burning flesh would have been overpowering. Marble pillars supported cedar beams where carcasses were hung for skinning.

At the western end of the inner temple was the enclosed Holy Place, raised, roofed and containing one golden lampstand, a table and an altar of incense.

This was the most enjoyable part to sketch, I had the doors open so I could draw the seven-branched lamp inside.

In the western half of the Holy Place, separated by a double veil was the Holy of Holies, entered once a year by the High Priest who presented sacrificial blood to atone for the sins of his nation. It was built of pure white stone richly decorated with gold, and was absolutely empty. No furniture, no graven image or picture. This stunned non-Jews, because every other faith had idols and pictures of their gods. The doors were adorned with veils embroidered with purple flowers, and a golden vine, its branches hanging down from a great height.

The temple was run by ritual and tradition. At first light the nominated priest climbed the tower to wait for dawn to reach Hebron, then the first sacrifice was made of a sacrificial lamb, to the sound of three shrill calls from silver trumpets.

I didn't draw any lambs, or blood, but I went back and added a few more grapes to my hanging vine.

A second lamb went to the chop every afternoon, two more

every Sabbath, with a few goats and rams thrown in on Passover and festivals when the blood of a quarter of a million lambs ran out of the temple sewer into the Kidron brook, turning it red. And that was just for starters, pilgrims came all day, every day with their first-born animals - even big ones like oxen. It must have been disgusting, and no wonder Jesus didn't go in for sacrifice. If a Jew had sinned he could be let off by smearing sacrificial blood in the temple. The sinner placed his hand on the animal as it was slaughtered. Lovely.

The point seems to be that the God of the Jews was an angry, vengeful God who needed constant appeasement by blood. And he was pretty un-approachable, only one man ever got close to him, on an annual basis. But I could appreciate the sense of awe and holiness the temple must have inspired, and the design alone may never be surpassed. Small wonder that the Jews fill pages of websites with battle plans and strategies to reclaim this piece of holy ground for their God. Tragic really. In roughly 32 CE Jesus predicted the temple would be destroyed, and it fell to the Romans only fifty years later.

I pulled out my little gospel and decided to make a chart of the places relating to Peter in Jerusalem. The last few chapters make pretty depressing reading. Jesus and the apostles seem to have spent the last few days travelling between the city and Bethany, probably because it would have been tough for thirteen blokes to find lodgings during Passover.

They spent most of their time in the temple, and then of course the Upper Room.

I searched on the web but found the references confusing, there's a lot of Catholic stuff about the Virgin Mary's last sleeping place, and David's tomb. I felt my archaeological antennae waking up and knew most of this is later detritus on top of the real thing.

The upper room was probably an unusually large one, built near the tomb of David. There's a lot of speculation about who owned it, but Mark doesn't mention that, so I don't think it's important. Jesus told the disciples to follow a man carrying a pitcher of water who would lead them there – and that's a good landmark as women always carried the water. If the men had known the place already, he wouldn't have given cryptic directions. Whatever, it was probably a simple room with a low table and cushions, you leaned on your neighbour as you ate in a reclining position.

I could picture it, the full moon slanting in on an angle, green on the white stone. A lamp burning, its bright spark floating in olive oil, the crenellations and towers of the city set out against the starry sky. Jesus predicting Judas' betrayal and sharing his last meal with the men, his last cup.

And Peter's famously daft promise, 'Even if everyone else betrays you, I will not. If I have to die with you, I'll never disown you.'

Taylor had told me Peter dictated this gospel to Mark and it really moved me that he put this bit in. Because if I was dictating I'd have changed it to make myself look good, putting the denial in the mouth of Thomas or Andrew, or better still leaving it out.

It suddenly occurred to me - this is a pattern of the gospel, it's humble, kind of pointing you to Jesus and away from the other characters. That's why Susannah is invisible, lost to history, gone forever if I hadn't dug up her shard.

Jerusalem
CE 32

I returned home with Salome and Mark to make our final preparations for Passover supper. Because she can afford paid help, there's little for me to do in the house, and my mind kept wondering back to Jesus in the temple, and I ached for his presence. When I'm with him my world is full to the brim and running over, but when we're apart I feel lost. And it's not just because I'm a girl, I know Dad is exactly the same. Ever since Jesus came, Dad is restless and morbid when he's separated from the Master.

Zebedee had brought our lamb back from sacrifice in the temple, Salome skewered it on pomegranate wood making sure she didn't break a single bone, and it was already in the oven roasting, no part of it touching the oven sides. Just as our people have done for centuries, since Moses ordained it, before the flight from Egypt.

But this year I have no peace, and did a terrible thing, slipping out of the house as the sun was setting, because I longed to watch the last light upon the white marble of the inner temple, setting alight the golden spikes on the Holy of Holies. I wanted to be near to Jesus' Father, because I wasn't eating Passover supper with Jesus or Dad.

I daren't leave the city gates which are locked early for Passover with their heavy bars, so I stood on the esplanade beneath the outer temple and watched the sun going down. In the fading light, oven fires on the Mount of Olives stood out, glowing like hot rubies outside the hundreds of Passover tents, pitched for the week. The Mount was easy to see on the far side of the Kidron valley, with olive trees among the rocks and the first wild poppies between white donkey tracks. Half way up its side I saw the Garden of Gethsemane, a walled oasis among the olive presses on the Mount.

Suddenly the loud imperious Roman trumpets sounded from Antonia, signalling the changing of the guard.

A smell of roasting lamb pervaded the air, and I imagined the quantity of ovens containing thousands of sacrifices. A great sadness fell on me and I wondered how many more lambs must be slaughtered, how many more pointless rituals must be observed before our hearts are ready for God's Kingdom? However much blood is shed, it will never be enough.

Sun-down was only minutes away and I knew I had to be indoors in time, so I lifted my tunic and ran swift as a messenger to the house of Zebedee.

Salome was furious, 'Susannah, what in Elijah's name are you thinking? The sun is set. Come in and sit down.' She looked hot and flustered.

During supper I felt really low, and Mary and Salome didn't say a lot. The psalms were sung and rituals observed, although they didn't mean anything to me this year.

But I'll never forget what happened afterwards. The food was cleared, but I couldn't settle and offered to finish the cleaning so the maid could leave. The family had all retired to their beds.

Suddenly there was an almighty banging on the outer door, enough to wake the dead in a tomb. I rushed to the door and unbolted it.

In the street I saw Philip, one of the twelve, his hair dishevelled and breathing in huge gulps, 'Judas has gone to the chief priests. We need Mark to help us fight off the temple guard. Gethsemane, quickly!'

There was no time to ask him what he was talking about. I bounded to the upper rooms and whispered for Mark, 'Cousin, come quick, Jesus needs you.'

None of the family seemed to have heard the noise at the door, and only Mark appeared from his bed, 'What's going on Susa?' he hissed.

'I don't know, just fetch your cloak and come.'

As we ran I tried to get some sense out of Philip, 'What on earth has happened?'

'We ate Passover in an upper room in the city, and Jesus accused Judas of betraying him, and he left in a temper.'

'Jesus?'

'No, Judas. Bartholomew told us Judas has been in contact with the priests since we arrived in the city, and they've given him money to arrange for Jesus to be arrested.'

'What's Judas thinking of?' I hissed, though I knew the answer already. He's trying to give Jesus the chance to prove himself, to go before the Sanhedrin and demonstrate his miraculous power.

'The Master's in trouble,' Philip went on, 'Antonia is full of re-enforcements because the Romans are anticipating a riot, Pilate himself is here this year. We need every pair of hands to fend off the guard and get Jesus away in time.'

We had reached the city wall.

'We can't get out – the gates are locked.' I said, stating the obvious.

'The wall can be breached here – that's how I got to

210

you,' Philip said, and he lifted Mark by the legs and tipped him on top of the wall.

'Damn this tunic,' I cursed, 'have either of you got a knife?'

Philip threw down a small blade. There was no time to think, and I ripped a wide strip, four spans wide from the hem of my tunic. My legs were completely naked.

Then Philip hoisted me up beside Mark, 'Sorry Susannah, forgive me for touching you,' he apologised.

Dropping down from the other side of the wall was easy, and we joined the path to the Kidron bridge and ran fast as arrows toward the Garden. My breath was quite gone, and I leaned against the wall to steady myself.

A low voice barked out of the darkness, 'Drop your weapons, we are armed!'

Philip replied, 'It's me Andrew, I've brought Mark.'

I stood still and waited for my chest to quieten. In the heights and hollows of the garden, whited sepulchres gleamed in the moonlight like shrouded ghosts. Beneath each olive tree a pool of shadow fell. The moon hung directly above us, touching the ridge with a golden-white haze, painting a shadow of every tree against the rocks. It was as though the very earth was brooding before a birth.

I could make out the men clearly now - beyond Andrew were Bartholomew, Thomas, Matthew, the other James, Thaddeus, Simon the Zealot and Matthias, all curled on the moonlit ground sleeping.

'Where's Jesus? And Dad?' I asked.

But I saw them before Andrew had time to answer, raised higher than us, the white shapes of Dad, James and John sleeping a little apart from Jesus who was prostrate on the ground.

'Is he hurt?' I yelped, moving towards Jesus.

'No niece, he's praying, and weeping. He's completely inconsolable.'

I let out an involuntary cry and tried to run forward. But Uncle Andrew seized my arm, 'No Susannah. Not this time. He asked to be alone.'

As he spoke I heard the sickening sound that can't be mistaken, leather soles studded with nails ringing on the stony path. An entire Roman guard of more than twenty men was heading down from Antonia toward the garden. As they approached we could identify the Chilliarch of the twelfth legion in front – he commands the entire Jerusalem cohort and is Pilate's deputy.

The apostles would be powerless against this. Tagging behind the Romans were a straggle of armed temple guards, looking like a bunch of boys beside the legionaries. I understood how much they must fear Jesus if they needed to send an army like this.

In horror I saw Judas Iscariot at the head of the march. 'They've arrested Judas!' I cried, and then in a wave of nausea I understood. He was walking free. He was actually leading the guard toward Jesus. His Lord and Master.

We stood paralysed as the guard entered the garden. Jesus stood.

Everything happened so quickly, first Judas stepped forward and kissed the Master, saying 'Rabbuni,' and I thought everything must be fine after all. But with the quickness of lizards, the temple guards seized Jesus by the arms, and as they did it, Dad lunged forward with the strength of a bear, wrenched the sword from a guard and slashed at him madly.

Jesus yelled then, 'Am I a common thief, that you send

legionaries to capture me with clubs and swords? Let me go! Day after day I have gone about openly and you never laid a hand on me.'

Dad was braying like a wild creature and carving through the men with his weapon.

The Roman guard had stood back until now, but they'd had enough. The Chilliarch gave the order, 'Seize them!'

As one body, the legionaries sprang forward towards Dad, James, John, all of us. Mark leapt to my side and covered me with his own cloak, then ran towards his older brothers to defend them. Andrew seized my arm and pulled me to the road.

'Let go, let go!' I yelled, biting him on the arm, 'I will *not* leave Jesus, aaaaargh' and he covered my mouth with his hand, picked me up and ran. The Romans only followed us as far as Kidron brook, then abandoned us, they had got what they came for.

Andrew took me as far as the wall, where he set me down, 'Wait here for Mark, do not move. We will find somewhere to hide,' he hissed, and disappeared into the night.

I cried like a baby, howled and mewed as I watched the tail end of the cohort marching back to their barracks in Antonia. Jesus wasn't with them - he was in the hands of the temple guard whose torches were just disappearing through Potsherd gate, the route that avoids the wealthy quarter and would cause least disturbance. None of the twelve, or eleven now, were anywhere to be seen.

Out of nowhere I saw a figure scrabbling to me wearing nothing at all, not even his under-garment.

'Mark!' I sobbed. I still had his cloak.

He was tired, but completely cool-headed. Taking the

cloak from my out-stretched arm, he wrapped himself in it, 'They grabbed me by the loincloth and held on to the linen, but I managed to wriggle free. Your Dad and my brother John have followed Jesus. They'll have taken him to the High Priest's palace, and as John's a priest he'll be admitted by the Portress. Where are the others?'

'They've scattered, Andrew left me here and said he was going to hide.'

'I can't believe they've abandoned Jesus. We must follow Susa.'

He took my hand, and we helped each other over the wall, like a couple of babes, him without underclothes, me naked from the thighs down. I was glad of the darkness covering our long walk to the palace beyond Zebedee's house in the south-western corner of the city. I felt dazed, confused, lost.

The palace gates were locked of course. Mark knocked and told the portress he needed to speak with his brother. She closed the gate and there was a long pause. Then she came back and let Mark inside. As he disappeared, he motioned for me to wait.

There was nothing to do but sit and pray. I tried to calculate the passing of time, but it was impossible, though we must be in the third watch of the night. As I waited I thought I could see the first streaks of lighter grey in the sky, surely it couldn't be almost dawn? The stars were fading one by one. Then I heard the sound of the first cock crowing.

My stomach sank. I dreaded the new day, the first of Jesus' captivity, and I prayed for the delay of dawn. But three shrill blasts from the temple confirmed morning was come, and I saw the pink of sunrise above the Mount of Olives. Then the cock crowed for the second time.

A shudder went through my very soul, and I tried to imagine what they were doing to Jesus inside the palace. The High Priest is second only to Pilate here, and I'm sure the truth isn't what he wants to hear.

At last the palace gate opened and Mark re-appeared. He looked absolutely terrible, and shook his head as he came to me. 'Don't ask,' he whispered.

Then the gate opened again and I was shocked to see Dad emerge. I rushed forward, and was checked by the sight of him stumbling blindly. He was like a rock that had been severed from its foundation, crumbling before our eyes.

'Dad! Are you drunk?' I called.

He let out a blood-curdling yell.

I shouted, 'Dad, tell me, Dad, are you hurt?'

He reeled away from the palace, tripped and collapsed on the flagstones, his whole body rent with sobs. 'Jesus, my Jesus?' he was crying in anguish.

Mark stepped forward and touched my arm, 'Leave him Susannah, come away. He denied he knew Jesus.'

'What? What?' I said in confusion.

'In there. He was by the courtyard fire with the servants, and they challenged Simon Peter that he knew the Lord. He tried to deny it but they recognised his accent and knew he was a Galilean. He denied it again but someone had seen him with Jesus and accused him. So he denied it more hotly. That's when the cock crowed for the second time.'

'But Jesus will understand,' I protested.

'No, apparently he predicted your Dad would deny him before the second cock-crow, and Simon Peter promised him it couldn't happen, he would never do it.'

I let out a sob, 'Dad, don't!' and ran to his prostrate figure.

'Dad, don't do this to yourself,' I begged, kneeling on my bare knees in the dirt beside him.

He raised his wet, furrowed face and I saw he was utterly broken, 'The Master saw me, he looked down at me from the gallery, bound up with cords, he *heard* me do it. *Leave me*,' he howled, 'I'm not worthy to be called your father. I wish I was dead.' And he staggered to his feet and made off into the city streets.

Last night's tour of Temple Mount left me cold. So today I opted for the Church of the Holy Sepulchre, built on the site of Golgotha. And it's ghastly. I defy even the imagination of a JRR Tolkein to strip away the idolatry and embellishment to reveal what was real.

I was utterly unmoved by the site, even by the pieces of Calvary bedrock which have been exposed beneath an altar. But I was moved by the stupidity of man.

I'll admit right now I've been touched to the core by everything I've found out about Herod's Jewish temple. Everything but the slaughtering.

So why has this Christian site been polluted with graven images and ornament so clearly un-necessary in the Jewish Holy of Holies?

What went wrong? For the first three centuries after the crucifixion, the Jerusalem sites were left alone, Peter and the apostles never attempted to revere the places associated with Jesus. They were focussed on the coming of the kingdom, and telling the world the truth.

Then something changed, and humanity took over. A battle began between Turk and Christian that continues to this day. Muslim-Jew, Christian-Muslim, Greek Orthodox-Catholic.

Though I was un-moved by the sepulchre, I was stirred by the ladder. Outside the main church entrance, a little ladder rests against an upper window. It looks old, and it is. Been in the same position since 1860, when it was used to reach some monks who were imprisoned inside. But the battle over who has the right to move and touch objects on the church, has meant no-one has been allowed to take it down. For 140 years.

I was moved all right, to belly-aching guffaws.

And the story of the key had the same effect. Four different groups of Christians fight for authority of the church, and they've established battle lines over different parts. In the 12th century CE, the Muslims stuffed them by taking away the church key.

Eight centuries later, the ten-inch metal key is still held by the same Muslim family. This went on until 1999 when for safety reasons approval was given for a second door into the church. But it hasn't been opened, because no-one can agree who will have the key.

I sat on the pavement and stared at the ladder as I mulled this over. What in God's name would Jesus say about all this? The bloke who said buildings and status count for nothing. Who loved everyone he met, but loathed hypocritical Pharisees and priests. He'd do more than turn over a few tables here I reckon.

The place pissed me off so much I sat and shut it out by reading my little gospel of Mark to the end. Unfortunately it's a bit thin on length, Mark doesn't exactly waffle. But the power of the last few chapters blew me away. It's so real, and fresh, shocking. It seems Jesus knew what was coming to him, and even though fear nearly crushed him, he went through the trial and crucifixion because it was what God ordered.

When I put the gospel away I knew I'd had it with the modern shrines, and headed for the Holy Land Hotel. Whenever I've been on the web in the last two days, images of it keep popping up. Images of the mind-boggling scale model of Jerusalem in 66 CE, temple and all. It's huge.

And I'm not ashamed to say I wept over it. Sat outside the model city walls and let tears run down my cheeks. It's beautiful, miraculous, perfect.

In a way it represents everything an archaeologist like me is born for, the chance to let the past live again. But it's more than that. I'm out of my depth here because I've never read the Bible, but I've definitely heard the phrase 'New Jerusalem' meaning heaven.

And hey, if heaven has got the real version of this model, I'd like to be there.

I spent more than an hour looking at the temple alone, then searched for the model High Priest's palace where Jesus would have been tried, and found the upper city where Zebedee lived. Excitement just took over and I rushed about finding the Pool of Bethesda, how beautiful is that? And the Antonia fortress, and the city gates.

That was when the sun went in. It hasn't rained here since March, and I haven't read a newspaper forecast since I found the shard. But undeniably the sky was turning blacker and blacker. A woman told me they've had amazing thunder-storms across Europe in the last few days, and it wasn't long before we heard rumbling.

I love thunder and lightening, it reminds me of very early childhood under the bedcovers when Mum and Dad were still together.

The site started to clear of tourists immediately, which was an unexpected bonus. Within ten minutes the heavens opened and I had the place almost to myself. And the feeling of the hot rain poured over my head like healing oil.

Suddenly I realised I hadn't seen Calvary, the site of the crucifixion. I located it on the 'You are here' map, and decided to go the way Jesus would have walked to the cross.

The rain was coming down in buckets now, and nothing on my body was dry.

I reckoned Christ would have been held in the High Priest's palace until he appeared before Pilate whose residence was at Antonia, and from Antonia to the cross. So I started at the fortress, on the north-west corner of the temple and followed the main thoroughfare towards the gate nearest Calvary.

It wasn't far, the real life journey wouldn't have taken long.

Unless you had the cross-beam of a crucifix on your back. And unless you had a crown of thorns pressed into your skull, sixty lashes on your naked torso, and hadn't eaten for twenty-four hours. Then it would be the longest walk on earth.

I stepped on to the rocky hill of Calvary. Exposed, outside the city walls.

Then a bolt of pain shot to my core. Susannah might have seen it. No!

She mustn't see it.

I looked at the rock of Golgotha, the place of the skull, and imagined what she might have seen. And every sinew in my body steeled with adrenaline wanting to protect her from a sight fit for hell.

And the thunder broke over my head, rain so hard it stung my face and neck.

So they killed Jesus. They put the bloody son of God to death, the bastards. They hammered nails through his wrists and hung him from a Roman crucifix, the most painful form of death ever devised by man.

And my Susannah watched, oh God of all, please no.

I fell to my knees on the model and hugged the ground, weeping, 'Oh baby, baby, I'm sorry they hurt you.' I was talking to Susannah, but to Jesus too. The man I never looked for but who has come after me.

The sky was riven with thunder and sheet lightening as I reached my personal Calvary.

Jerusalem
CE 32

I haven't slept, and have no hope of ever sleeping again. When Mark and I returned to his home, the family was just stirring.

Salome was sitting at table with a curdled milk, looking only half-awake.

Our appearance must have shocked her, not only our attire, but our staring, white faces.

'Mark, you look dreadful, and Susannah!' she cried, putting her fingers to her mouth, 'you're almost naked. Who did this to her Mark?'

'She did it Momma. The worst thing in the world has happened. They arrested Jesus in the garden of Gethsemane before dawn, took him to the High Priest's palace, and Peter denied he knew him, and the men are all fled.'

'Slow down, Mark, please. Start again.'

I tried to tell Salome the night terrors. As I spoke she stood from the table and paced the inner room anxiously.

'We must do something, we've got to help him. Where's John?'

'Still inside the palace. He's our only hope of defence for Jesus.'

Just at that moment the outer door burst open and we heard John calling as he ran in, 'Momma!' he cried with a great sob, and though he's seen at least twenty-four summers, he took hold of her as if he were still a suckling child.

He couldn't speak for sobbing.

Salome held and rocked him from side to side,

smoothing his black hair with her slender hand, 'Sssshhhhh,' she soothed.

After a while John let go and sat down, 'It's over Momma. They won't let him live.'

'What?' I screeched. Arrest was one thing, but it has honestly never occurred to me that Jesus is facing anything worse than imprisonment.

'I was there at the trial, if you can call it that. They woke the entire Sanhedrin from their beds and brought them to the palace to hear the case against him. It's gone on all night since the arrest. They're rushing everything through before the Sabbath.

I stayed until the end, when they dragged him off to Antonia to stand before Pilate. I haven't the smallest hope, because they've accused him of blasphemy, which the Romans couldn't care less about, but they're telling Pilate it's insurrection, that Jesus set himself up as a King to rival Herod or Caesar. Pilate can't run the chance of Jesus causing a riot, it's his job to keep the peace this week.'

Salome was very edgy, 'But what evidence have they got? He can't be accused without evidence.'

'Several false witnesses were produced, but they all contradicted each other. Jesus refused to speak or answer any of the charges, he was silent all night. So eventually they asked him the direct question - is he the Messiah, yes or no? And he said yes.'

Salome and I took a sharp intake of breath.

'Oh no,' Mark said, turning away from his brother.

'So the High Priest tore his robe and the rest was a formality.'

We stood in silence, the four of us, there was nothing we could say. Over and over in my mind I wondered why he hadn't defended himself, when he has spent the last three years answering stupid questions. Why would he do that?

Then Mary of Magdala came into the room, looking just like a bridal virgin in her fresh clothes, stretching and yawning lazily as she woke to a new day. I would have given up the entire lake of Galilee to spare her what she would know in a moment. If only I could take it from her. But none of us who love him can be spared the pain of this. We just have to support each other, and help Jesus fight for his life.

'Take us to him,' Salome said at once.

We made a sorry party, Salome and her two sons, me with Mary, hurrying through the morning streets in frightened silence.

John led us to Antonia through the outer temple courts. We couldn't get any closer to Jesus than this, standing on the Court of Gentiles pavement, looking up the flight of steps that lead into the fortress, the way Romans come whenever there is trouble in the temple compound.

We knew Jesus would be tried in the praetorium - Pilate's official temporary residence when he's away from Caesarea.

It was obvious we weren't the only ones thinking of Jesus. At the top of the flight of steps we saw a gaggle of temple priests and scribes, lurking outside the fortress doors. John bounded up the stairs two at a time and spoke to them. I saw him waving his arms, shaking his head, and throwing his head back in disbelief. Then he returned to us, slowly this time.

'They won't enter the praetorium in case they defile themselves - they're more concerned about their ceremonial purity than the morality of killing the Son of God.' He turned his back on us and paced away, toward and away again.

Then he announced, 'From this moment I am no longer a priest in the temple of God,' and he tore a rent in his cloak, ripping the fabric with the strength of a bear.

Salome groaned and put her head in her hands.

'Mother, I can't wear a title that's been so shamed.'

I couldn't contain my fear any longer, 'John - find out what's happening in there. Please!' I begged him.

John was calmer now, and I saw a look of resignation on his face. He mounted the steps and spoke again to the priests, and before long they disappeared inside Antonia. While we waited, the temple court was filling up with petty daily business. People were behaving as if today were any other day, unaware that the foundation of our world has cracked in two.

While the morning sun warmed us, we saw groups of pilgrims forming, and it wasn't long before word started to get round that Jesus was in trouble. I knew this was what we needed, now the people would rally to support him, even cause a riot, until the authorities were forced to release Jesus. That gave me an idea, I ran to the largest group, 'Have you heard the Romans are holding Jesus in the praetorium? He's before Pilate. We must do something.' I looked at the men as I spoke, and waited for their promise of help.

But none came. The tallest man spoke without looking at me, 'I said he was trouble from the start, didn't I?'

'Carrying on as if he was a prophet - he had it coming in my opinion,' said another.

'What do you mean?' I asked, 'He's the Messiah.'

'Blasphemy!' a woman shrieked and pointed at me. It was hopeless, so I moved to another group.

'We must help free Jesus,' I begged them.

'Help a trickster? You're mad,' said a girl not much older than me.

Another man said, 'I knew it was only a matter of time 'til he was exposed.'

Salome touched me on the shoulder, 'Susannah, leave them, they're not worth it.'

I seized her open arms, 'But we must help him, he needs us,' I wailed, 'I don't care if no-one does anything, I'll keep fighting for him.'

A fat Jew shouted to me, 'If he was the Messiah he could save himself - he wouldn't need the help of a foolish bit of a girl like you.'

Salome held my wrists as I flailed towards him. 'Leave it!' she ordered.

Our attention was diverted by noise coming from Antonia. A stream of legionaries was emerging from the fortress on to the gallery above the northern colonnade. I ran forward to Mark and Mary.

Then a trumpet sounded and a man who must be Pontius Pilate appeared, robed in the crimson toga of authority, edged with gold, a purple sash belting his white tunic. No-one in the temple court could be ignorant of this man's reputation, he's notorious for cruelty and barbarism, worse than most Roman prefects.

I looked up at this man who held Jesus' fate in his hands.

The Court of Gentiles was filling up rapidly, like wine pouring into a shallow bowl. The crowd was pressing forward now, as one predatory body. We hardly ever see a Governor in person and this was a sight to remember.

My heart was beating as if I had a bird inside my chest.

The trumpet sounded again, and Pilate spoke loudly, first in Latin, then Greek with a bit of broken Aramaic, 'People of Jerusalem.'

The crowd pressed forward toward Antonia. Everyone was looking up at the gallery.

'People of Jerusalem, the Sanhedrin has brought a prisoner to me for trial. They say he must be executed. But I find no case against him.'

I clapped my hands to my face and gasped. I loved this man, at this moment, I loved Pontius Pilate with all my heart. Jesus was free.

'The Sanhedrin tell me Jesus says he is King of the Jews. I will not execute him for that.'

A loud voice shouted up from the crowd, 'We have no King but Caesar!'

I was completely stunned to hear such blatant falsehood and yelled, 'Hypocrite!' but the crowd took up the shout, 'We have no King but Caesar!'

Pilate waved their words away in the air, as if they irritated him, 'As it is Passover I will make a special concession and release a prisoner, then you cannot say Caesar is ungenerous. Shall I release Jesus?'

He was trying again, Pilate didn't want to murder Jesus, I could tell he didn't want to do it.

There was more activity on the gallery, and with utter horror, I watched two centurions lead a prisoner into view. Behind him was Jesus.

The centurions lined them up for us to look upon. A common criminal, burly, rough, beside the Lord of all the world.

I hadn't seen Jesus since the arrest. He was naked except a loincloth, his arms tied behind his body. But he stood like a lion.

'Release Barabbas!' a voice piped up from the crowd. Then, 'Release Barabbas,' the people echoed.

Pilate lifted his arm in impatience, 'Barabbas is a common brigand – he robs from Jews like you. Are you stupid?'

The crowd shouted louder now, 'Release Barabbas!'

A shrill voice beside me was yelling, 'Release Jesus! Release Jesus!' I turned to see Mary of Magdala, tears streaming down her face, arms outstretched toward Pilate. I screamed with her, Salome and Mark too, our four small voices crying out for Jesus while a thousand drowned us out.

Pilate lifted his arm again, 'So what shall I do with Jesus?'

For a moment the crowd was silent. Then a lone voice muttered, 'Crucify him!'

I screamed, as if I had been stabbed, 'No! No!'

But the people took up the chant, quietly at first, then as one murderous voice, 'Crucify! Crucify, CRUCIFY!'

Pilate turned his back on us and began to shout above the din. As the chanting ceased I heard his words, 'Be it on your heads - I wash my hands of this. I find no guilt in him.' And he disappeared into the fortress.

Jesus stood beside Barabbas, unmoved, utterly still.

'Jesus!' Mary yelled, 'My Jesus!' He didn't try to look for her, and the centurions led him away towards the praetorium.

Before Mark or Salome could stop me, I leaped up the steps to Antonia and spread my body against the heavy wooden doors, pressing until the rivets hurt my flattened face. This was the nearest I could get to my master, and I cried, called for him within the fortress, 'Let me in, let me in,' I wailed hopelessly, until at length the doors were unbolted from the inside.

But they weren't opening for me.

Instead, the huddle of temple priests, scribes and Pharisees came out, followed by John, and the doors were slammed and re-bolted in my face.

John was white as new marble.

We gathered around him like lambs before slaughter, shepherd-less.

'They have scourged him,' he whimpered. This spelled the end, the third degree of Roman beating is used only before crucifixion. It alone is enough to kill.

'They pressed a crown of thorns into his flesh, and dressed him in a purple robe to mock him. It's over. All we can do now is pray.'

Mary fell to her knees and Mark began weeping and kicking the stone steps with his bare toes. He kicked until they bled, 'I'm going to fetch the men,' he choked, 'maybe one of them can help.' And he left us, I assumed he would head for Bethany.

'When John?' Salome asked flatly.

'Straight away, before sunset. The Sabbath is coming,' he replied, 'so they'll act quickly.'

Mary had turned and was making for the door out of the temple. Salome and John ran after her.

'Where will they take him?' Mary asked John blankly, her face devoid of emotion.

'Out from Antonia to the place of the skull, beyond the wall,' he said.

She moved quickly.

Salome called, 'Susannah must be protected from this, she's little more than a child.'

'We must stay together,' John replied.

A hoard of people were pressing out of the temple, along the wide streets towards the main western gate out of Antonia on the city side. We were carried along by the crowd, catching on to each others' cloaks to keep together. I had no feeling, my body and soul were completely numb. But I never stopped praying, 'Father save him, Father spare Jesus, Father stop this madness.'

He is still alive, there's still hope.

A Roman guard was already on the streets, but we couldn't see what was happening.

John pulled my cloak, 'This way, we'll go behind Herod's palace and get ahead of the crowd.'

We rejoined the road between Antonia and the Genath city gate. Moments later the first centurion appeared on horseback, behind him a legionary with a notice on a pole. Red words in Latin on a white background - *Jesus of Nazareth, King of the Jews*. Behind him two criminals, great cross beams of a Roman crucifix lashed to their backs. And behind them Jesus. Blood running from his hair, open gashes from neck to waist.

I couldn't move, speak, think.

He staggered nearer, so close I could almost touch. Lifted his unfocussed gaze to mine. As our eyes met, the anguish in his face intensified to torment. Slowly, he shook his bleeding head at me and mouthed, 'No!'

That was the last thing I remember.

* * *

I woke in Salome's arms. I didn't know where we were.

'Salome, I had the most awful dream. They were crucifying Jesus.' Then with a sickening realisation I saw her ravaged face and knew it hadn't been a dream.

'Sssshhhhh,' she murmured.

'Where are we? Take me to him!' I demanded.

'We're at Towers pool outside the city. You fainted,' she said. 'He doesn't want you to watch.'

The dam burst inside me, 'I don't care what he wants, I don't care what he wants, I don't care,' my voice came in gulping sobs, 'I care. I care, I care.'

Suddenly through my pain I saw an image of him, grasping my arm in the temple as I gazed at the sanctuary. He had begged me not to watch what must happen, and had told me to remember. If it was the last gift I could give him, I would be obedient.

Salome must have seen my face change, 'I want you to wait here baby,' she said, 'beside the pool. I'm going beyond the corner to the foot of Golgotha. I will come for you. Pray, pray.'

She left me and I curled into the smallest ball and covered my ears with my arms. Trying to blot out the blood-curdling baying of the people. The Jewish bastards who pray in every synagogue across this land for God to establish his Kingdom on earth. Who claim that God is their King, and who I've just heard proclaiming they have no king but Caesar. I am a Jew, I despise my people.

As I crouched, the swifts screeched and circled in the joy of a spring noon. At a little distance from me, three centurions lay down to eat their lunch of bread and cheese, talking and relaxing.

And a few cubits away, God was dying.

Even from here I heard taunts of 'Save yourself,' and I

pressed my ears tighter and sobbed one of Momma's lullabies. In my heart I held the bleeding face of my Jesus and rocked it to rest. They can drive nails through his feet, but they can't stop me loving him. He is safe in me.

At the sixth hour, a wind began to blow, whipping dust from the earth into my face, tugging at my clothes.

Later, the sky began to darken, to grey, charcoal, black. I have never seen such blackness.

Then a scream went up from Golgotha, like the roar of a dying lion, and a clap of thunder rent the air. He was gone. I knew it instinctively. And the rain came down, like jugs of well-water pouring over the ground, soaking me, washing the world.

He is gone.

Jerusalem
15th July 2003

After crying so much beside the Jerusalem model, I slept like a baby last night, well more like a drunk actually. This morning I was at the university library before it opened, pacing up and down the street, waiting to log on and find answers to the endless questions I've asked since yesterday.

The bottom line is this - I need to know whether Jesus was real, whether he was crucified, and by default this will confirm Peter was real, and therefore Susannah. I have to know.

Eventually an old codger opened the library doors, then the door to the IT research room. Eventually a young woman powered up the computers, and at last I had a connection.

Today I searched on 'tomb jesus Jerusalem archaeology.' I've learned to put in 'archaeology' to prevent google finding all sorts of trash about Holy Land tours and holidays.

Pretty quickly I found a great site that pulls together all the archaeological evidence uncovered in Jerusalem. Because as far as we professionals are concerned – the Gospels don't count. Funny that, we accept the writings of Josephus and Tacitus and the rest, even though the oldest hard copy is at least 700 years later than the date of writing, while we have one tiny fragment of Mark's gospel dated 70 years after it was written. Which I suppose is like finding a letter today from a soldier in the first world war, and doubting its authenticity. But that wouldn't be religious so it's different.

This is what I found – here are my notes,

- 1961 – discovery of the Pilate inscription in Caesarea – commemorating a temple he built to Caesar – his title PONTIUS PILATE PREFECT OF JUDAEA, exactly as used by the gospel writers.
- 1968 – discovery of 1st century CE body of crucified male – with nails through feet, proving gospel record as true, transforming opinion of scholars who said crucifixion with nails couldn't have worked. Humble pie etc.
- 1990 – discovery of Caiaphas' tomb – chief priest 18 – 36

CE who tried Jesus. Inscription JOSEPH CAIAPHAS, title as used by gospels and by Roman historian Josephus.

- 2000 – discovery of ossuary (stone coffin) inscribed JAMES SON OF JOSEPH, BROTHER OF JESUS.' Inscription dated to 63 CE, limestone confirmed as first century, quarried in Jerusalem.

Conclusion – archaeology has revealed the tomb, the persons and events attested in the gospels. They are proven as factual and accurate. But faith in Christ depends on a historically empty tomb.

And no way am I going back to the Church of the Holy Sepulchre, built over Calvary and the traditional site of the tomb. So I picked up my notes and headed out to Gordon's Golgotha. I love that name. It's so Monty Python.

And it's worth a visit. Serene, peaceful, almost holy. A garden, planted with tasteful flowers, a sepulchre, an empty tomb. First century definitely, probably not built by Joseph of Arimathaea - the bloke who provided a resting place for Jesus' broken body - but atmospheric certainly.

I sat down in the morning sun and leafed through my web printouts.

Jewish tombs were pretty solid. Hewn out of natural rock, and sealed with a huge stone. Diggers like me have uncovered numerous first century tombs around this area. The seals are usually round, set on edge and rolled into a groove at the mouth.

When Romans were required to seal a tomb, they attached a cord across the circular stone which they secured with wax stamped with the seal of Imperial Rome. To tamper with the seal was to defy Roman authority, and risk the death penalty. Guards were placed at the tomb mouth – who would also be executed for falling asleep on duty.

Obviously when Pilate ordered the guard to the Jesus tomb, special care would be taken. This bloke had predicted he would rise from the dead after three days. And if you want to believe the entire Roman guard fell asleep simultaneously while a couple of apostles undid the seal and removed the stone, that's fine with me.

Or if you think Jesus wasn't really dead and - despite his scourging, crucifixion and 72 hours fast – rolled the stone away and sneaked past the Roman guard, then that's OK too. Because it still makes him Super-man.

But what impressed me most as I sat in the garden, is the change in Simon Peter after the fateful Sunday morning. The guy who (whatever slant you put on it), let Jesus down big-time, then abandoned him to run to Bethany where he lay in hiding. A few days later he suddenly stood up, and claimed he had met the risen Christ. Then he preached in Jerusalem and Rome, for heaven's sake, the most anti-Christian city on earth, until they crucified *him*.

Something took away his fear, and that can't have been a stolen corpse.

I lay back, stretched and closed my eyes.

That's when it hit me. My mother! Today is the 15th July, I looked at my watch in a frenzy, it was twelve-fifteen, and I had promised to meet mother at noon.

Legging it to the street, I hailed a cab, and told the driver to risk life and limb to get me to Caliph bar, Betzalel. I needn't have bothered asking - Jerusalem taxis drive like that anyway.

I fell out of the passenger door and ran inside blindly, checked the entrance, restaurant and back again. Nothing. I grilled a waiter.

'A woman has just left. She waited thirty minutes. You just missed her.'

Running into the street, I looked left, right, left again. For the first time she had put herself out for me, come all the way to Jerusalem from Brussels and I was late.

I leaned against the bar window and pressed my head back in despair. She's right, I'm a total bloody failure.

'Ben?'

I opened my eyes.

'Mum!'

'Oh Ben, it's good to see you.' She didn't touch me, we never touch.

'I'm *so* sorry I'm late, I got distracted.'

'It doesn't matter,' she said, but it did. She knew it, I knew it. 'Shall we go in?'

I followed her sheepishly.

She ordered drinks and picked up the lunch menu. 'What are you having?'

'Anything. You choose.'

Watching her eyes run quickly down the printed page, I analysed her as if we didn't know each other. Her neat, almost obsessive tidiness, not a highlighted, straightened hair out of place. Her linen suit pressed and tailored. As ever, she looked expensive, fashionable and very clean. I could see myself in the mirrored wall opposite, hair uncombed and too long, khaki tee shirt faded and old. A mess basically. But genetically fifty per cent the same as the woman facing me.

She asked the waiter for two lobster salads. I hate lobster but didn't tell her.

'So how are you,' she asked, meaning - it's been so long, you never write.

I paused before I was trapped into giving the usual compliant answer. Trapped into another pointless, meaningless interchange about nothing at all. Instead I said, 'Mum, it really matters to me that you've come today.'

She smiled coldly, 'So much so, you forgot to turn up!'

I paused again. Don't bite Ben, don't. 'Actually, the reason I'm late is partly the reason why it matters.'

She looked faintly dis-interested. Maybe she's afraid of emotional declarations.

'I read about the shard,' she said, reaching down into her bag. She pulled out two newspaper clippings, unfolded and smoothed them onto the white cloth. 'I'm very proud of you.'

'Can I see?' The first was the Daily Telegraph, 'Simon Peter – the ultimate evidence', the second from the Mail, 'UK Digger hits the jackpot.'

I scanned the columns quickly. All a bit melodramatic, and they both had the same ghastly photo of me in 1987.

'There are lots more like these, and plenty of TV coverage

too. What I don't understand is why you had to run away? Just when you'd started to be a success.'

So that's how she sees it. 'But it wasn't like that, it would take too long to explain.'

'I have the time.'

'When I understand, I promise to tell you the whole story. In a nut-shell, finding the shard began a burning need to find myself. And Susannah.'

'And what have you discovered?'

'About me or her?'

'Her.'

How predictable, I thought. 'Nothing, and everything. That she was real. Funny, but she's made me think about the past a lot.'

Mum looked uncomfortable and flicked imaginary specks from the linen cloth. Then the waiter brought two enormous salad platters.

I pushed the lobster to one side, 'I've thought about little Joe.'

Mum visibly froze, 'Don't Ben, please.'

'But he was my only brother.'

'He was my second child.' She paused, still as an icon in the Holy Sepulchre. 'I had a third child, so you have a sister too.'

'What?' I stared at her, fork midway between table and mouth. I could see she was debating whether to say any more. 'You mean a half-sister? You had a baby with Mario?'

'No, with your father. When I left home in 1970 I was pregnant.'

I was speechless. A tremulous silence dropped into the space between us, and it was her job to fill it.

'Dad asked me to leave when he discovered I was having an affair. It was my boss at the council offices. You were seven or eight at the time, the affair started after I lost little Joe.'

An image of Mum's office, a white façade, her black stockings and buckled patent shoes flashed up from the murky depths of memory.

236

'I suspected I was pregnant but didn't know for sure. I told my boss the baby was his, though dates made that impossible, and asked him to leave his wife. He didn't of course.'

She moved a piece of cucumber half an inch, and then back again. 'So I was pregnant and alone. Dad may have had me back but I never dared ask, and in 1970 it was very tough to be a single mother. So I flew to Rome and took a job in the tourist board. I wore my wedding ring and told everyone my husband was planning to join me when he could find work. I rented an apartment in the city centre, and the baby was born five months later. I named her Anna and gave her up for adoption immediately.'

Thoughts raced through my head - I have a thirty-two year old sister. I have a family.

'After her twenty-first birthday, I decided to trace Anna and managed to make contact. She's beautiful, still lives in Rome, and has a husband and two gorgeous boys. She's a solicitor. I didn't know whether she would accept me, but finding her is what matters. So you see, I have my own history.'

Thoughts raced through my head, I felt sorry. For years I've resented Mum for not being there. But I didn't know anything about her life.

'I'd like to meet Anna,' I said.

'Maybe that's your right. I'll give you her address and leave it up to you. I've tortured myself with the dilemma – should I tell you, and your father? She's his child after all.'

I looked across the table and saw a stranger, not the child-hating monster of my imagination, but a victim, and I leaned forward and laid my hand on hers.

Date 15.07.03
To boogyhen@onetel.co.uk
From taylordenton.arch.instit@hebron.com
Hi Ben, I'm back. Can we meet up for lunch soon?
Love T

Date 15.07.03

To taylordenton.arch.instit@hebron.com
From boogyhen@onetel.co.uk
Hi there, I'm in complete shock after a meeting with my mother. Yes, let's lunch tomorrow, as long as you're not bringing holiday-man.

B

Date 15.07.03
To boogyhen@onetel.co.uk
From taylordenton.arch.instit@hebron.com
Hi again, It's only fair to tell you Steve (holiday-man) and I are now an item. But obviously that doesn't mean we can't be friends.

Love T.

Date 15.07.03
To taylordenton.arch.instit@hebron.com
From boogyhen@onetel.co.uk
Not obvious from where I'm sitting. Maybe catch up with you later, when I'm next in the area. I'm off to Rome shortly.

Ben.

Jerusalem
CE 32

Throughout the Sabbath I was sick, and lay in my bed at Salome's home, vomiting every few moments. In a way I'm glad I was too ill to think, it shut out the pain for two nights and a day.

Mary and Salome cared for me, bringing hot wine, wet cloths for my forehead, and clean pots. I've never been so ill, Salome believed I was dying, and I hoped she was right. Sometimes I've wondered whether Jesus' Father was protecting me from the pain of remembering yesterday.

But I don't want any more to do with the God of Jesus, Moses or Abraham. And I don't want any more to do with my Jewish faith. I just want Jesus, ache from the loss of him that hurts more than my wretched belly.

After the Roman executioners had confirmed death, Pilate agreed the body could be given to Joseph of Arimathaea for burial, Salome says he's a kind man, who took it to a brand new tomb he has hewn from the rock near Calvary. Pilate set a full Roman guard at the entrance and sealed the tomb, so we weren't even able to perform the last rites of anointing.

Over and over again I ask myself the one question – Why in God's name didn't Jesus save himself. He could have done. He raised Lazarus. He could have used his father's power. Why?

And I never want to see my father again. He's the worst of men, a snake, a traitor. He's safer holed up in Bethany because if he was anywhere near me I'd tear his tongue out with my bare hands. At least that way he wouldn't be able to betray Jesus again.

I'll never forgive him for running away. Or Uncle Andrew. Or any of them. They're worse than Judas, at least he's had the courage to kill himself from the guilt of betraying Jesus, the rest of the men just fled and hid.

So much for the twelve, only John is left with us women, who were never called apostles. I have nothing to hope for now but death.

Part Three

Home

Rome
17th July 2003

I touched down in Rome at 15.30. The flight took a chunk of my cash, but there's nothing left for me in Israel. I'm so disappointed, because in my dream Susannah promised I would find her in Jerusalem. And I didn't. All I have is my imaginary image, a slender young woman with olive skin and fire-bright eyes that see right inside your skin.

Before we said goodbye, Mum gave me the phone number of my magically appearing sister. Mother really did come all the way to Jerusalem to have lunch with me, and I put her in a taxi for the airport after dessert. It's the first time she's made an effort like that and it moved me.

I've been trying to work out why she never kisses or touches me. In airport departures today I watched loads of families saying goodbye. They all kissed. Or hugged, or both. I've been trawling the memory banks and I don't think she ever kissed me goodnight in the eight years we lived together. So how do I know she loves me? Obviously she's never said. Sounds pathetic, but I've got this knotty pain in my chest from wanting her to hug me. I need to get a grip.

And I refuse ever to think about Taylor again. She led me on from start to finish. Making me think I was an interesting person, lending me the gospel - which I'm keeping now just so I won't have to contact her again. And imagining she could move in with coca-cola man and still flirt with me. She needs to grow up.

I called Anna's number as soon as I came through baggage handling. The phone rang for a long time. Then I heard, 'Salve! Anna Alvarez.'

I struggled to say five words in Italian, 'Non parlo italiano molto bene.'

'That's OK, are you English?' She spoke with a beautiful soft accent.

'Er yes.'

'Can I help you?'

'Um, I'm a relative from England, and I wondered could I pop in for a coffee as I'm in Rome for a while?'

'Yes, certainly. When would you like?'

I paused.

Anna continued, 'I am at home today from the office. If that would be OK?'

'Yes, fine, thank you.'

She gave me directions in perfect English. Clear, kind.

I hung up and panicked. Her apartment was a twenty minute taxi drive from this spot. And I only found out she existed two days ago. The old Ben would have done a runner. In fact he would have intended to make contact but never bothered.

I hailed a cab, gave the address and said the second prayer of my life as the car hurtled through the streets, 'Dear God, if you're there, make this OK mate.'

Anna's apartment block is in an old street, the building plastered and painted warm pink. Window boxes balance between wooden shutters, and spill over with geraniums and hibiscus. I could live somewhere like this.

I paid the cab and paused at the front door, smoothing my unruly hair, patting my old combat trousers. But they need more than a pat to make them acceptable. What if she finds me disgusting, what if she thinks I'm a con-man?

I knocked quietly and waited, planning to leg it if she didn't hear me right away.

But the door opened at once. And I nearly dropped down dead when I saw inside. Standing two feet from me was a woman the spitting image of Susannah. My Susannah. Dressed in a cream shift dress with a yellow stone at her neck, and looking at me with compelling eyes, was the most beautiful girl I've ever seen. And I couldn't help it, the tears just came.

'Come in,' she said, so gently.

'I'm sorry, what must you think of me?' I wept.

'It's OK. Madre called me last night. You're Ben. Welcome home brother.' And she embraced me, in spite of my sweatiness, my uncut hair and hot face. She pressed her cheek to mine, and I breathed in her cinnamon scent. She is beautiful and she's my sister.

Anna led me upstairs and indoors, into a dreamy living room that opens over a central courtyard with lemon trees. A low table was set for two with a pot of coffee and a jug of iced water.

'Sit down,' she smiled, 'and relax.' I watched her olive skin as she poured us both an espresso.

'This must be such a shock for you,' she said, passing the cup as elegantly as an Edwardian hostess. 'I have known of you for a long time, since I was twenty-one or so, and always hoped to meet you, but Madre had not told you about me. It is so difficult of course, because of our Padre. Do you think he will meet me one day?'

I could listen to the softly rolling vowels of her Italian accent all day. 'I'm sure he will, after the shock wears off.'

There was no longer any doubt in my mind that we share the same Dad, Anna's mouth and nose are miniature versions of his.

I said, 'I've never had a family because my – I mean our – little brother died before Mum left home.

'Little Joe, yes. Madre hates to speak of him, the pain is still too bad. I think her marriage to our father broke down after our baby brother died, then she began the affair with her boss. I was conceived in the last days of the marriage. I often wonder what my life would have been like if she had stayed in England and we had grown up as a family. You, me, together.' She looked wistful. 'I have two boys,' she said suddenly, and rose to fetch a photograph from the bureau.

Two energetic, smiling black-haired faces laughed out of the frame at me. My nephews.

'I am a solicitor, and my husband works for the government. The boys are on holiday with my parents - my adopted parents - this week.'

'How do your parents feel about our mother?'

'They were afraid at first that they may lose me, but they brought me up, and now they know Madre is different, more of a friend. It was very hard for me to understand that she had given me up, but she had no choice in those days. I am an only child in my adopted family. Famiglia is so important to me. To all Italians. Now we have found you, I can never let go.'

She stood and put her arm around my shoulder, 'You have suffered, I see that in your eyes. You have been very lonely.'

And of course that made me cry again, but she was fine about it.

'Are you single?'

'Unfortunately yes, I just haven't met the right person since my divorce. Until last month when I found someone in Jerusalem who was just my type. Except she was far too attractive. She's American, and it turned out she was only messing with me. But hey, I don't care.'

'Of course you care, that is silly. And why do you say she was too attractive? You are handsome.'

I laughed at the archaic word.

'Tall, slim,' she went on, 'lovely eyes, a very open face. And so strong. She has missed a fine man.'

Anna's reassurance hit the spot, her words flowed straight through my veins to my starved heart, and spread a new glow.

She laughed, 'You see, I need to learn how to treat you as a real brother, I should tease you and argue, no?'

'Hey, not yet,' I smiled. My eyes rested on a decorated image of the Virgin Mary in an alcove, 'Are you a Catholic?'

'Yes, and you?' she asked.

'Not really. A bit confused on that subject. But I've got a big interest in Simon Peter.'

'Our Saint Peter, the first Pope. You must see the Basilica. I shall take you there.' She looked at me eagerly and I watched her expression change to love, 'We have a lifetime to be brother and sister,' she said, 'fratello and sorella, I am so happy Ben.'

Jerusalem
CE 32

My fever must be making me delirious, my mind is confused. This morning, after another long night of sickness, I woke to find Mary of Magdala shaking me and gushing, 'I've seen the Lord, I've seen Jesus!'

Salome burst in behind her, and I've never known her like this, frenzied, wild with excitement, 'Susannah, it's true, he's alive!'

'Is this a dream? What are you saying?' I stammered.

Mary seized my hand and pulled me upright on the mattress, 'This morning, before first light, Salome and I went to the tomb to anoint Jesus' body with spices and oil. We were waiting in the shadows until the sun rose, wondering how we would get to the body, but terrified of asking the guard to let us in. The place seemed eerily quiet, and as we crept nearer, we knew something was wrong because Pilate's guard was nowhere to be seen.

When the sky lightened to grey we could make out the entrance to the tomb, a gaping hole, the stone rolled aside. This was terrible, because we knew the Romans must have moved the body to a secret location. Dawn was near, but we were terrified of entering the tomb, stepping into the blackness. Salome hung back but I needed to see Jesus so badly I took a deep breath and crept inside.

Susannah - this will sound crazy, but inside the tomb it wasn't dark. I screamed when I saw a stranger, a young man sitting on the ledge where they had laid Jesus' body. He was dressed in white and the soft light seemed to be coming from him. I leaped out to Salome and he called to us gently, 'Don't be afraid.'

Eventually we tiptoed through the entrance together, holding each others' sweating hands.

He spoke again, 'There's no need to be shocked. You're looking for Jesus of Nazareth who was crucified. But he isn't here, he is risen. This is the place where his body laid.'

We looked at the slab and saw the linen cloths and shroud were lying there. And Susannah, this is the oddest part, they were still in the shape of a body, wrapped round and round, but empty. They hadn't been unwrapped, so Jesus' body must have lifted out of them. I don't think I could have believed the man, unless I'd seen the cloths. And he commanded us to go and tell the apostles, 'And Simon Peter, you must tell Peter.'

We were scared out of our wits, and just ran out of there.'

Salome butted in, 'And I came straight to find Zebedee, to take him to the tomb.'

'While I stayed in the garden,' Mary went on, 'a few cubits from the tomb, because I needed to cry in quiet to try and make sense of it all. That's when I met him.'

'Who?' I yelped.

'I was streaming with tears, and saw this man a little distance from me, and assumed he was the gardener. But he called my name and then I realised it was Jesus, I held him, Susannah I held him! He is warm flesh and blood, he showed me his scars. He's resurrected. And I'm ordered to go to Bethany and tell the men, because he will appear to them there.'

I jumped out of bed and started to dress.

'What are you doing?' Salome barked.

'Going to Bethany, to wait for Jesus.'

Mary turned to my aunt, 'She has such faith, look how she doesn't doubt what I've seen. I suspect the men won't be so open.'

'You're going nowhere,' Salome said sternly.

My temper erupted at last, 'Don't you DARE try to tell me what I will or will not do. I am going to him, and nothing in the Promised Land will keep me from him. *NOTHING.*' I was pulling her robe with my nails and screaming like a wild beast.

'Stop!' Mary shouted. 'Stop right now! He said you are to return to Galilee and wait for him there.'

I let go, and stood still as a marble statue, 'What?'

'You are the only other person he mentioned by name. He said, 'Tell Susannah she must return to Galilee and wait for me there."

My tears came like a flood, so hard and deep that I retched again, and Salome and Mary had to lift me on to the bed.

When I woke again, Mary had left for Bethany.

* * *

Since Mary met Jesus, life has gone from bad to mad.

As soon as my traitor of a father heard Mary's story he ran the short distance from Bethany and visited the tomb for himself. It was still early in the morning when he arrived at Zebedee's house to tell us.

Salome told him I refused to see him but he burst into my room. He was looking terrible - grey, ravaged by guilt and grief. I rolled toward the wall and wouldn't look him in the face.

'Susannah, I've seen the Master!' he pleaded.

I put hands over my ears and pressed my nose to the

cold wall.

'Susa, listen to me, I want you to share this.'

'Go away. Go. Away. For. Ever.' I spat the words one at a time. 'I hate you.'

'Don't do this to me. I'm broken enough already.'

'You could never be broken as much as you deserve.'

Even with my back to him, I could hear that although he'd seen Jesus, Dad seemed dejected. 'Daughter, you've said enough. Mary's right,' he went on, 'Jesus must be risen. The grave cloths prove it. If someone had taken the body, the linen would be gone, and even if they'd stripped him it would be unwound. I can see he's been lifted right through the cloth.'

I turned just enough to peep through the blanket. Salome laid her hand on his shoulder, 'But Peter, that's wonderful.'

And Dad began to weep again, soft rivulets that ran down his face and glistened in his lined skin, 'I hate myself, how can I live and look on him? How can I live after betraying the only person I truly love. I'm unfit to be called apostle.'

I snapped, 'You're right.'

'Susannah!' said Salome angrily.

'It's the truth,' I went on, 'You let Jesus down, betrayed everything he stood for. Think of the times he stood by you, patiently supported you when you were stupid and stubborn. I don't know why he picked you to follow him. Or Andrew, any of you, a bunch of useless, treacherous fishermen!'

Dad wiped his face over and over with his cloak, 'She's right. I can't sleep because every time I close my eyes I see him standing on Caiaphas' balcony, looking down at me as the cock crowed. His eyes, the love in them.' He couldn't go on.

Next day we heard Jesus had appeared to two Galileans on their journey to Emmaus. And after that he met with the eleven in their locked room at Bethany. Mark came back and told us all about it.

But I wasn't pleased for them. My heart is full of bitter anger, against Dad, even Jesus. I ache to see him, I was at the crucifixion, while the men hid in shame, so why doesn't he appear to me who loved and stayed by him? What makes it worse is the resurrection must be true, because so many people have seen him now, and the number grows every day. I'm going back to Galilee, not because he told me to, just because it's home.

I hate everything about my life, but I miss Momma and the lake. And if Jesus doesn't love me enough to appear to me, then I won't love him either.

Capernaum, Galilee
CE 32

Thirty-six days have passed since they killed Jesus. And I don't believe in him any more. I've been home for thirty of them, and life has returned to normal. In fact it's better than before. I have Momma and Joseph, Gran and Miriam.

We don't have any money, but I'm working hard and forgetting what's happened. I don't think about my madness any more, the two years when I thought Jesus was the Son of God. Because he wasn't. He was a family-wrecker, a home-breaker, and because of him I've lost my Dad, and most of the men in my family.

I used to have such a strong bond with Dad, and I've been remembering everything bad that Jesus did. He sent his own mother and brothers away empty, he put crazy ideas into the men's heads, and ruined their livelihoods.

And he had me under a spell for too long, because that's what I've realised, he was a magician after all. Still working his trickery from beyond the grave. Because what kind of Messiah would be executed as a common criminal under the Romans for heaven's sake? I've thought about the prophets' words, and they don't fit Jesus. He isn't the one. And I don't care what Miriam says, or Gran. We've agreed not to talk about it, just bake bread, sweep and work. Which is fine.

This morning Momma asked me to take a message to the hired hand. I walked the shepherd's paths toward Magdala. It was the way I went with Jesus that day. Which isn't important.

Afterwards I cut across the fields to the lump of basalt where we sat the night I followed him. I wanted to be sure I could go there without feeling the old madness again. And I could. I sat looking across the water towards Hippos and felt nothing. Nothing at all. He had promised my love would shine like the city on the hill. How wrong was that? I don't love anyone any more. And never will.

I breathed in the scents of the last spring flowers. The blood red scarlet anemone, pink flax, crowfoot, and blue iris. And the white rose of sharon, called lily of the field. I was all right with that, I could look on a lily and feel nothing.

I watched a pair of black and white kingfishers sitting on a twig, their eyes toward the water. Then they flew, suddenly startled.

My eye caught movement on the path.

I turned my head and my breath stopped. Heart flew into my throat. Hands to mouth. His name wouldn't come.

'Lily, my Lily,' he said.

Striding forward with one huge bound, he scooped me up from the rock, and hugged me so hard my weak legs lifted from the ground.

My scream wasn't of joy, it was an agony too deep for words.

And all the time I screamed, he held me, smoothing my veil, rocking me like a baby.

When he set me down my whole body was quaking. We sat in silence until I could breathe, his arms around me.

'Why did you betray me Lily?' he asked very gently.

'I didn't. Judas betrayed you, and Dad, and the other men.'

'Why did *you* betray me Lily?' he asked again.

'I never did. I was there until the end, I stayed with

you, I did honestly!'

His unyielding blue eyes bored into me.

'They denied you, went into hiding, ran away to Bethany. But I didn't.'

He looked down at the ground and spoke in a low voice, 'You were the only one who stopped believing in me. I don't say this out of blame, I have never blamed you, but to show you the faults of others are no worse than yours.'

'But how can you forgive Dad?' I sneered. 'How can you come back from the dead and appear to him, the one who denied you three times, said he didn't know you, and hid in a hole because he was so afraid of arrest? Why didn't you come to *me*? I was the one who stayed, saw your blood running down, saw your……eyes….'

The flood finally came. The agony of remembering his walk to Calvary broke over me and I clutched him like a woman possessed.

He cradled me tightly to restrain my shaking limbs, and spoke healing words, 'I never wanted you to see it my love. It is over, finished. I am with you forever. Forgiveness is the only way. You must forgive Dad.'

'I can't, don't make me. How can I?' I sobbed.

'The same way I forgive you. Look at these Lily,' he said, opening his palms to me. I saw the scarred marks of the nails through his two wrists and flinched.

'I bore these nails for you. If you had been the only person in the world I would have died just for you.'

I looked at him with astonishment.

'I bore the pain because I forgive you.'

'But you didn't come to me. All the men have seen you, and Mary, Salome.'

He didn't reply, just looked at me with fire in his eyes.

'I'm sorry,' I blurted, 'I'm sorry. I was so jealous you'd appeared to the others, I tried to stop loving you, blamed you, hated you for dying. Forgive me for betraying you, forgive me Jesus.'

'Betrayal in the heart is the same as betrayal in the high priest's palace. It's time to uncover the meaning for you, the deeper meaning that has been hidden from all men until now. You know the scriptures Lily.'

I nodded slowly, my eyes transfixed on his beautiful face.

'Remember how God initiated the Passover in Egypt, when every Jewish household was told to mark their door with the blood of a lamb. When the angel of death passed over in the night, he could not bring the plague to a single house marked with that blood.

I am the Passover lamb Lily, dying at Passover as the final perfect sacrifice. If anyone believes in me, the angel of death will pass over them, and they will live for ever in my Father's Kingdom. My sacrifice is acceptable to God, in place of your death. The death of all the world.

Just before I lost consciousness on Calvary I called out to my Father, 'My God, My God, why have you forsaken me?' And He didn't answer me Lily. For the first and only time since I was born in Bethlehem, my Father withdrew from me.'

Jesus' voice began to rise to fever pitch, 'I couldn't feel Him, He was gone from me, and I called out for Him in the agony of my pain, and my need. But He left me, and at that moment I knew what it is to be truly human, to be living apart from the Father.' He let out a cry that pierced my heart.

'It was hell. And I went to the grave separated from

Him.' His voice changed again and softened, 'The Father has accepted my sacrifice in place of your death. He laid your sin on me. And at the moment I went to hell, the veil of the temple in the sanctuary ripped in two, rent from top to bottom. Do you know why?'

I shook my head in stupefaction.

'Because now it isn't just the High Priest who can enter God's presence once a year, the new covenant is here, God-with-us, He is with every man, woman and child. This is the beginning of the Kingdom.'

As he spoke, scales fell from my eyes and everything Jesus had ever said and done began to have new meaning. A new happiness dawned inside, not the fluttering kind, but a deep and gentle certainty.

I stood to my full height and took his precious hands in mine, 'Stay with me!'

He twirled me round in the sunlight, until a giggle bubbled out of me and I ran through the grasses, knowing he would chase, until I let him catch me.

He laughed and I knew this was heaven.

We were together for a few precious hours while he shared many things with me. At last he said, 'I must leave you now, but only for a little while. My Father will send his spirit to be with you until the end times. You will not see me again in this world Lily, but you will feel me daily. I ask you to stay in Capernaum and build my church in your father's home. And in Bethsaida, Magdala, throughout Galilee. Many will come, hundreds upon hundreds of believers. Every one is part of my flock. Feed my lambs.'

'Don't go. I love you,' I pleaded, but I felt utterly peaceful inside.

'I will stay here on our rock, and you will walk back to Momma now. It will be easier for you that way.'

I held him tenderly, like a lover, and stood to take my final draft of him. His creamy-olive skin, muscular fore-arms, blue eyes, his heart.

I would not look back. And as I turned to head home, I knew he was behind, watching me for the last time.

Rome
20th July 2003

Date 20.07.03

To boogyhen@onetel.co.uk

From taylordenton.arch.instit@hebron.com

Ben, I miss you, sorry if I messed up and said the wrong things. You weren't just a digger to me, you were a friend, soul-mate. Please call me soon,

Love T. x

I've had such a good time with Anna. She's a genuinely wonderful girl, and I'm just chuffed to bits that we're related. She gives me hope that as we're created from the same gene pool, I might have the makings of her in me.

She's a senior partner in her legal firm and just phoned them to say she's taking time off to be with me. No holiday form or permission required, she simply *told* them. The boys are still with the grand-parents and her husband is in Turin on business, so I've had her all to myself. I feel good walking beside her, because she's gorgeous, but there's none of the complication and fragility of a sexual relationship.

Last night we sipped aperitifs at a pavement café, ate fresh pasta in a trattoria, and saw the Sistine chapel. Anna knows everything, better than the best guide. She made me throw a coin into the Trevi fountain – it's supposed to guarantee you return to Rome.

I protested, 'But of course I'll return, we're family, and I'm going to be hard to shake off,' I said, hanging on to the coin.

'Ah, but I want to be certain of you,' she laughed and shook my hand until I let the coin drop and splash.

The day before yesterday we saw the Colosseum, then Nero's golden house, and shopped for a whole new wardrobe for me on the Via Condotti. Anna has this vision of me as some kind of cool athlete in designer linen.

'Your clothes are all wrong Ben, you dress like a university student in a gap year. And what are these?' she laughed, picking at my leather bracelets with her elegant nails.

'They're part of me. This one hasn't been off my wrist since 1991.'

'And it shows. We are going to find your true image,' she promised, taking my hand.

I wouldn't let anyone else do this to me, certainly not Carys, or any wife for that matter, but I've loved being her mannekin. Standing obedient as a well-trained Labrador in sumptuous changing rooms, letting her hold up linen pants and crisp Italian jackets in front of deferential salesmen.

My only problem has been at the till.

'Anna, stop it, you can't pay for these,' I've protested.

'So how much money are you earning right now?'

'You know I'm not.'

'Then enjoy it. Or if you can't, watch me enjoy myself. I have too much money Ben, and I want to do this. Please?' and she tilts her beautiful oval face imploringly. I can't resist her.

When we went to St Peter's Basilica this morning I looked and felt like a new man. A couple of gorgeous Italian women clocked me as we were buying our tickets – as if they fancied me. I could get used to this.

The Basilica is horrible in the same way that the Church of the Holy Sepulchre is horrible – but I wouldn't dream of saying that to my sister. It's a site heavily revered by all Catholics as the place where Peter was crucified.

'Now I give my guided tour,' she began breathlessly as we stepped inside from the burning heat of the hottest summer on record.

'You love this church don't you?' I asked her.

'But of course, it is very holy. Beneath us is the garden of Agrippina the mother of Caligula who built a circus in her garden, the very circus where emperor Nero later tortured and murdered early Christians for sport. He massacred thousands, using gladiators and lions and worse. But they still believed, to the end.'

'Hold on guide, I need dates. I'm an archaeologist, I like

dates. And evidence.'

'Ah, I am not so good on evidence. But dates yes. Caligula was Emperor just after Jesus was crucified, and Nero from about 60 AD.'

'60 CE' I corrected her, we don't say AD any more.'

'This is my tour, and I say Anno Domini, the year of our Lord, I don't care what you atheist historians say. We date our world before and after Christ, and that is how it should be.'

I smiled at her passion and certainty, she's getting under my skin.

'The exact spot in the circus where Peter was crucified is beneath this altar. And his tomb there.'

'How do you know?'

'Because they excavated in 1950 and found the first century tombs and remains of Christian burials.'

'But they didn't find any conclusive evidence did they? No inscription, bones or finds?'

'Oh Ben, even if they dig up the very crucifix itself, you still need faith to believe in it. That's no different to every part of God's story on earth. The very earliest tradition preserved that Peter lived and died here in Rome. Yes there are manuscripts that confirm Peter living in Rome, but papers are not conclusive. The gospel only tells us Saint Paul travelled to Rome as an old man and does not specify where Peter ended his life. But we have the Acts of Peter.'

'Is that part of the Bible?'

'No, a second century compilation of stories about Peter that didn't make it into the New Testament. I will buy you a copy at the Basilica gift shop,' Anna promised.

'Hey, I can afford a book,' I laughed.

I flicked through the slim volume as we sipped iced coffee beside the Spanish Steps.

'Must you read that now?' Anna asked teasingly.

'Yes,' I protested, lifting the book closer to my face.

Anna flicked a sugar packet across the table toward me. When I ignored that, she began tapping my leg with her foot.

I smiled at the incongruous image, a stylish Italian solicitor was trying to irritate me into talking to her.

Looking up, I felt the thirty year void between us melt away, we were a kid brother and sister at a street café, vying for each other's attention. It was one of the best moments of my life. Up until now.

I soon found the part referring to Peter's martyrdom, 'What's this? It says Peter asked to be crucified upside down?' I said in horror.

'He refused to share the same death as his Lord.' Anna replied, serious now. 'He felt it would be too much honour to die the death of Jesus.'

'Too much honour to be nailed to a crossbeam, with four inch nails ripping through your wrists and ankles while your chest collapsed? What are you talking about? So Susannah's Dad was hung upside down?'

I could feel tears pricking my eyes, and hoped people would think they were watering in the bright sunlight.

'Yes Ben, that is what we believe. He had dis-honoured Jesus in life, but honoured him in death. That is why we cherish him, the rock on which Christ's church was built on earth, he lived bravely and ended faithfully.'

'But Susannah had already lost Jesus,' I whispered, 'she'd already seen him executed. And you're saying she lost her Dad that way too. It isn't fair Anna, I want to kill the bastards that did this to her.'

My sister pulled her chair alongside mine and put her small arm around my shoulder. 'God is just, He will make all things well.'

'He'd better,' I cried, 'He'd damn well better.'

Capernaum
CE 51

Almost twenty years have passed since Jesus went back to the Father - I've reached my thirty-fifth year. But he's still with me, in every breath of wind over Galilee, just as he promised. Our family life is quite broken up, and yet we're utterly happy. Gran died peacefully soon after Jesus appeared to me in Galilee, and Momma is an old woman now, just like a widow, since Dad is away all the time. He preaches the truth all over our land, Jerusalem is his home, but he has stayed for long periods in Jaffa, Caesarea and Lydda.

Momma spends many months in Jerusalem with Salome and Zebedee, and Dad sleeps with her there, but he's gone at first light into the market place and temple courts, teaching and healing in Jesus' name.

It's many, many years since I was restored to him. For months I had dwelled on Jesus' words that I had to forgive Dad. But I couldn't do it, not even after Jesus had appeared to me, not even after I understood the reason for the crucifixion. My bitterness stayed inside my chest like a hard nut I'd swallowed which pressed on my heart. When Momma mentioned him, I changed the subject.

Then one summer day he came home to Capernaum without warning. I was seventeen or eighteen years old.

I was on the roof airing clean blankets, and saw him far off on the road from the south. At first I wasn't sure, then I recognised his stooping strength, the bear-like power that couldn't be any one but my Dad. For a brief spell I felt a gush of love, and wanted to run along the road to greet him, then the old hardness came back.

So I stayed on the roof while Momma and Miriam whooped and fussed him downstairs.

'Is Susa here?' I heard him ask in his deep, throaty voice.

'Of course.'

'No different?'

'Towards you? No, I don't think so,' Momma replied.

I was wondering how I would come down from the roof without passing him. But then he went out again towards the shore.

I took the opportunity to slip out and hide in the old potting shed, empty of catch now, as it had been for a couple of years. Dad's idle nets stood in piles, no longer smelling of fish or lake. As I fingered the cord, my eyes closed and I saw him aboard, tossing the throw net in a graceful movement, just like a bride's skirt sinking to the floor at the end of the wedding dance.

'Susannah?'

I turned in shock.

'Dad!'

There was complete silence as I stared into his brown eyes. He didn't say anything more. I knew this was my chance, the moment when I had to choose, finally to forgive or to hate. And I still hated him, still saw the man who had failed. In my mind I called to Jesus, 'Help me, I can't forgive him. Help me!'

Suddenly it was as if Jesus was in the shed. I knew he wanted me to hold out my hand to Dad. Just lift it. But my arm felt so heavy. I tried to imagine it wasn't Dad in front of me, and half raised my hand, the palm uppermost.

That's all it took. Dad fell forward and seized me saying,

'I love you, if you knew how I've hated myself for failing, Susa,' he cried, 'but it has helped me work for him, because if he can turn a sinner like me around, then there's hope for anyone.'

I pressed my face into the coarse fabric of his travelling cloak, and breathed in the unique, wonderful smell of my Dad, the fresh air and scent of his skin. The smells of girl-hood, when he was all in the world to me. 'I'm sorry Dad, I love you, I'm so glad you're my father.'

His humility and passion were enough to break a heart of stone. And he melted mine. As we held each other in the place we had worked side by side since I was a toddler, the hardness in my chest undid, and he became my Dad again. Flawed, blustering, penitent. Once more I was Susannah, Peter's daughter.

* * *

To this day, he tells everyone the stories of how he failed Jesus, and uses himself as the ultimate example of how God can turn a sinner around.

When he last came home – how many months ago, I don't remember? I asked him, 'Dad? Did you ever miss our past life, the fishing and the family?'

He laughed, his grainy laugh of old, 'Susa, my daughter, I have no time to miss the past. There's so little time to tell the world of Jesus before he returns in glory.'

'But Dad it's almost twenty winters since Jesus went to the Father. He may not return for twenty more.'

'But we never know when, be sure it will be when we least expect, we must prepare the people so they choose to believe in time.' He paused and looked very grave.

'What is it Dad?'

'There's something I must say to you Susa. The Lord

has called me to preach to the Gentiles.'

'Yes, I know that.'

'In Rome Susa.'

'In *Rome*! No Dad, no. Absolutely not. You are *not* a second Daniel - fodder for the lion's den.'

'Claudius is a kinder emperor than Caligula was, I must go where the Lord sends me, and his lambs are suffering in Rome.'

'But you know Claudius' son is a brute. Nero could succeed his father at any time, and there won't be a live Christian in Rome then.'

'All the more reason to hurry. I've prayed over this Susa, and Mark will come with me as usual. I'll write you from Rome so we can make arrangements for your betrothal!'

And we roared with laughter at the old joke, that shrinks the years which have separated us, and take us back to the blessed times, when Dad and Uncle Andrew were fishermen, and Jesus lived among us.

Momma came in just then, still as slim as the day Jesus came, 'Simon Peter, we've got to do something about the meeting house here. Miriam and Susa can't cope with the numbers of pilgrims much longer.'

'It's true Dad,' I added. 'This place was built as a home, not a church. It's bad enough in the week, but you should see the crowd on the Lord's day.'

'Then it's time for our family to move out,' Dad replied. I'll have a word with Zebedee about you girls moving into his old quarters, and we'll get this house plastered. Done out properly, with little lamps all around the walls, and a new table and chairs so you can celebrate the last supper properly.'

'Plaster! And how will we pay for that Simon Peter?' Momma smiled, shaking her grey hair.

'He will provide, my love, he always does,' Dad said, drawing a bag from beneath his cloak. 'Salome sent this for our church. There's enough here to pay for plastered walls and a ceiling, with a few aureus left over.'

'You're kidding?'

'Please don't speak of it to anyone, but Salome has been giving to our work since the first Pentecost. She had a vision of little churches all over our land, this was years ago, fifteen or more. Not synagogues, but plain rooms where the last supper will be celebrated and the stories of our Lord told over and over. And it's time to build them. What do you think Susa?'

I closed my eyes for a moment and remembered. 'Jesus asked me to stay in Galilee and work for him. Yes, I will build a church in Magdala, and Bethsaida.'

'Beware the Pharisees my love,' Dad warned, 'I'll be praying for your protection.'

Momma was whirling round our central room with her broom, 'I shall have plaster, and little lamps, this place will be clean enough to lick the floor, oh Simon Peter it's going to be perfect.'

And it was of course. I've been as good as my word and set up a meeting house for the Christians in Magdala – when I asked Mary to lead the church she was as happy as the day she went to the empty tomb, and now I am moving on to Bethsaida, Dad's birthplace, to set up a new meeting place and my new home.

Rome
CE 59

Though I've committed the rest of my life to working in Galilee, I've worried so much about Dad in recent years that I had to risk a journey to find him. I've prayed about it long and hard, and finally arrived in Rome yesterday – after a journey much less eventful than Paul's. No shipwreck, no arrest, just calm seas and glorious excitement. Fear of Nero almost prevented my journey, but I would have risked worse to reach Dad. The emperor is only twenty-two years old, but he's already committed enough evil to fill fifty lifetimes.

I met Dad at the house of Coponius – a Roman believer who shelters many new Christians.

When we saw each other, the years rolled back and beneath the stooping shoulders, I saw the burly fisherman of half a century ago.

'Susannah!' Dad roared, with one of his old bear hugs, 'You're grey around the temples, and even more like Momma. Such a beauty from an old brute like me!'

Mark rushed forward to hug me, 'You still have the eyes of a girl.'

'But I'm more than forty Mark, you goose.'

'Pity you never married Susa, you were always the loveliest in our family.'

'Saddle-querns, what nonsense! I always told Dad I wouldn't marry, and stuck to it.'

Mark dropped his voice, 'It's dangerous here Susa, we meet in secret and leave signs for believers so they know where and when to meet for worship. Nero's getting worse. It's harder and harder for Peter to speak openly in public.'

I turned to Dad, 'Then write it down Dad. Have you ever written the stories of our life with Jesus?'

'There's no need to write them love, I can speak better than I read.'

'But that's only while you're still alive Dad. You're not getting any younger and Nero is closing in on you, think how people will treasure your words if they're preserved for future generations.'

'Jesus will return soon love, there's no need to waste time scribing when I can be teaching face to face.'

'Dad you're maddening. We don't KNOW when Jesus will return. At least pray about it.'

'You know I can't write, never have.'

'But you can dictate.'

And he walked outside, putting an end to our discussion.

I've been in Rome for three months, helping with services, praying over the sick, and administering alms for the poorest believers. It's hot, smelly and dangerous work, and I've longed for the peace of Galilee. My home and my life's work. Now I've seen Dad's all right, it's time to return.

Last night when I came back from market, I heard Dad speaking in a soft voice from the inner room. Quietly, so as not to disturb him, I peeped through the archway. There I saw him, huddled under his robe, head in hands. He seemed to be praying, and Mark was sitting opposite, absorbed in writing onto a sheet of papyrus. Beside him on the ground were several more rolls, reed pens, and blocks of ink cake.

I heard Dad say, 'We took the boat to the territory of

the Gergesenes on the other side of the lake, and when we disembarked, a man with an unclean spirit came out of the tombs towards Jesus. He lived in the tombs and no-one could restrain him any more, because even when they had fettered him, he was strong enough to break the chains.'

My stomach flipped as I watched my dear father, the flawed fisherman with a heart as big as Canaan, remembering the very day when I had begun to love Jesus. He was dictating with closed eyes, not looking up, and Mark copied every word faithfully with his reed pen.

Dad was writing our story.

Bethsaida
63 CE

When I last saw him after the resurrection, Jesus had said goodbye to me. Afterwards the men saw him taken away to the Father, and we never expected to meet again until he comes in glory. So last night was a thrill and a shock.

I was really tired at the end of the Lord's day, and hadn't finished clearing the meeting room until well after sunset. The church in Bethsaida has been more blessed than the hopes of my wildest prayers. We meet in the house of Rufus, the same centurion who believed in Jesus so many years ago. He has retired from service in the Roman army and returned to Bethsaida to make his home. Rufus never lost his faith, and though he's almost eighty years old, he's active as ever, his booming voice leading us in song and praise. Our church is famous throughout Galilee, and we have many pilgrims asking to see the spot where Jesus walked on the lake, and fed the multitude. The crowds love to hear me speak of the past, and just as people did in his lifetime, they focus on the miracles rather then the message. Gently I teach them about the Kingdom, using the stories Jesus taught me.

Each week I'm certain our numbers are growing, and it now takes the entire Sabbath to bake enough bread for the Lord's supper next day.

It's hard to keep count of the years, and Momma's no longer alive to help me, but I must have passed my forty-sixth year - my bones feel older than that. Whenever I'm tired or sad, the lake is my comfort, and last night I walked the southern shore-path toward my childhood home of

Capernaum. To find the rock where I once sat with Jesus, to think and pray in quietness.

I nestled among the reeds where the waters lapped against the rocks, and must have fallen asleep at once.

But something woke me with a start. My heart was beating in my chest like a tabor, and for a moment I felt afraid. Then I heard, 'Lily!'

No-one has called me that for thirty years – it had to be, it couldn't be!

I turned and saw the shape of the one man on earth I have ever truly loved, adored, worshipped.

I was too happy to cry out, and sank to my knees, breathing in shallow gasps.

'My little one, it seems a long time to you since we met. But I have watched over you every single day. The Father is very pleased with you Lily, well done for building my church.'

I looked up into the shadowy face and my words came breathlessly, 'My Lord and my God! Why are you here? Have you come in glory?'

'Not yet. I want to show you something my love,' Jesus went on. 'Look across the waters at our city, the light on the hill.'

I raised my eyes to Hippos on the far shore.

'What I'm showing you will seem strange, but watch and remember,' he commanded.

As I stared at the lights of the city, the image began to blur and swim toward me.

'Am I dreaming?' I asked.

'No Lily, you are seeing what will come to pass. Things I must show you to sustain you through the suffering ahead.'

As he spoke, the lights got larger and I saw the image of Nero, just as he appears on the current coinage. In his hands he held a pitcher of water which he was throwing over the lights of Hippos, but as fast as he emptied the pitcher, it refilled. The quicker he poured, the further the lights spread, across the entire eastern shore of the lake. Suddenly I was able to see as far as Rome, as though I were an eagle soaring above the land. Nero threw great quantities of water, while the lights spread beyond Rome to lands whose names I would never know.

The image faded as suddenly as it had begun. Hippos returned to normal and I was aware of the quietness around us, and soft moonlight.

'What does it mean?' I asked.

'The lights are my church, and Nero is my persecutor. What you have seen will come to pass ~ Nero will try to extinguish my name, but he cannot stop my church from spreading. I am the light of the world Lily, and you must never be discouraged. When trouble comes, as it will, remember tonight. You are safe in my Father, and Simon Peter is safe too.'

Then he threw back his hood and I realised the light wasn't coming from the moon, but from his face, emanating from inside him. I was awe-struck and looked at the ground as tears began to come.

'What is it love?'

'Don't be angry, it's just ~ I want you back as you were, human, real, ordinary. Then you were my Jesus, now you're not.'

And he laughed, the old belly laugh I had missed 'til it hurt. Suddenly he was mine again, and my world was full to the top, and running over. When his laugh subsided, he still smiled, 'And you *shall* have me back Lily. Everything that is good about this world is already in heaven. Be patient, it's all waiting for you - your job on earth is almost done. Sleep now, I will sit here while you rest.'

And I fell into a deep sleep with my head cradled against his side.

TO SIMON PETER, FORGIVE THE
PAPYRUS DAD, I HAVE NO BROKEN
POTSHARDS! GREETINGS IN THE
NAME OF JESUS WHO WILL PROTECT
XANTHIPPE WIFE OF ALBINUS, BUT I
URGE YOU WITH THE CHURCH OF
BETHSAIDA TO RETURN TO US
BEFORE AGRIPPA HEARS OF HER
CONVERSION. GREETINGS TO MY
COUSIN MARK, DO NOT REST UNTIL
HE HAS WRITTEN EVERY WORD
ABOUT YOUR TIME WITH THE LORD.

Rome
10th August 2003

This afternoon I said goodbye to my sister before boarding my flight to Heathrow. It was the hardest goodbye of my life. I've been accepted by her boys and become part of the family, the family I never had.

We were standing outside departures.

'What will you do when you get to England?' Anna asked me.

'I'll catch up with Dad, trawl the job ads, make a fresh start.'

'Where will you stay?'

'Dad'll put me up for a while. Then I'll go to Tnymaes. It's gorgeous in the autumn. I'll be fine, honest.'

'Come back soon,' she pleaded, touching my face. 'And promise you'll come for Christmas – a big Italian family natale. It will be wonderful.'

'I don't want to spoil your plans.'

'You *are* my plans. Promise me.'

I hugged a 'yes' and turned quickly to walk through security. I decided not to look back, the old Ben would never look back.

But something inside was tugging at my ribs, urging me to turn my head.

As I reached the security gate, I looked towards my sister.

And I saw a slender, girlish figure, dressed in cream linen with a yellow scarf at her throat. Anna, Lily, my Susannah. A lump thumped into my mouth. My search is finally over.

Kent
20th October 2003

"Jerry and Carys are delighted to announce the birth of their son, Thomas, delivered safely on 16th October 2003, weighing 7lb 3oz."

In her own hand, Carys had scrawled across the bottom, 'Second name Ben. Jerry didn't like it, but I insisted. Hope you won't mind. Love C x'

Tnymaes, Bird Rock
6th November 2003

It's so good to be back. I've been trying to work out when I was last here, and haven't managed, but it's a long while.

I arrived three weeks ago, and before I could get through the front door (the only door) I had to find my scythe and hack down a forest of nettles. The garden has pretty much disappeared, although the teasels are doing well, and the cottage is darker than I remember, because the trees haven't been lopped.

Inside was damp and cold, but I got a fire going - good job the log store is under cover, and I've spent the time having the biggest sort out in forty years.

I've strimmed the garden, dug out the worst of the weeds, pruned over-hanging branches and had a major spring-clean indoors.

And I've put aside the old romanticism and called the electricity board to install two heaters and an electric cooker. I'm considering a washing machine, but funds are getting low.

My sister would be impressed by my efforts, because although I live out of a fifteen-pound rucksack for most of the year, Tnymaes is packed to the gunwales with years of flotsam and jetsam.

Sorting my old photos has been the most stressful part. Years ago I dabbled in photography and bought some expensive kit, taking rolls and rolls of film wherever I went. But once I'd developed the photos I didn't know what to do with them, so I have boxes, bags and crates full of negs and pictures. Since the divorce I haven't used the camera much, and haven't had the heart to look at the old photos.

It took me four days to sort them. We've had a bit of an Indian summer here so I took every container into my strimmed garden and tipped out the whole lot. Black bin bags to the left, 'keep' pile to the right. And I won't pretend it hasn't been painful. Mixed up with the photos I've found letters from Carys, old birthday cards from my Nan, and a black and white picture of baby Joe's grave. And sack-loads of really bad photos. Snaps of trenches, backs of diggers who I can't even remember, empty views, birds that are just too far away to make out.

And wedding photos. Me in a navy suit, Carys in a dreamy designer dress. Mum on one side smiling falsely, Dad looking sheepish.

The 'keep' pile was really small. When I'd finished, I biked into Tywyn and bought a few frames for the best pictures. One of me in my first trench, Mum holding baby Joe, a perfect view of Galilee. They look all right on my walls.

Yesterday was the first time I began to feel concerned about the future. I've been searching the professional journals for a job, but nothing has grabbed me. I love it here, but there's no work, no way I could earn an income. In bed last night I sort of prayed, 'Hey mate, if you're still there, I'd like the next forty years to be a bit more, fulfilling. And I don't know what to do next. Thanks. I mean Amen.' I said it out loud which I think is the right way, the old Ben must be laughing fit to drop.

But this morning I woke feeling low. Empty, with nothing to look forward to but Christmas. And fabulous as she is, my sister isn't going to fill the big need inside my soul. I chopped a mountain of logs to replenish the store, then went indoors to make lunch.

This place is the far side of the back of beyond, so I don't get many callers. Even the postman has to use a map. So when there was a knock at the door I had a shock. Who knows I'm here? Anna? The only other person who could find me is Carys.

So I opened the door gingerly and came face to face with a gypsy. Rings on every finger, grovelling expression, a basket of heather. I peered through the trees looking for her Mercedes, but that would be parked out of sight.

'Buy one for good luck sir,' she grinned.

Usually I'm a soft touch, can't say no to pushy types.

'It's lucky heather, let me pin one on your shirt,' she encouraged.

'Er no. Thanks.'

'Go on sir, to bring you good fortune and protect you from evil. That's got to be worth three quid hey?' She was trying to poke me with the pin.

I pushed her arms away, repeating, 'I said no. Thanks.'

Immediately her face changed from sun to thunder, 'Then go to hell mate. I can curse as well as bless. A curse on this place.' And she turned her back.

Slamming the door, I watched her out of sight through the tiny window. I won't deny I was spooked, and wished I'd given her the three quid just to stop her cursing me. I was so bothered, I pulled my little Gospel down, and looked at Taylor's inscription inside the front cover, '*Find peace.*'

I couldn't think of a single time when Jesus had cursed anyone, even when they told him to bog off. So I just put my hand on the text and closed my eyes, hoping the curse wouldn't work.

That's when the door knocked again.

I swore under my breath and ducked down beside the bookcase. Scared she would try the door.

Another knock.

'Go away. Go away,' I whispered under my breath.

The handle turned slowly and I saw a crack of green light as the door opened. That did it, I leaped to my feet ready to punch her lights out. I wasn't going to be scared of some corny crystal-gazer. I seized the door and threw it open.

Standing in front of me was no brown-faced gypsy, but a slim, tanned woman with eyes as blue as tea-cups of Californian ocean.

'Taylor! God in heaven what are *you* doing here?'

She was holding a bottle of wine and car keys.

There was a split second of silence as we stared into each other's shocked faces.

Then 'Ben?' she asked quizzically.

And for the first time in my life, as if it was easy as winking, I pulled a woman into me. Wrapped her beautiful body inside my digger's arms, and let my face fall into her hair. And I just couldn't help a sob rising, choking my breath.

The ground seemed to come up to meet me, I didn't plan to kneel. We dropped right there in a little pool of forest light on my door-step, and held on to each other like drowning rats.

She was crying too, and between my tears I heard her weeping, 'Why did you run away?'

'Because I was scared. Stupid and scared, I've never felt like this before.'

'Oh Ben you silly, silly idiot. I tried to make it so obvious.'

'But holiday man!' I said, pulling away and staring into her mascara-smeared face.

'I was trying to make you jealous, I've regretted it every day.'

'Jealousy doesn't work with me, I was crushed.'

'I know, I know that now.'

Suddenly I had a rush of panic, 'But why me? Why are you here?'

She smiled, 'Because you've got a perfect body. Because you're needy, real. Because of love.'

Love. That word. I don't know what it means, but I know what I'm feeling right now. And it's totally bloody wonderful.

She giggled and wiped her face, 'How ridiculous is this? Kneeling here. Aren't you going to invite me in? I've only travelled a few thousand miles for this drink.'

After supper we sat by the fire, Taylor's back nestled into my body.

'We hardly know each other,' she said.

'But it doesn't feel that way.'

'You certainly cost me a fortune in emails!' she laughed.

I watched the flames licking the base of my logs, curling around them and rising into the chimney.

'I've never felt so happy,' she said simply.

My body tensed, 'Look, what happened when you arrived,' I stumbled, 'I don't want you to think I'm, you know…'

'Keen?' she finished for me.

'Exactly.'

Taylor sat up and turned to face me head on. She looked

even more lovely in the firelight. 'So if you're not keen, what *are* you then? Exactly.' Her voice was harsh and edgy.

Thoughts raced through my confused brain. Old Ben was doing overtime. The words scared, excited, unconfident came to mind.

Taylor's eyes were frightened, 'I've travelled half way round the world to find out what you feel, and think I have a right to know.'

'Hey, can't be more than a quarter of the world from Jerusalem to Cardiff,' I joked. It was all I could manage, and my heart sank to the flagstones. I'd done it again.

Taylor looked as if something inside her was coming apart.

Then for some unknown reason I saw Susannah. As real as the log basket she was standing beside. I could tell she was waiting for me to speak. And I had a sense that someone else was there with her in the shadows.

I could feel her urging me on, 'Say it Ben, say it!'

There was no way left for old Ben. With relief like a huge weight falling away, I shoved him aside and laid my hands on Taylor's shoulders, 'Do you want the truth?'

She nodded sadly.

'I love you, really love you. Please stay with me, and never leave.'

Taylor put her arms around my waist and looked up at me as though she couldn't believe her ears.

I glanced towards the log basket. And just before she disappeared for the last time, my Susannah smiled.

FORGIVE ME, I HAVE NO PAPYRUS. GREETINGS IN THE NAME OF JESUS TO SUSANNAH DAUGHTER OF SIMON PETER. THE LORD WILL PROTECT ME FROM THE WRATH OF ALBINUS AND I MUST STAY IN ROME. MY BLESSING TO YOUR CHURCH AND TO MARY AT MAGDALA, MAY THE LORD'S WORK CONTINUE TO FLOURISH.

MARK SCRIBES FOR ME, I WROTE TO THE CHURCHES OF PONTUS & GALATIA REMINDING THEM WHAT THE LORD HAS TAUGHT ME THROUGH YOUR LIFE, THAT WOMEN DESERVE RESPECT & UNDERSTANDING AND ARE CO-HEIRS WITH MEN. YOU WERE WISE WHEN YOU SAID JESUS IS A LIGHT SHINING IN A DARK PLACE LIKE HIPPOS ON THE HILL. HE IS THAT LIGHT, AND THE MORNING STAR THAT RISES.

FOR THE LORD'S SAKE I AM WILLING TO DIE, BUT AM NOT WORTHY TO SUFFER THE SAME DEATH AS HIM. AGRIPPA WILL SEAL MY FATE.

MARK LEAVES ROME FOR GALILEE TOMORROW WITH THIS LETTER AND THE MANUSCRIPT OF MY LIFE WITH

OUR LORD, AND OF HIS DEATH AND RESURRECTION.

GROW IN THE GRACE AND KNOWLEDGE OF OUR LORD AND SAVIOUR JESUS CHRIST. GLORY BE TO HIM NOW AND FOR EVER! UNTIL WE MEET AGAIN IN HIS KINGDOM, SUSANNAH – PETER'S DAUGHTER. AMEN.

Footnote

All Bible references from Gospel of Mark New Jerusalem version except final page, Matthew chapter 28 verses 16-20, Author's translation

Bibliography

Archaeology and the Galilean Jesus by Jonathan L. Reed, Trinity Press 2002
Archaeology in the Holy Land by K M Kenyon, Ernest Benn
Temple, Jerusalem by W E Stinesburg, New York, Abingdon
Handbook of Life in Bible Times by J A Thompson, Inter-Varsity Press 1986
The Land Jesus Knew by David Roberts, Eagle Publishing 2001
Epistles of St Peter and St Jude, Cambridge University Press

Principal Websites

www.bibleplaces.com
www.israel-mfa.gov
www.unonaha.edu
www.galileeguide.com
www.gospelcom.net
www.bible-history.com
www.us-israel.org
www.bib-arch.org
www.jewishmag.com

Also by Helen Wilkinson

Dying to Live

The acclaimed biography of Fran Burke, who gave up treatment for leukaemia to have the two children she longed for.
Her heart-wrenching story has been described as gripping, moving and life-changing - this is a book with a truly happy ending.

'This book is a gem' - Sharon Hendry, The Sun

The Missing Peace

'This book, aimed at 8-12 year olds, is a fascinating read and has a "can't put it down" quality. The characters come to life from the first page.
Set in the seaside holiday village of Dunwich, the book is tightly structured, intriguing and with a great twist at the end. I *thoroughly* recommend this book.'

Marion Field - Candle & Keyboard

'Wow! What a book! A beautiful story that hangs in the mind and heart for days after reading it. Helen really gets inside a child's mind and the mystery lasts right to the end.'

Jennifer Rees-Larcombe

'A truly beautiful story - it had me in tears. I was hooked.'
'Leaves you feeling you have been part of a magical experience.'

"I give you my peace, a peace you will never find in the world. When you have heard this, go out and tell the good news to everyone. Find new followers in every country and teach them what I have taught you.

And know that I shall be with you always, to the end of time."

Jesus